The Detective Joanna Best Mysteries
Book 1

The Code of Monte Christo

Cenarth Fox

The Detective Joanna Best Mysteries
Book 1
The Code of Monte Christo

First published in 2018 by Fox Plays
www.foxplays.com
www.cenfoxbooks.com

Cover design by Oliviaprodesign

ISBN 978 0 949175 16 8

Dictionary of Australian slang/language

Some of the Australian words and expressions found in this novel.

arse - backside, posterior
barney - a fight, argument
bollocking - being reprimanded
bummer - no go, not an option
Centrelink - government department, Social Security equivalent
cossie - a costume usually for the stage
cuppa - a cup of tea
dobbing in or **dob in** - to squeal, snitch or rat on someone
doos - South African derogatory expression (not an Aussie word)
drongo - a dill, a stupid person
gobsmacked - mightily surprised
loo - lavatory, toilet, bathroom
Mum, Mummy - Mom, Mommy
panto - a pantomime (more common in the UK)
petrol - gasoline
PM - Prime Minster
pub - public house, hotel
Puffing Billy - steam locomotives on a tourist railway
rego - car registration, number plate
Sat Nav - a GPS, a navigation system in a vehicle
shagger - a promiscuous person
silly-billy - a stupid person
soft-soaper - someone who butters up another person
spark - an electric train (as opposed to a diesel or steam train)
sunnies - sunglasses
Tassie - the state of Tasmania
The Apple Isle - the state of Tasmania
tosser - a loser, a selfish person
tradie - plumber, electrician, carpenter, etc.
Tullamarine (Tulla) - international airport at Melbourne
uni - university
Up train - train to city, **Up platform** – platform used by Up trains
VCAT - a lower court, Victorian and Civil Administrative Tribunal
Vegemite - popular food (a spread) and a happy person
yonks - ages, a long time

The Scottish Pharmacist

There was once a pharmacist in a small Scottish town who
had the unenviable task of telling senior couples from
Ohio and elsewhere that the Mr Smith they were seeking
did not live at this address.
The pathetic people had crossed the Atlantic hoping to
discover what had happened to their life savings.
They were victims of online fraud. The address the
scammer gave was that of a pharmacy in this lovely
Scottish town.
Nice place to visit, mind.

Catfishing

The falsifying of an online identity to trick a victim into a
romantic relationship.

A Common Email
(as writ)

Hello and good day.
My name is Edward, and I am contacting you for partnership by
reason of the significance of your Nationality, which concerns
claim/transfer of Approximately 21 Million US Dollars in a fixed
deposit account left by a deceased Boss and Friend for onward sharing
between you and I in a ratio to be agreed.
Kindly get back to me as soon as you receive this email for complete
details as time is of the essence giving that we have less than 2 month
period to achieve this.
Regards
Edward

To Chadwick
For endless love

1

HE YELLED, SHE SCREAMED and the violent domestic kicked off. Passengers scattered. The Clifton Hill Up platform was packed and a scratching, slapping, shrieking barney got people moving. Did it ever?

'Shut up, you stupid bitch,' yelled the bully to his girlfriend. She taunted him. 'I can smell her on you,' she spat. He slapped her hard. She slapped him harder. Round 1 kicked off.

Waiting for her train was commuter, Senior Constable Joanna Best. Once she would have worn her police uniform to and from work with the Force keen to make its members known to the public. Alas, in these days of terrorism, police officers (and the military) are discouraged from flying the flag. Mind you, Jo was in uniform albeit hidden beneath a light coat, her hat inside her bag.

With immaculate hair and mirror-like shoes, Jo had a date with an interview panel following her application to join the Victoria Police Homicide Squad.

She was on time for everything important, and as she'd set her heart on joining Homicide when only a slip of a girl, today's interview was super important. Grandfather, John "Robbo" Robertson, Pop to Joanna, was once the head of the Victoria Police Homicide Squad, and the tales he told his teenage granddaughter thrilled her. She wanted to solve murders.

Her interview was at police HQ in the city. She planned to catch the train at Clifton Hill, alight at Southern Cross Station and then wander across Spencer Street arriving with time to spare.

Suddenly her plans went out the window. She was a cop, and cops respond to incidents such as the nearby serious assault.

The fighting lovebirds were into the screaming and spitting round. A couple of bystanders tried to intervene from a safe distance.

'Piss off,' screamed the bully at the would-be peacemakers.

Jo removed her coat revealing her uniform, and had no trouble moving through the crowd. She reached the boxing-ring just as the male shoved the female who fell. Referee Best yelled.

'Hey! That's enough of that.'

The furious male turned to deal with another interfering do-gooder, stalled when he saw the police uniform then resumed his aggression.

'Stay out of this, pig.' He raised a threatening fist.

Jo dumped her coat and bag, and prepared to respond. 'You're under arrest for assault and ...'

Stupidly she thought her words and uniform would win the day. It didn't. Everything happened in a flash. The man, with a hidden six-pack, grabbed Jo's jacket and heaved. The jacket screamed, as did the woman on the ground, as did the chorus of gawping onlookers.

'Right,' yelled Jo trying to break his grip, 'you're under arrest for assaulting a police officer.'

The thug released one hand and threw a punch. Jo ducked enough for his fist to miss its target, her face, but not enough for it to miss her beehive cum French roll hairdo. *Big mistake, buddy.* Jo had spent ages setting her hair, and to have it wrecked before an all-important interview flicked Jo's Kung Fu switch.

She grabbed his free hand, twisted his arm causing him to scream, spun him around, and kicked his feet from under him. He headed south and only just used his free hand to stop his face leaving an impression on the platform. Jo knelt on his back, fumbled for her cuffs, and struggled to restrain him. Two passengers helped by kneeling on the offender. He spewed vitriol. Commuters applauded.

'Thank you, folks,' said Jo to her deputies as she cuffed the thug, and felt proud until a member of the public lost it. The bullied woman swapped sides, now choosing to defend her abusive boyfriend.

'You bitch,' she screamed and started grabbing and tearing at Jo's head, inflicting even more damage to the once meticulous hairstyle. This was beyond the pale. The woman continued slapping Jo while her partner hurled abuse and imitated an angry steer at a rodeo.

More passengers chose to sit or kneel on the male, allowing Jo to deal with her new attacker. It wasn't easy.

The woman grabbed Jo's shirt, and a ripping sound meant the garment changed from radiant to ruined. Jo used her self-defence

2

skills, outpointed the female, and with plastic ties, fixed the woman's hands behind her back. She joined her partner in spitting abuse.

Great. So now Jo's jacket, shirt and hair were not fit for purpose, she had two people under arrest, and her Homicide Squad interview loomed large. The 0755 from Hurstbridge rolled in on time.

Shit.

She put on her coat to cover her uniform fiasco. That wouldn't help at the interview. She couldn't leave the prisoners, so called her colleagues who promised the nearest patrol pronto.

Then there was movement at the station as the travelling public upped and left. And as the Hurstbridge Up spark took its audience to town, Jo guarded two growling bandits, who sat on a platform bench.

Great work, girl, but you look a mess, and your interview awaits!

Jo's blood pressure crept higher. *I can't be late today.* Finally, the cavalry arrived and removed the sparring partners. Jo was free to go. But what about her appearance and mode of transport?

She couldn't front the interview like this. Should she go home, change then call a cab? But what if she couldn't get a cab immediately or at all? Being late, or not turning up for this interview, meant she could kiss goodbye to her dream, a career as a homicide detective.

An Up train from Epping arrived and she took it. She had a plan. Passengers in the crowded carriage looked at her with suspicion and alarm. They knew nothing of her heroics. There was even blood on her face thanks to a slap from her female punching pal.

On board, Jo called a colleague, Constable Tammy Grimes, and whispered her situation. Grimes was off duty, the same height and weight as Jo, and agreed to grab a spare shirt and jacket and meet Jo outside Police HQ in town. Tammy lived in a city apartment so could walk to the rendezvous in ten minutes. With a quick repair job in the loo, Jo might still make her interview.

The walk from Southern Cross Station was tricky. Hundreds of worker bees, heading to offices and shops in the city, stared at the woman with the bloodied face and messy hair. Jo's thoughts raced.

Will Tammy be there? Can I complete a makeover in time?

Tammy was there and felt for Jo. 'Sorry, pal, but you look like you've been in a pub brawl.'

'I have, on a railway station.'

Tammy gave Jo the clothes, still in their dry-cleaning wrapping, and a can of hair spray. Jo could have cried. 'You're a saint,' she said and hugged her friend.

'Good luck,' said Tammy. 'Let me know how you get on.'

A sheepish Jo entered the building. The officer on duty gave her a wary look. Jo showed her ID, interview letter, and change of clothes.

She wanted the *Ladies* and the chance to perform a makeover miracle. In the loo, she had her first decent look in a mirror and nearly died. Staring at her was a drunk after a night on the tiles.

She removed her ruined jacket and shirt, and washed her face. The hair was her major problem, or so she thought. The repair began. She was going well until she glanced at her watch. 'Shit!' She panicked. A Homicide Squad detective needs to be calm and in control of the situation.

She made an executive decision, combed out her fractured French roll, and went for the ponytail with a squish. Her makeup needed a touch up, and soon she was presentable.

Perhaps this less formal look is better anyway.

All that remained was to slip on her new shirt and jacket and then all would be good. Oh no! Tammy and Jo were the same height and weight but Tammy's back was more narrow and Jo's bust was bigger. Disaster. Jo struggled to button up the shirt and only just made it.

Great. I look like Barbara Windsor in Carry on Camping.

Perhaps the jacket would cover a multitude of sins. No, it only made matters worse. The jacket had to be done up but its buttons were straining, threatening to escape. Wouldn't that be perfect? A high-ranking police officer, in the midst of conducting a job interview, is hit in the eye by a flying button from the interviewee's jacket, under which her breasts threatened to burst forth and sing.

She was about to surrender, and utter an expletive when the door opened and a middle-aged police officer entered. They nodded, and Jo observed the woman's hair and uniform were immaculate.

'Morning,' said the new arrival and disappeared into a cubicle.

Jo struggled, trying to make the garments less suggestive. She went red pulling on abdominal muscles and holding her breath.

The woman came out of the cubicle and washed her hands. She turned to Jo. 'Are you all right?'

'Fine,' she lied. 'My uniform was trashed in a violent arrest, I've borrowed a colleague's shirt and jacket, both of which are too tight, and I can only hope the senior officers about to interview me don't think I moonlight as a stripper gram.'

'Well depending on the senior officers, that might be an advantage.' She smiled and left.

What a shame. No one could have prepared better. Jo could have been on time, looked terrific and given a professional interview. Instead, she was stressed, tarty and prepared for failure.

If you fail to prepare, you'll prepare to fail.

'Be yourself,' said Pop. 'Don't try and impress people, let your natural personality win them over.'

Jo sat in the corridor and pondered Pop's advice. An officer appeared. 'Senior Constable Joanna Best,' he said. This was it. Weeks of rehearsing answers to every conceivable question now came down to the next 20 minutes. She gave herself a pep talk. *Don't blow it, Jo.*

She entered the room and saw three men, seated ready to grill her. *Are they staring at my chest?* Then a fourth member arrived. She just happened to be the highest-ranking female officer in Victoria Police, and the woman Jo met in the loo. Senior Constable Best hadn't recognised her. What a cock-up. Could things get any worse?

Someone else had an interview that day or rather that night. Well, not so much an interview as an audition. The Belgrave Players were an amateur theatre company in Melbourne's Dandenong Ranges, and one of their main activities was performing a murder mystery play where the audience travelled on the famous tourist steam train, Puffing Billy.

Passengers loved the night train, chatted to the actors en route to the venue, hopped off for a slap-up meal, enjoyed the mystery play, and then took the train back to Belgrave.

The "someone else" in this tale is Larry Devine, the auditionee who hoped to join the local thespians. Larry was an actor of many years standing who once lived and loved in this area with *loved* being the key word. Larry had a colourful past, a reputation. In short, he was a love rat or, in old-fashioned terms, a bounder and a cad.

More than 30 years ago, in the Dandenongs, Larry began seducing local females. His behaviour gave him the moniker, Lothario Larry.

He'd love 'em and leave 'em. Today you'd call him a bastard and, were he a public figure, his name might well feature with the #MeToo.

In theatre groups in and around the hills, Larry would act on stage then seduce women off, under, over and behind the stage. He was a professional whisperer of sweet-nothings, and once he found a new love, he'd dump his current beau without warning or regret. For Larry, there was always a back-up bird in the wings.

His seduction of women proved dangerous with the constant risk of a serious assault from enraged fathers, mothers, husbands, wives, brothers and boyfriends. When enough irate folk joined forces to enact rough justice on the randy actor, Larry reckoned new pastures were all the go, so set sail for Tassie.

He lived on the Apple Isle for decades where he continued playing Don Giovanni, only to return briefly for his old man's funeral. When his dear old Ma pegged out last month, the phantom shagger decided to return to his roots—family and female.

He was an only child, and his widowed Mum left him her entire estate including a charming abode in Selby near Belgrave. Overnight, Larry became a man of property. He figured no-one would remember his long-ago sexual escapades in the hills, so returned to the Dandenongs to enjoy his retirement.

When he read about the Belgrave Players, he decided to tread the boards again, rocked up to the rehearsal hall, and introduced himself. The director and committee members were too young to know of licentious Larry or his extra-curricular activities, and so watched and cheered as he gave a brilliant audition. New actors were always welcome, and especially anyone with talent and testicles.

'Well, Larry Devine,' said the young director, 'you are the answer to a maiden's prayer.'

Boy, was that an unfortunate choice of words. Larry grinned. He'd already sized up the female talent in the room and liked what he saw.

'One of our actors has dropped out, so how would you like to play the murderer in our next mystery?'

Larry's grin got cheesier. 'My pleasure,' he oozed, and the phantom philanderer was back where it all began.

Gentlemen, lock up your daughters.

Jo left the Homicide Squad interview feeling as flat as a football supporter whose team had just lost the grand final by a point, with the winning goal kicked by a former player of their team after the siren.

Bugger.

She panicked when she saw the female officer on the interview panel, worried about her "June is busting out all over" top, and did exactly the opposite to what her grandfather had advised. She was pushy, acted unnaturally, and generally made a dog's breakfast of the most important interview of her career.

At home, the first person she rang was her grandfather. 'I blew it, Pop. Sorry, but all your fabulous advice got lost in ...' She choked and started to cry.

'Hey, none of that,' replied the snowy-haired retiree. 'Put it behind you, lass, and get back on the horse.'

Jo struggled to speak, holding back the tears. 'Thanks, Pop,' she mumbled. 'Love you, mate.'

As the tears broke free, she hung up before he could reply. She didn't ring her mother who would have been cautiously proud, albeit worried, to have her daughter follow in Pop's footsteps. There were reasons why Jo didn't ring her father.

Sadly, she was ashamed or sad or dead set flattened to speak with anyone. She needed sleep before her night shift but instead put on joggers, a leotard and shorts, and went running.

When she arrived for her shift, wearing a uniform which fitted like a glove, she was acting. Her brave face and cheery grin covered her misery. Missing out on the job was bad enough. Missing out because her uniform got damaged as she performed her duty—and bloody well too—made her sick to the core.

If only that couple were on an earlier train. Sometimes life sucks.

She wandered into the station, greeting her fellow workers. They asked about her interview. She lied. Her bravado kept her going.

God, I hope I don't cry.

She was due on patrol so headed outside when her sergeant called.

'Oi, Best, where do you think you're going?'

'Sarge?' she replied.

'You're off, Senior.'

'Right off,' grinned a young cop.

Jo was confused. Her sergeant continued.

7

'No shift for you tonight, me girl. Go home and get some kip.'

Colleagues grinned. Jo's confusion increased. 'What's up, Sarge?'

The officer in charge explained. 'Early start, Senior Constable. 0800 hours, six months' probation at Homicide.'

Stunned didn't begin to describe Jo's mindset. She started to shake. Her brain would not, could not compute that last statement.

'Homicide?' she mouthed.

'That's what they said. Probation starts tomorrow.'

The grins of her colleagues, their back slaps, congratulations and good wishes rendered her speechless. She even hugged colleagues she didn't like. It was a mix of pandemonium and overwhelming joy. Finally, things settled and she looked for an explanation.

'Don't ask me, Senior Constable,' said her sergeant—now former sergeant. 'I got a call from some woman at HQ who said you were to cease work here immediately and report to Homicide first thing tomorrow.' He handed her a printed email confirming the phone call.

'But I gave a shocking interview. I blew it because my uniform was torn during that arrest in Clifton Hill, my face was a mess, and I had one seriously bad hair day.'

The sergeant offered her a clipboard with a form attached. 'Sign here,' he said. 'And if you don't, get out on patrol.'

Everything stopped. Everyone watched. Jo paused and looked around. A sea of expectant faces stared at her. Suddenly she snatched the clipboard and scribbled her signature with a flourish. She handed back the clipboard, raised her hands in the air, and roared.

'Yes!'

2

CORNELIUS 'CONNIE' KRUGER WAS A LOT LIKE Larry Devine. Both targeted women, although while Larry worked at seducing them, Connie craved their cash. He used soft words to persuade women to divulge their banking details. Like Larry, Connie moved house once his exploits caused problems. He was a South African who moved to Melbourne, Australia to defraud females. King Catfish was now an Aussie, pitching his romance scams to wealthy women.

Many victims of romance stings never talk about their experience. Once scammed, they remain silent, being shattered and embarrassed by their catastrophic mistake. You don't trumpet the fact you handed over most, if not all your money to a con artist.

The stats about romance frauds are frightening. We know the number of victims and the amounts of money involved are both on the rise. We know it's mainly women who suffer, and that many are intelligent with love overriding the intellect.

Connie was good at finding possible victims. He called them his bunnies. He reckoned once he shone his headlights in their eyes, they froze, being ripe for the plucking.

His knowledge of social media was first class, and his ability to strike up a relationship with lonely women was brilliant. He groomed his bunnies.

So as Senior Constable Joanna Best swapped her uniform for plain clothes to join the Homicide Squad, and become Detective Senior Constable Joanna Best, Larry Devine and Cornelius Kruger were busy in their respective areas of expertise—philandering and scamming. Apart from being complete bastards, the one thing these two men had in common was a future date with a certain policewoman.

It was the Best of times.

Norma was 41, and recently widowed. Her loving husband left for work three months ago and didn't come home. He sat on the lavatory, pitched forward when his heart malfunctioned, and came to rest blocking the cubicle door. Attending to him took time, and some deft climbing by an agile paramedic. It was easy for the coroner. Death by natural causes, move along, nothing to see here.

Norma, named after Norma Jean Mortenson, aka Marilyn Monroe, was now the sole owner of a prestigious house in Albert Park and a healthy bank account. Despite her wealth, Norma was desperately sad.

Lonely, wealthy widows were the preferred category for Cornelius Kruger. Norma ticked all the boxes.

Her social media postings announced her loneliness. She wasn't blatant in her search for companionship or preferably love, but a clever scammer like Connie knew the signs. Norma's posting on a web site where people advertised their loneliness, told Connie that here was a woman ripe for exploitation. When he discovered her wealth, the poor woman was bumped up to first class, becoming a priority target.

Connie followed his proven procedure, and invented a new persona. Meet Australian Special Forces Officer, Mike Trenchard.

Now photos are super important in hooking a victim, and if the woman can see the man who replies to her post, she's far more likely to respond. But Connie was no oil painting and, of course, wanted to avoid recognition so naturally used a false name and picture.

And what a picture. Mike was handsome. Yes, it was a stolen photo, and Norma Jean could have saved herself a truckload of misery and cash had she simply run Mike's pic through some facial technology software such as Google Cloud Vision.

To do so would have revealed Mike Trenchard to be the late Glenn Baird, stockbroker, former Australian Army Reserve officer, and polo player from Portsea. But Norma Jean was lonely and fell for the photo and the story of the man on her screen. Connie wrote.

Hi Norma Jean,
I was knocked out by your lovely photo and knew I just had to respond. I too am looking for companionship after my darling wife tragically died from cancer last year.

The lush orchestral strings began playing tearjerker music in Norma Jean's mind. She was hooked. Her post had uncovered a gorgeous looking man, a professional soldier risking life and limb for Queen and country, and widowed like her. The wife he dearly loved had been cruelly taken from her man, dying far too young.

He's good, is Kruger. Norma Jean wrote back.

Hi Mike,
Thank you for your wonderful reply. I was touched by your story and would love to correspond with you some more.

Connie purred and moved to the next stage.

Hi again, Norma Jean,
May I call you Norma? Your photo suggests a fun-loving girl just like my favourite actress, Marilyn Monroe.

Now that was luck, well an educated guess, but boy did it hit the sweet spot. Scammers like Cornelius Kruger get better with age and use every trick to ingratiate themselves into the victim's heart. He delivered on the blarney, but then switched subtly to the practical.

It's much easier for me to contact you by email because I'm currently serving overseas—can't say where for security purposes. Would you be happy to chat by email? Later we might even try Skype. My email address is mikeos1@bigpondoz.com.au.

Norma Jean, now just Norma, was struck.
He loves my photo. He called me a girl. He wants to share emails. I'm so excited.

Getting the victim off the dating web site and on to email is a major gain for the scammer. Their chances of being monitored or traced are reduced than when communicating through a dating site.

Norma couldn't wait for her next email from Mr Wonderful. They exchanged several. But Connie knew how to draw her in then lock her in. After a while, he delayed making contact. Norma would turn on her laptop first thing every morning, and delight in reading the flattery from her newfound love. But suddenly, nothing arrived.

She worried then stressed. *Has Mike been killed? Has he gone out on some dangerous mission and been captured by the enemy? Right now, is he being horribly tortured by some crazed terrorist?*

Not exactly because, as it happened, Connie was playing golf for a week on courses along the mighty Murray River. When the bastard sent his next email, he was all apologies.

My darling Norma,
A thousand apologies for my failure to write. I've been on a secret mission, and had no contact with the outside world. I've missed your witty and loving emails and hope you are well and happy.

She *was* well and happy now that Mysterious Mike was back online.

And so it progressed. Norma was a perfect victim because she had few friends or family members in whom she felt happy to confide. Every Friday she had coffee with a girlfriend who was such a gossip, Norma decided never to tell her anything about her personal life.

Mike started to reveal more of his back-story. The drip feed method worked well. The scammer will rarely offload a ton of information in one hit. Slow and steady is the way to go.

I hope you won't mind me telling you this, darling girl, but I have a tricky family situation and you are the only person I feel comfortable talking to.
I have a seven year-old son called Simon who has cerebral palsy, not so bad that he can't do most things and, of course, he's the light of my life. But being away from home so often, my late wife's parents have been caring for him, and now they want to make the move permanent. Sadly, I don't get on with my in-laws and the thought of me losing Simon is just too hard to bear. I don't mind telling you, my love, I've been crying a lot of late.

God he was good. To some he was as subtle as a sledgehammer. To a woman with a smitten heart, he was "my hero".

Now many people would see this as grooming and preparation for a scam, which it was. But remember the victim is vulnerable and emotionally involved, the scam is very much a slow and gentle process, and when the photo of Simon, Mike's disabled but gorgeous little boy appeared on Norma's screen, she was smitten. Of course it was another fake photo—but a good one.

Connie's method was simple—win their heart and the mind and banking details will follow.

Norma not only wanted to be with Mike in every possible way, she wanted to become an instant mother. She was childless, although not for want of trying, and here was an amazing situation. Norma couldn't believe her luck. She could marry Mike, become an instant mother, and be able to look after darling Simon thus saving her man's family.

Look, dear reader, I could go on with the rest of this story but I think we all know how it's going to end. Long story short, Norma paid six grand to enable the non-existent Simon to have a life-changing op in America, and then $24K as a part deposit on a property Mike claimed he'd signed for, and which would be their home in the Blue Mountains as soon as Soldier boy finished his current tour of duty.

A couple of times he was coming home and Norma couldn't believe they would actually meet in person. Would they hug and kiss in an instant? Would he love her as she loved him?

She counted the days until her new man, the war hero, would touch down. Then disaster struck as Mike was re-posted at the last minute and his flight cancelled. The excuses were powerful with as much detail as military protocol allowed. Of course, it was all bullshit.

Now to date, all Norma's "donations" were peanuts. I say peanuts because first prize in the scam-of-the-year lottery was about to be awarded. This was where the real skill of the scammer came into play.

Connie created a situation where the victim herself suggested a course of action. He would never say, "Hey babe, why don't we open a joint account and pop our savings in together." That was far too obvious. No, the scammer allows the victim to think they're running the show. A notion is floated; the victim gets an idea, and can't wait to share it with her man. So Norma suggested they set up a joint account and Mike "reluctantly" agreed.

And to "prove" Mike was such a good guy, once the joint account was established, Connie deposited ten grand. It was part of the money she'd already handed over. He set a sprat to catch a mackerel.

He trusts me. This wonderful man trusts me, thought Norma. She transferred her life savings, and then it was Good Night Vienna.

It's hard to imagine the reaction of the victim when the sting is discovered. The heartbreaking finale began. Norma deposited $150 grand plus change, and everything disappeared including Mike.

At first Norma thought it was a mistake, then she endured disbelief, until finally, the penny, well much more than a penny dropped. Norma was being tortured. The account was empty and Mike wouldn't reply.

Where are you, my darling man?

Her emails bounced. The Australian Armed Forces don't reveal private details of their serving officers, and it wouldn't have helped if they did. Mike didn't exist.

Connie moved on. His Norma Jean account was erased.

Who could Norma tell? The police? Yes, but there are so many scams and many of the crooks are overseas. Could she tell her family and friends? She could but the embarrassment and shame would kill her. Could she hire a private detective? Yes, but most likely that would be throwing good money after bad. And now she was broke anyway.

The wretched woman suffered on multiple fronts. Which was worse? The loss of her entire savings? The death of her love affair? The sheer embarrassment of having made a fool of herself? The end of her dream of becoming a stepmother? The physical pain just thinking about her stupidity? How about all of the above?

It's fair to say Norma entertained thoughts of suicide.

Ah, Connie, you are a mega-bastard. Will you ever get your comeuppance? And who, pray tell, is next on your list?

3

JO COULDN'T SLEEP. By the time she got home from her interrupted night shift, it was too late to call Pop or her mother so she made coffee and flopped on the settee. She pondered.

How the hell did I get accepted by Homicide? My interview was a disaster. And I've never ever traded on Pop's name. Why am I in?

She set two alarms to ensure she wasn't late on her first day.

Again she travelled by train, and this time wore civvies. If anyone needed a cop, Joanna Best was an ordinary citizen. In the words of Sergeant Schultz, "I see nothing, I know nothing".

On the train, she still thought it was all a mistake. *The Homicide Squad think I'm someone else. There was a major clerical error.* Then she remembered her outfit. *Surely, they couldn't forget my Carry on Constable clobber?*

She entered the Homicide Squad building and Reception.

'Good morning,' said Jo identifying herself.

'Hello love, welcome to Homicide. I'm Beryl.' She handed Jo some paperwork. 'Just fill in this lot and I'll get you a temporary pass.'

Jo completed the forms. The place seemed deserted.

'Am I the first one here?' asked Jo.

'Oh no, everyone's in a meeting; double homicide overnight.'

Jo felt sick. Her first day, she was early and yet she was late.

'Please, where do I go?'

Beryl pointed. 'Through those doors and first on the right.'

'Thanks.'

'Good luck, love.'

At the door, Jo waited. *Do I knock and enter? Do I wait?*

15

She heard voices and people moving. The door opened and a squad (that would be a *posse* in the US) of detectives poured forth, dispersing in different directions. Most ignored her although a couple of males gave her the once-over. No-one spoke and she was reluctant to ask for help. Then a woman appeared and stopped.

'Are you the new detective?'

'Senior Constable Joanna Best, ma'am.'

The woman turned her back on Jo and called into the room. 'She's here, sir. I'll take her with me.' And with that, the woman headed down the corridor. 'Come on, Detective,' she called with Jo scrambling to keep up. 'And don't ever call me, ma'am. It's Sarge or Billy.'

The woman was Detective Sergeant Deborah 'Billy' Hughes, 38, an experienced homicide detective who was definitely one of the boys. Some unkind colleagues described her as ballsy.

She got the nickname Billy from her first sergeant who knew the name of every Australian Prime Minister. So Constable Hughes became Billy, after PM Billy Hughes, who once belonged to six political parties, although not at the same time. Three of them chucked him out.

In the car park, several police officers reached the car, and Billy slipped behind the wheel. Jo went to open the front passenger door but was beaten to it by a male colleague. 'In the back, Detective,' he ordered, 'brains before boobs.' The man was all class.

Detective Senior Constable Stephen Payne sat in the front. No welcome, no excuse me, and no introduction. Payne was a law unto himself. Jo slipped in the back, and was joined from the other side by another colleague, and one cut from a very different cloth.

He offered his hand. 'Hi. Senior Constable Charlie Baldwin.' His smile was as warm as the strength of his handshake.

'Jo Best,' she replied and returned his smile.

'I think you mean Detective Senior Constable Best, Jo Best,' grinned Baldwin. She glowed at the sound of her new moniker. This wasn't a dream and she struggled to lock her seat belt as the car accelerated.

Jo wanted to ask a dozen questions but decided to button her lip. The rude DSC got in first.

'So, first case, hey, Detective Best?'

'First day, first case,' said Jo.

Payne wanted to give her a hard time.

'Only two rules to follow when we get to the murder scene. One, don't enter, and two, regarding evidence ...' Payne stopped speaking as Hughes negotiated a risky overtaking.

'Keep your hands in your pockets,' said Jo.

This floored all three detectives, and especially the experienced Billy Hughes. 'How the hell did you know that?' She twigged. 'Of course, you're Robbo Robertson's granddaughter.'

Jo felt chuffed. From Pop, she knew the importance of not contaminating a crime scene, and he was still remembered.

Hughes continued. 'I never met the old bloke but his reputation is legendary. If you're half as good as your grandfather, Jo Best, you'll do all right.'

'So nepotism is alive and well,' sneered Payne.

'Ignore him,' said Baldwin. 'He's Payne by name and nature.'

'Yeah, shut it, Constable,' said Billy to the man beside her.

Payne scowled. Baldwin looked at Jo and winked. She nodded and mimed, "Thanks". They drove in silence. Finally, Jo decided to risk asking a question. She'd missed the meeting and didn't want to arrive at the crime scene knowing almost nothing.

'Did I hear this is a double homicide?'

Hughes replied. 'Two bodies but we won't know if they're homicides till we get there.'

Jo grimaced. *Elementary mistake, Watson; never assume.*

'Apparently there's an absence of blood and guts, Senior Constable,' oozed Payne. 'We thought we'd break you in gently.'

Hughes ignored Payne. 'Couple in their 60s, well off, and dead in bed is all we know. No immediate suspect. So now, Jo Best, as your colleagues will attest, if you help me, your future is rosy. Get in my way and you'll become extra keen on a transfer. Got the picture?'

Jo knew what to say. 'Sarge.'

'Billy speaks,' said Payne, and Baldwin gave Jo a thumbs up.

They arrived at a prestigious home in nearby Elsternwick. It was a touch akin to *Midsomer Murders* in that the setting seemed more important than the crime.

Uniformed officers had taped the front of the property, and one stood guard. The four detectives approached with Jo in the rear. The others flashed their ID and were nodded through. Jo had the temporary pass provided by Beryl in Reception and was stopped.

Baldwin looked back and told Hughes who called. 'She's with me.'

The uniformed officer nodded and Jo followed along the drive which seemed to go on forever.

At the front door, a uniformed officer with a clipboard was writing the name and rank of every police or forensics' officer in attendance. The other three detectives suited up and Jo was asked for her details. Her name was listed and she felt great, at last a part of a team of investigators. Then disaster. Only three Teflon boiler suits were available and Jo was the one without a chair when the music stopped.

'Wait here,' said Hughes. 'Check the outside.' She headed indoors.

'Yeah, go smell the roses,' said Payne who disappeared. Baldwin raised his eyebrows at Jo and followed his colleagues.

The officer with the clipboard looked up the drive. 'Here's trouble.'

A middle-aged woman walked, almost stumbled towards them.

'Good morning, Doctor,' said the officer.

'What bloody time do you call this? I don't get out of bed before lunch, and certainly never before my second caffeine fix.' She stopped and looked at Jo. 'Who the bloody hell are you?'

Jo hesitated then replied in the most polite voice possible. 'Who the bloody hell is asking?'

The uniformed officer gasped fearing the worst.

The middle-aged woman glared at Jo then roared with laughter extending her hand. 'Doctor Gabrielle Strange, pathetic pathologist.'

Jo shook her hand. 'Detective Senior Constable Joanna Best, deranged detective.'

More raucous laughter exploded from Strange. 'I like you, girly. Be careful or we shall become the best of friends.' She looked at Jo. 'Where's your fancy costume? And where's the stiff?'

Jo explained that the bodies, plural, were inside and she, being new, was outside due to a lack of protective clothing.

The wobbly pathologist needed help putting on her own protective outfit after which she departed. Jo looked at the officer. 'Is it okay if I have a look around the garden?'

'That's what your boss said,' she replied, and Jo went exploring.

The garden was magnificent. Police tape was attached to bushes beside a French window, which looked to be the point of forced entry.

Jo remembered Pop's advice and kept well clear. But by leaning in she was able to see footprints in the garden bed. She thought there was something unusual about the impressions. *They look odd.*

Around the side of the house, she looked for anything which might be helpful. Seeing nothing, she turned to leave when someone called.

'Excuse me.' An elderly woman peered through a gap in the hedge, which acted as a fence between the adjoining properties.

'Good morning,' said Jo.

'Has there been an accident?'

'Possibly but I can't say until we've finished our investigation.'

'Are you the police?'

Jo produced her ID. 'Detective Senior Constable Best, and you are?'

'The nosy neighbour.' Jo grinned. 'They say you're old when the police all look so young.' Jo liked her. 'Looking at you, young lady, I feel like I'm a hundred.'

'Well you've certainly got your wits about you ...' Jo invited the woman to identify herself.

'Winifred, but you can call me Winnie.'

'Hello Winnie, I'm Joanna but you can call me Jo.'

'Do you fancy a cuppa, Jo?'

'Is the Pope a Catholic?' Winnie cackled. 'I'll just tell my colleague where I am.'

Winnie pointed. 'You can squeeze through the hedge by the bird feeder. Come round the back.'

'Thanks,' said Jo. She informed the keeper of the rolls, and soon sat in Winnie's overcrowded kitchen, which housed enough knick-knacks and cookbooks to open a cookery shop.

The tea simmered, and the homemade biscuits were scrumptious.

When Jo returned to the murder location, her notebook contained what she hoped were useful facts. Winnie was a chatterbox, and Jo was desperate to contribute to the case.

Hughes, Payne, Baldwin, and Dr Strange emerged from the house. The sergeant wanted a summary.

'So your initial diagnosis, Doctor, is a natural death by heart attack for the male, and murder by suffocation for the female,' said Billy.

'All preliminary, Sergeant, as well you know. Nothing confirmed without a PM,' replied the pathologist. She started to remove her protective clothing and stumbled. Jo moved in and helped her. 'Thank you, my dear. You're the only gentleman present.'

Hughes gave orders. 'Stephen, supervise the removal of the bodies after Forensics give the word. Charlie, supervise uniform for the door knocking. We meet at HQ at noon.' She headed back along the drive.

'Sarge?' called Jo, not knowing what to do.

'You're with me.'

Jo jogged to catch up as Payne stirred. 'Ooooh, teacher's pet.'

Strange looked at Payne with disgust. 'God, you're a dickhead.'

Driving back, Jo told Hughes about her interview with Winnie.

'Good initiative, Senior. Get anything useful?'

'I think so, Sarge, but ...'

'Save it. Unless it needs immediate action, presenting to the group is best. It saves multiple reporting, and re-telling can mean you change things, and that's dangerous.'

Another lesson learned, thought Jo.

Hughes gave her the basic details of the scene inside the house then, back at the office, left her to find a desk and settle in. The meeting began at noon with the four detectives who went to the crime scene plus DI Pierre Richelieu, the OIC (Officer in Charge) of the investigation, DI Grant Steele, the head of the Homicide Squad, and 3 other detectives Jo had never met. She struggled to remember names.

Richelieu chaired the meeting and Jo thought she was in love. Well, at least with his voice. With a name like Pierre Richelieu, the DI had a silky smooth French accent and the bluest of eyes in which she might go swimming. He began and then stopped to apologise.

'I am so sorry. I 'ave not mentioned our new member of staff. Mademoiselle Best, vous êtes les bienvenus.'

The others rolled their eyes, and one groaned as Jo blushed. That settled it. She *was* in love. Billy Hughes began with an overview.

'Husband and wife, David and Larissa Hall, found dead in their bedroom by their cleaning lady at 0830 hours this morning. Approximate time of death, midnight. The bedroom had been ransacked. Sign of forced entry in the front garden. Only son, Gavin, flew to Sydney on business early this morning. Lives with his boyfriend and both have been told of the situation. The son arrives back at Tullamarine around 1630 hours this afternoon.'

'So is this a double 'omicide?' asked Richelieu.

'Too early but it's either a double homicide or a murder/suicide.'

'PM report?' asked Richelieu.

Payne replied. 'Dr Strange's preliminary report tells us the male suffered a heart attack, and the female was suffocated.' Then Payne flicked the sarcasm switch. 'As usual, we'll get her final report in the fullness of time.'

'Right, what else?' asked the OIC.

Hughes explained. 'The bedroom was trashed possibly by the intruder or intruders to cover their tracks.'

'A neighbour advised the husband had heart problems,' added Baldwin, 'and took medication.'

'CSOs (Crime Scene Officers) have collected prints and DNA, and will process same in due course,' said Hughes.

'Door to door?' asked the former Parisian.

'Quite a few not home, sir,' said Baldwin. 'Some mentioned the husband's health problems and that the son was a visitor.'

'Anything else,' asked Richelieu?

Jo froze. She had things to say but feared they'd be useless and she'd make a fool of herself. Hughes looked at her.

'Senior Constable Best?'

Jo had no choice. 'Yes, I interviewed a next-door neighbour.'

'Which side?' This came from DI Grant Steele, the serious, no-sense-of-humour boss of Homicide.

Steele was a psychiatrist's dream. He enjoyed being a cop but enjoyed winning promotion even more. He craved power and was never happy standing still. He pondered career paths. Which would get him to the top faster? Who were his opponents in rising within the ranks? He didn't like bright underlings. They might show up his weaknesses. Jo Best was a potential danger.

She was thrown by his question. 'Ah, North,' she blurted and stopped. Everyone stared at her. Payne willed her to fail. Jo took out her notebook. 'The woman's name is Winifred Gray, known as Winnie, and believes there was trouble between the son and his now dead parents, over his relationship with another man.'

'So the son's gay?' snapped Steele. Baldwin winced.

'I have no idea, sir, simply reporting what the neighbour said.'

'Is that all, Senior Constable,' asked Richelieu. He never snapped.

Jo looked at her notes, saw her comment about the odd impression of the footprints by the window, and decided she wasn't brave enough to go there on her first day. She didn't fancy ridicule. 'Yes sir.'

'Merci, Mademoiselle, your initiative does you credit.'

Jo blushed again and wanted to disappear through the floor. Payne's hatred simmered. Steele observed.

'Right,' continued Richelieu, 'we await reports from Forensics and Dr Strange. We resume door knocking for the not-at-'omes this afternoon and evening, and we interview the son when 'e returns today. What about the cleaning lady? 'as she made a statement?'

'She has,' said Hughes, 'with only the basics of finding the bodies.'

'Then another interview, Sergeant, s'il vous plaît.' Hughes nodded.

Richelieu looked to see if any other comments were to be made. He was about to close the meeting when interrupted by his superior.

'What about the son's boyfriend? He might be a player.'

'Thank you, sir,' said Richelieu, 'we follow up on the boyfriend.' The DI indicated the meeting was at an end. 'Merci ladies and gentlemen, 0800 tomorrow, s'il vous plaît.'

Just as the meeting broke up, Steele made his third and final comment. 'And well done Detective Senior Constable Best.'

Everyone stopped. Silence dominated. Jo had no idea what to say and so said nothing. Steele left and others followed.

Baldwin sidled up to Jo and whispered, 'A little tip, Detective. Beware of bosses who are tossers.' He raised his eyebrows and left.

Jo felt concerned with a pinch of fear. She collected her bag and notebook and headed for her desk.

So far so ... no, let's wait and see.

4

CHLOE REDMOND WAS THEATRE MAD. She got the acting bug in high school and joined the Belgrave Players aged 16. She auditioned for everything, painted sets, made costumes and props, and generally gave her life to the mighty Thespis. University student Chloe lived with her mother, Simone, a single-mum who too was once a performer.

The theatrical daughter came home from rehearsal and flopped on the settee. Her mother watched TV, or rather the TV was on and Simone just happened to be in the room.

'Good rehearsal?' asked Simone.

'We have got the best cast ever,' said a tired but excited Chloe.

'That's not what you said last week.' Simone went to make tea.

Chloe called. 'We've got a better script, a great new actor, and that director is dead set brill.'

Simone spoke louder. 'Is that your Mr Young and Gorgeous?'

'That's him.'

'So, any progress on his eligibility?'

Chloe entered the kitchen and started on the cake her mother had baked that afternoon. 'That's a bummer, I'm afraid.' Simone looked at her daughter. 'He's gay, Ma. I think he's in love with the leading man.'

Simone sorted teabags and milk. 'Plenty more fish in the sea, my girl. When do you open?'

'Two weeks, and the train's booked out already.'

'Great. So who's this fantastic new actor?'

'He's terrific; only started tonight but boy can he act.' She ate more cake. 'But he's old, even older than you.'

'Charming. Thanks for nothing.'

'He's an old version of Tom Cruise. His name's Larry Devine.'

A deep chill exploded in Simone's body. Smash! She dropped the kettle and boiling water splashed free. Simone screamed in pain. Chloe screamed in fear. 'Mum!'

Boiling water hit Simone's foot albeit covered with a sock and fluffy slipper. It was panic stations in a Belgrave kitchen. Chloe helped her mother to sit.

'Cold water,' shouted Simone, 'quickly!' Chloe rushed to turn on the cold tap. She grabbed a saucepan. 'Under the sink,' yelled her mother. 'Get the bucket.'

Chloe half-filled a bucket with cold water and helped her mother place her scalded foot therein. Neither had any idea about first aid and particularly about burns or scalding.

'Better?' asked the daughter.

'A little,' replied her mother.

Simone's real pain was mental. Her mind suffered torment when she heard that Lothario Larry was not only still alive but now back in town. That man ruined her life.

After Chloe went to bed, Simone sent a text to long-time friend, Colin Grubb. He was older than Simone, and lived alone in nearby Belgrave Heights with his pooch, Brunel. Colin was retired and spent his waking hours working on the tourist railway running through the hills from Belgrave to Gembrook. Colin was a guard on Puffing Billy.

The reason Simone and Colin knew one another and the only thing they had in common was Larry Devine. Simone's text went as follows.

Help! Devine's back and in the Belgrave Players.

Simone thought Colin would be asleep and wouldn't see the text until morning. She was wrong. Her phone rang and she grabbed it.

'Just a sec,' she said, and closed the kitchen door.

'It can't be true,' said Colin. 'How do you know?'

'Chloe told me.'

Colin's shock soared. '*Chloe* told you?'

'She's in the Players. I got such a fright I dropped the kettle and splashed boiling water on my foot.'

'Christ! Are you okay?'

'It stings but I'm fine.'

'What the hell is he doing back now?'

'No idea.'

'He must be pushing 70.'

'He's joined the theatre group. Colin, he's acting in a play with Chloe. You've got to help me. I can't believe this is happening.'

'Is he in the Puffing Billy play?'

'Yes, in their next show.'

'Jesus, I'll be working with him.'

There was a long pause before Simone spoke.

'Colin? Are you there?'

'Yeah, still here.'

'What can we do?'

'He must think he's been forgotten.'

'He hasn't, not by me.'

'Or me. Does Chloe know?'

'No, and she must never know.'

They both took a breather. Then Simone remembered. 'Of course; his mother died. It was in the local rag. Long-time Selby resident Harriett Devine died aged 96.'

'She's left him the house.'

Another pause as both continued in shock. Something in their past, something terrible, had been pushed aside, and remained repressed for decades—until now. Now it raised its ugly head and boy was it ugly.

Simone struggled to breathe. 'I've just had a terrible thought.'

'Don't say it. Don't even think it,' almost ordered Colin.

Simone couldn't help herself. 'But what if she likes him? What if he still does what he did before?'

'Simone, stop!'

'What if he seduces his own daughter?'

She collapsed on the floor, and fought to mute her screams and wails. She must never wake Chloe, or let her see her mother like this.

Colin was beside himself. His hatred for Devine mingled with his concern for Simone. He yelled into the phone.

'Simone? Simone?' She couldn't hear him such was her despair. He ended the call and sent a text.

I'm on my way.

He ran out of his house leaving his dog Brunel barking. Colin raced back and released him. Brunel fancied a midnight adventure. They piled into Colin's car and drove to Simone's house in Belgrave.

'Now be quiet,' Colin warned his dog. They walked to Simone's back door where she waited. All three sat in the kitchen with the doors closed, and Brunel on his best behaviour.

Simone's face was a mess. She'd stopped crying but the after effects of the shocking news were clearly visible.

'I'd make a cuppa but I'm scared to boil the kettle,' she whimpered.

'Forget it,' said Colin. 'What do you want to do?'

Simone had confided in Colin, because Colin had once confided in her. Both shared a burden, two separate horrible events in their lives, both caused by Larry Devine.

He had seduced the teenage Simone and fathered Chloe. Simone's parents wanted the whole thing covered up and sent Simone to her uncle's farm outside Benalla in rural Victoria. Chloe was born in the Benalla Hospital. Simone refused to say who the father was, chose to keep her baby daughter, and never spoke to her parents again. Larry departed for Tassie not knowing he became a father.

Colin's younger sister, Brenda, had learning difficulties, a condition once described as being simple. Larry got her pregnant. The distraught girl had an abortion, and was so distressed she finished up in a secure facility where she later killed herself. Larry knew nothing of this.

It was easy to understand why Simone and Colin loathed Larry.

Colin was angry but more worried about his friend. 'Simone?'

She was distressed. 'What?'

'I said what do you want to do?'

'What I've always wanted to do,' she replied, 'kill the bastard.'

There was a long pause before Colin spoke without feeling.

'Okay, let's do it.'

Simone's jaw dropped as she stared at Colin. Brunel didn't like the silence and barked. Both adults immediately shushed the canine. He wasn't used to reprimands in stereo, and fell silent.

'Colin, are you serious?'

'Too bloody right I am. If he thinks he can waltz in here and start where he left off, then of course I'm serious. He trashed your life, mine and others, and while destroying people's lives is one thing, coming back here and rubbing our noses in it is way too fucking far.' He looked a tad sheepish. 'Apologies for the language.'

'No apology needed.'

They fell into thinking. Brunel grew nervous.

Simone spoke. 'We shouldn't even think about killing someone.'

'What, you don't want him dead?'

'I do but I'd like him to suffer first.'

'Too easy,' said Colin. 'Listen, I've got a plan.'

On the same night that Chloe told her mother about Larry Devine, Nina did pretty much the same thing to Jason Bartholomew. Nina was the wardrobe mistress for the Belgrave Players, and Jason the technician who looked after lighting and sound.

Jason was 25 and lived with his divorced mother, Heather. Nina was 56 and lived with a house full of cats. She got a lift to and from rehearsals with Jason. They pulled up outside her home and, instead of thanking Jason and hopping out, she didn't move. He looked at her.

'We need to talk,' she said, and Jason switched off the engine. He was surprised and a little worried. This was not like Nina.

'Is something wrong?'

'That new actor, Larry Devine, I know him, knew him years ago.'

Jason waited for more information. It didn't come.

'And?'

'I'm not sure I should be telling you this. I've thought about it and I'm in a real mess.'

'Did he do something ... not nice?' Nina nodded. She was struggling. 'Well, with due respect Nina, that's really none of my business. I mean, if you want a good listener, that's fine but ...'

'He did something nasty to you too.'

Jason stopped. He stared at Nina. The silence continued.

'Are you going to tell me?' he asked.

She nodded then began. 'A long time ago, Larry Devine lived here in the Hills. He was a sweet talker and I fell for his charms. I was 16 and my strict parents told me I was never to see him. I did and my parents threw me out. He told me he wanted to marry me but Lothario Larry the Liar wasn't called that for nothing. He dumped me and moved on to someone else. No big deal; it happens all the time. But in my case, my father disowned me and my mother, bless her, did as she was told.'

'That must have been really tough,' said Jason.

'It was. My parents died and I missed both funerals.'

27

'I'm sorry.' He wondered what else she would say. 'What are you going to do? Will you stay with the company? Has he spoken to you?'

She laughed. 'He wouldn't know me from Adam. Jason, it was 40 years ago. I was pretty then. Look at me now.'

Jason struggled to reply. Nina was the cat woman of the Hills. Her long hair was streaked with grey, she never wore make-up, and her homemade clothes were functional, speckled with cat fur, and hid whatever body shape existed beneath them.

'So what has Larry Devine done to me?'

Nina didn't speak. Jason was thinking. His parents divorced when he was a baby. He never knew his father. He twigged.

'My parents?'

Nina nodded. 'They split because Larry had an affair with your mother.' More silence. 'I couldn't bear it if you told your Mum about the wonderful new actor and she heard his name from you.' The same silence returned. 'I hate hurting you but even more, I couldn't bear your mother being hurt.'

'It's okay, Nina, and thanks.' He thought aloud. 'I've wondered why Mum has these bouts of depression, why she won't talk about my father, and maybe now I know.'

'Your poor mother was devastated when your father left. I know she loved him and her guilt must have been horrendous. Of course it takes two to tango, but why would Devine seduce a happily married young woman. He did it for fun, because he could. He didn't care who he hurt. And she blamed herself for robbing you of a father. Now, out of the blue, back comes the cause of her misery.'

There were deep breaths from Jason. 'I'll have to tell Mum.'

There were deep breaths from Nina. 'It's your decision but you don't want her to hear it from someone else.'

'Is there anyone else in the company who might be affected?' Nina didn't answer. 'Nina?'

She nodded. 'Larry's victims know their soulmates.'

'So?'

'If I tell you, you must promise to never say a word. Promise?'

'I promise.'

Nina hesitated. 'People Larry has hurt have shared their secrets over the years. Chloe doesn't know this but Larry Devine is her father.'

Metaphorically, Nina slapped Jason in the face. He gasped.

'But I've seen them laughing and joking, fooling around at rehearsals.'

'The thought of them fooling around doesn't bear thinking about.'

Jason twigged. 'Bloody hell.'

'I can't imagine how Simone will react when she finds out that bastard is not only back in the Hills, but in the same company as her daughter, *their* daughter.'

'Jesus,' gasped Jason. He fancied Chloe but thought she was far too beautiful and classy for him, a Mr Average lighting geek.

They sat in silence. Talk about a major news story.

'Would you like me to tell your mother?'

'No. Thanks for the offer but I think I should do this on my own.'

'Tell her you heard about Larry from me. She'll understand. I hope.' She paused. 'I'd better be going.'

He was still in shock. 'What are you going to do?'

'Something I've always wanted to do—kill Larry Devine.'

Jason imitated a goldfish. Nina pointed to his open mouth.

'Now you promised you wouldn't tell anyone about what I've told you. Jason?'

'I won't.

'Promise?'

'Why would I tell anyone? I'm going to help you kill him.'

5

'YOU CAN SIT IN, DETECTIVE.' Jo was shocked. Hughes gave the new homicide detective, the opportunity to be part of an interview with a key person in what was probably a double homicide. What a break. Baldwin winked at Jo and Payne clenched his fists and stood.

'I'd like a word, Sarge?'

'Certainly Detective. Just the one?'

'In private.'

'The answer's the same, Stephen. I choose who sits in on interviews, with Billy's decision being final, and no constable's correspondence being entered into. Is that all?'

Payne fumed.

Hughes set off, calling. 'This way Senior, and bring your notebook.'

Outside the interview room, Jo worried. Hughes gave instructions. 'I talk, you observe. Take notes if you wish but your role is to listen and learn. Understood?'

'Yes, and thank you, Sergeant.'

Hughes snapped. 'I told you, it's Sarge or Billy.'

Jo nodded and entered the interview room for the first time as a homicide detective.

Gavin Hall was 32, a few years older than Jo, and hard to read. His parents were dead, both probably murdered, yet their only child exhibited little emotion. There was no sadness or gladness from Gavin. Jo wondered about badness. *Cold fish comes to mind. Is he involved?*

Hughes ran the show. 'Thank you for coming in, Mr Hall. I'd like to begin by expressing our condolences in this tragic situation.'

He didn't speak, only nodded.

'This interview is to establish what, if anything, you may know about the death of your parents. We appreciate your cooperation and you may leave at any time. If you wish to have a solicitor present ...'

'I'm fine,' he interrupted. 'Could we get on? I have two funerals to arrange and God only knows what else.'

Hughes paused. Jo admired her calmness. 'Of course.' Another pause. 'Can you think of anyone who may have wished to harm your parents?'

'No.'

He was firm, she was patient, and asked the question another way.

'Do you know of any enemies your parents may have had?

'No.'

Jo thought Hughes was subtly building pressure on Hall. 'How would you describe your relationship with your parents?'

'Strained.'

'Would you care to elaborate?'

'I'm gay, Sergeant, or as my parents would say,' he checked himself, '*used* to say, homosexual. To my father that was unnatural, and to my mother, daylight robbery.'

'Robbery?' asked Hughes.

'I'm an only child and have robbed my mother of the chance to become a grandmother.'

'But surely with same sex marriage and surrogate births, men can marry and even have children?'

'My parents bitterly opposed those things. They were proud voting *No* at the referendum on same-sex marriage.'

Hughes remained calm and professional. Jo enjoyed her style and filed it for future reference. Hughes tried another tack. 'When did you last see your parents?'

'I last saw them alive the day before they died.'

'When would that be, exactly?'

'Exactly, in the afternoon of the day before their bodies were discovered.'

'And where did you see them?'

'At their home.'

'And they were well?'

'Perfectly,' replied the son.

'And what was the purpose of your visit?'

'Habit. Despite our strained relationship, I continued to visit my parents ever since I moved out of home.'

'Even though you say you didn't get on?'

'Sergeant, please, you must know about the thickness of blood and water. The fact that my parents disapproved of my sexual orientation didn't stop them loving their son, or me loving them in return.'

Hughes half-smiled and again changed tack.

'Did your parents have a happy marriage?'

'Define happy marriage.'

Jo was fascinated. If this man was involved in murder, he sure had a way of making a detective's life hard.

'Were your parents abusive to one another?'

'Never.'

'What time did you leave your parent's home after your last visit?'

'About four as I collected my boyfriend in Fitzroy around five.'

'And can you account for your movements from then until 7 am the next day?'

'Account for your movements? Detective Sergeant, I think you've been watching re-runs of *Frost* and *Inspector Morse*.'

Jo watched Hughes out of the corner of her eye. Would Billy snap? She did a nice line in anger and sarcasm. No, Billy didn't even blink. Hall surrendered.

'All right, we went home, I cooked, we watched TV and went to bed. We share a bed, and both are light sleepers. Would you like further details or would that be too much information?'

She ignored his jibes. 'And you remained at home until you left at what time?'

'A cab took me to the airport for a 7.30 am flight to Sydney.'

Jo couldn't think of any questions and wondered where Hughes would go next. Then someone knocked on the door, and Baldwin entered and handed Hughes a sheet of paper.

'Just arrived, Sarge,' he said, smiled at Jo and left. Payne would've snarled. Hughes read the document then handed it to Jo.

'Mr Hall, what do you know about your mother's jewellery?'

He shrugged. 'She had a lot but what it looked like, I'm not sure.'

'Do you know a Mr Benny Ross?'

'I'm related to a Benny Ross. His father and my father are cousins.'

'And what do you know about the television reception in your parents' home.'

Hall mocked her. 'Really Sergeant, is there a prize for the right answer?'

Hughes gave a forced smile, announced the end of the interview, and turned off the recording machine. 'Thank you, Mr Hall. We'll be in touch when we need to speak to you again.'

They all stood.

'Is that it?' he asked.

'For now, sir. Detective Senior Constable Best will show you out.'

Walking to the exit, Jo studied the witness. He was short and wiry. Neither spoke until they reached the public entrance.

'Thank you for your time, Mr Hall.'

He said nothing and left. Jo didn't know if this behaviour was caused by grief, guilt or rudeness. She returned to the incident room.

A display board had photos of various people with names, dates and comments. There were detectives present Jo had yet to meet. When they called it a Squad, they meant it. Her favourite detective, DI Pierre Richelieu, got the ball rolling.

'Mesdames et Messieurs, s'il vous plaît,' he said indicating chairs.

Detectives took their seats and Jo found herself beside DSC Payne. *Bugger.* The room fell quiet and DI Steele slipped in and observed.

'New information, ladies and gentlemen,' said Richelieu. 'Two possible leads. First, a male cousin of the deceased man 'as been arrested for trying to sell jewellery known to belong to the dead woman, and second, last week, local uniform were called to the Elsternwick property by the deceased 'usband because of an altercation with a local tradesman.'

'What happened?' asked Hughes.

'A television antennae tradesman claimed Monsieur 'all refused to pay for work done. Said tradesman confronted Monsieur 'all who called police when the visitor allegedly threatened violence.'

Payne was his usual sarcastic self. 'So a tradie who's owed a few bucks bypasses VCAT and commits a double murder? Are we serious?'

'Thank you, DSC Payne,' said Richelieu. 'What news from Dr Strange and Forensics?' This was Payne's responsibility.

33

'Her preliminary report says the wife was suffocated by a pillow, and the husband died of a heart attack which may be suspicious.'

'Suspicious, how?' asked Hughes.

'He took something which was not his usual medication. The good doctor is running further tests but believes the drug he took is one likely to cause rather than prevent a heart attack.'

Richelieu summed up what others were thinking. 'So if 'e took the wrong drug deliberately then murder/suicide comes into play. If someone gave 'im the wrong drug, we 'ave a double 'omicide, ...'

'N'est-ce pas?' said several detectives on song, beating the DI to his usual comment.

Jo twigged. The DI was being gently mocked. She was starting to enjoy her new appointment. Richelieu ignored the stirrers and turned to Hughes. 'Your interview, Sergeant.'

'Yes, Senior Constable Best and I interviewed the son, Gavin Hall. He was at the house on the Sunday afternoon but has an alibi for the time thereafter. We are yet to interview his boyfriend.'

'So,' said Richelieu, 'we need a background on the TV technician, an interview of the cousin with the stolen jewels, and more work on the son and 'is friend.'

'Boyfriend,' said Payne.

Richelieu ignored him. 'Merci ladies and gentlemen. Crack on ...'

Several detectives spoke as one. '... s'il vous plaît .'

Jo laughed inside at the way her colleagues sent up the DI. What made him more attractive was the fact that he didn't seem to mind, in fact, took it as a sign of respect. Jo was having a good first day.

So far.

The main meeting broke up, and Hughes' trio of Senior Constables gathered around Mother Hen who allocated tasks.

'Charley, take some uniforms and follow up any leads from the house-to-house, and interview the pawnbroker who reported the stolen jewels. Stephen, get everything on the TV technician and the incident involving uniform.'

He whinged. 'But I've got the PM and Forensics.'

'Detective, you know I give the toughest tasks to my best officers.'

He knew she was being sarcastic, and hated her more. That hatred catapulted towards dangerous levels with her next comment.

'And Jo, you're with me to interview the boyfriend and the cousin.'

They broke up and Jo followed her sergeant until a voice stopped the women in their tracks.

'Senior Constable Best, a word.' DI Grant Steele waited.

'I'll meet you at the car,' said Hughes and she and the others left. Jo moved respectfully towards her boss. She didn't know what to say, so opted for silence.

Steele was neither tall nor short. His haircuts, tie knots and bowel movements were measured by theodolite. He was a man on the move with promotion his raison d'etre. His success came from qualifications, experience and ability, and a fourth ingredient, knowing his rivals. Being able to stymie, stall or side-track a rival was a major skill of this Homicide heavy. He had a contrived smile and produced it for Jo.

'I've not had the chance to officially welcome you to Homicide, Detective Senior Constable.'

'Thank you, sir.'

'I admit to being surprised at your recommendation having heard reports of your interview.' Jo felt sick. 'You arrived in a dishevelled state with a ruined uniform, and chaotic hair. You failed to recognize the most senior female officer in the Force, and wandered the building looking like a tart from a sleazy pub.'

'I do apologise sir, and can explain.'

'I expect my officers to look the part, Detective, and to prove their worth through exemplary policing and behaviour.'

Jo didn't know what to say. She settled for, 'Yes sir.'

He looked at her with an expression, a cross between distaste and dislike. 'You're on probation, Detective and that was your only warning. Next time, you're out.' He paused allowing his withering look to linger. 'Dismissed.'

6

SIMONE WAS SHAKING. It was breakfast time, the morning after she and Colin (and Brunel) discussed the appalling Larry Devine and his return to the Dandenongs.

Simone had struggled to sleep. There were issues far too important for any shut-eye. The man who ruined her life had suddenly returned, and now threatened her happiness—again. Worse, he was now a real threat to their daughter who didn't know Larry was her dad. Simone faced some tough decisions, her mind in turmoil.

Should she tell Chloe about Larry? Surely a child, now an adult, has the right to know the identity of her parents. And if Simone does spill the beans, how will Chloe react? Will she hate her mother? Will her love of theatre end knowing her father is standing next to her on stage?

But far worse was the possibility Larry might seduce Chloe. If she isn't told about her father, and lover-boy gets up to his old tricks, well, that just didn't bear thinking about.

Colin had suggested holding off telling Chloe for as long as possible. Simone remembered his words from last night.

'I've got a plan to get rid of that evil bastard, permanently. If it works, he'll never hurt anyone again and Chloe need never know her father was a rat.'

Simone was persuaded to say nothing to her daughter mainly because she couldn't bear telling Chloe the news.

She argued with Colin. 'Okay, but we need a plan to watch Chloe like a hawk at rehearsals and make sure Devine never gets her alone.'

'No problem. I know someone in the company who can be trusted.'

'Nina Rogers?'

'Of course, I forgot you victims stick together.'

'Every female who was hurt by Devine knows his other victims. It's a sort of silent community. We have an unwritten agreement never to talk about it.'

'Until he returns.'

Simone nodded. 'Until he returns.'

She made breakfast for her daughter. Soon Simone would drive Chloe to Belgrave station where she would catch the train to uni.

Chloe appeared. 'Morning,' she chirped and opened the fridge.

'Morning,' replied her mother with her back to her daughter.

'How's your foot, Mum?'

'It's fine.'

'Show me,' said Chloe bending for a better view.

'Chloe, don't fuss. The slipper helped. Eat your brekkie.'

Chloe drank her juice and tackled the toast her mother prepared.

'I had this really strange dream last night,' said Chloe.

Simone worried. 'Oh?'

'I heard voices and a dog barking then a strange car.'

'You've had too many late nights, young lady. When's your next rehearsal?'

'Sunday, and it's a long one. We do a full run and it's the first time the new guy gets to work with everyone.'

'What did you say his name was?'

'Larry, Larry something, I've forgotten but he's very good.'

Simone needed support. She leant on the bench as the stress became palpable. Chloe finished her breakfast and they left.

In the station carpark, Chloe kissed her mother. 'Bye Mum, see you tonight.' She ran for the train. Simone sat thinking, and was about to drive out when a car entered at a dangerous speed. Somebody running late was taking risks. The driver parked then trotted to the station.

Simone thought about giving him an earful and lowered her window. She froze. The driver in a hurry was one Larry Devine.

She hadn't seen him for ages, and even knowing he was back in the Dandenongs didn't make a difference. She knew him.

He shuffled to ensure he caught the train. For a second, Simone thought about driving straight at him. She put the automatic into Reverse and flattened the accelerator. She took her foot off the brake and her car jerked backwards.

37

At the last second, she slammed on the brake stopping just before hitting the now startled pedestrian.

'Hey!' he screamed fearing for his safety.

'Sorry,' mimed Simone with a hand wave to reinforce her apology. Actually, it was to hide her face. Wearing her sunnies, she felt sure he didn't recognise her. Why would he? Simone was one of dozens he humped and dumped, although not every union produced a child.

Larry would have had a few words but he was late and so hurried to catch the train. 'Oh God,' cried Simone, 'that's Chloe's train!'

She sort of relaxed when the train departed with an annoyed Mr Devine still on the platform.

Once home, and still trembling, Simone rang Colin.

'Good morning,' he said. 'Sleep well?'

'I've just seen him.'

'Who?'

'Devine.'

'What? Where?'

'At the station.'

'And?'

'I tried to kill him.'

Colin couldn't speak. When he did his voice was very soft. 'Did you?'

'No. I chickened out at the last second.'

'Stay there. I'm on my way.'

Brunel loved a ride in the car, and remembered Simone's place well. He was there a few hours ago. This time the dog was not under any barking restrictions.

Colin was desperate for news. 'What happened?'

Simone told him about her reversing routine in the station car park.

'And he didn't recognise you?'

'No chance.'

'Now listen, Simone, this is serious. I know you want him dead but the secret is to kill the bastard and not get caught.'

'I know.'

'We have to kill him in such a way the cops don't think it's murder.'

'If we kill him it *will* be murder.'

'But we make it look like an accident.'

Brunel was fascinated. He didn't understand all the words but reckoned his master had some amazing ideas.

'How do we do that?'

'I've got a plan.'

'I hope it's not one of Baldrick's cunning plans.'

'Ha, ha.'

'You do know that even talking about killing someone is conspiracy to murder.'

'Simone, if you don't want to do this, just say. I'll work alone.'

'No, no, I want to help you. I'm in.'

Simone remembered a part she played yonks ago in a play called *The Perfect Murder*. She wondered if she still had the script. Could they murder Devine and have it ruled an accident?

She cried silently. 'I should have told Chloe when she asked me.'

'Simone, what's done is done.' He stopped. A thought popped into his head. 'How old is Chloe?'

'Nineteen.'

'Well if Larry left thirty odd years ago ...'

'Oh please, I thought you knew. He came back for his father's funeral. He dropped into the theatre for old time's sake and met the desperate and dateless chorus girl.'

'No.'

'Yes. I was his final fling in the Hills.'

'Bugger me.'

'He probably would if you let him.'

'That man needs putting down. Who else has he fathered?'

'Don't ask. Years ago Chloe asked about her father, and I told her he was an itinerant musician I met at a drunken party, that we had a one-night stand, and I didn't even know his name.'

'You're a good liar.'

'She seemed to accept it. If she finds out about Devine, she'll hate me, and I'll lose her because I've kept quiet. She'll never forgive me.'

Her tear ducts got busy.

'Okay,' said Colin, 'let's take a deep breath here.'

Colin was no therapist. He was a damn good Puffing Billy guard but counselling weeping neighbours was not his bag. Simone couldn't stop crying. Brunel nuzzled her leg and became a perfect pal.

'Okay, here's my plan for the permanent removal of Larry Devine.' Simone wiped her face. 'I'll be in the guard's van. Somehow, on the return journey, I'll get Larry into the van, probably at Menzies Creek. I'll say he got drunk and attacked me. He opened the van to push me out. Luckily I came to and as we crossed the Monbulk trestle, I defended myself, we fought and he fell.' Simone gasped. 'Lothario Larry became Leaping Larry and it was rack off Romeo.'

'That won't fool the cops. Why would he jump?'

'He doesn't jump, he falls. I saw him. And of course you trust the longest-serving guard on Puffing Billy—Mr Reliable. The man who fell was evil, drunk, showing off, inexperienced, and trying to kill me. It was an accident.'

Simone shook her head. 'What if the fall doesn't kill him?'

'I'm glad you asked that question. Waiting below in her horseless carriage will be a certain lady, ready to accidentally run over the unfortunate man who just suddenly fell from the sky. The driver had no chance to avoid the falling object.'

'That's me?' He nodded.

A miserable Simone looked at him. She was thinking.

'So,' asked Colin, 'are we good to go?'

Simone stared back and held his gaze for some time. She nodded and said one word. 'Yes.'

Brunel wagged his tail. 'Great plan, Dad,' he barked.

7

THE BOYFRIEND opened the door. He was not expecting callers and certainly not two female Homicide Squad detectives. He was caught napping, figuratively and literally.

'Bradley Finch?' asked the senior detective.

'Yes.'

Both women produced their ID. Jo was rapt to have her own.

'I'm Detective Sergeant Hughes and this is Detective Senior Constable Best. We're from the Homicide Squad and making enquiries into the death of Mr David Hall and his wife, Larissa. I believe you know their son, Gavin.'

Bradley was nervous. 'Yes, he lives here, he's my boyfriend.'

'May we come in?'

Reluctant was a good word to describe Mr Finch. 'Do I have to?'

'Do you have to what, sir?'

Jo was interested in the man's body language, and wished she'd studied the topic to a greater degree.

'Talk to you. I never met Gavin's parents, and know nothing about their murders.'

'Who said they were murdered?'

Flustered replaced *reluctant*.

'Ah, I heard it on the news.' He gained some strength. 'And I assume Homicide Squad detectives don't investigate stolen cars.'

'Actually we do sometimes; we're ambidextrous.' He didn't react. 'Look Mr Finch,' said Hughes, 'your partner gave us a statement about his recent movements. We need to confirm those details. We can ask you the questions inside your apartment, or down at the police station. Which do you prefer?'

'You'd better come in,' he said without a skerrick of hospitality.

Jo knew her place. Listen and observe. But this was a new location. She wasn't in a police interview room. She tried her look-and-remember routine. This stemmed from a game she played as a kid. A dozen or so objects were placed on a tray and covered with a tea towel. The cloth was removed for a few seconds then the tray taken away after which the players would write as many objects as possible from memory. Jo played the game now. She subtly looked around then made a note of all she could remember. It looked like she was taking notes. She was but not from the interview.

Hughes went through a list of questions. They were all "open" giving the interviewee the opportunity to explain. 'Gavin told us he picked you up last Sunday afternoon.'

'He did.'

'What time was that?'

'About 5.'

'And where did you meet?'

'Brunswick Street oval. I play football and that's our home ground.'

'Soccer or Aussie Rules?'

'Aussie Rules.'

'So are you a star defender, midfielder or champion goal sneak?'

Jo absorbed her colleague's routine. Gone was the list of prepared questions. Now it was a friendly chat, and Hughes obviously knew the topic well enough to ask relevant questions. She was impressive.

'I'm a defender.'

'And I'm guessing Gavin's an onballer.'

Bradley scoffed. 'You're joking, he hates football.'

Effortlessly Hughes resumed the real questioning with a brilliant segway. 'And did he hate his parents?'

'Did he ever?' Suddenly Bradley wished he could take that back. Gavin had given strict instructions. 'Tell the cops nothing and even less about my parents.'

Hughes paused. Jo was impressed.

The woman is brilliant. She softened him up, hit him with a sucker punch then left him to stew in his own mess. What a teacher. I need to learn these techniques.

Bradley tried to recover. 'Look, as I said, I never met the parents. Gavin had problems because they couldn't accept he was gay.'

'We know that, Mr Finch, Gavin told us.' Bradley could have kicked himself. 'And we appreciate your helping us and him.' She turned to Jo. 'I think that's all we need to ask, Mr Finch, unless my colleague has a question.'

Wow, there's a change. *Listen and learn* had suddenly become, *join the party, Jo.*

She was thrown but soon settled. 'So who's the entertainer?'

Bradley looked confused and even Hughes was baffled. Jo pointed to a book on the coffee table.

'*Ventriloquism for Dummies*,' she said.

'Oh that's Gavin. He's been doing it for years.'

'Is he any good?'

Bradley nodded. 'Actually he is, seriously good.'

'And who's the art collector?' She nodded at the paintings.

'That's me.' He was proud and upbeat. 'I plan to open a gallery.'

'Good luck,' said Jo and looked at her boss, giving a small nod.

They were becoming a team. They stood and went to the door.

Hughes spoke. 'Thanks again, Mr Finch. We'll let you know of any developments.'

They left and Bradley closed the door.

What will I tell Gavin? Will I tell Gavin?

Driving back to HQ, Hughes put Jo under pressure. 'Was he lying?'

Jo worried about being wrong or making a fool of herself.

'Not about the ventriloquist or being an art-lover.'

'I agree. Nice work, Detective. Now describe his body language.'

'Defensive.'

'Why?'

Jo hesitated. This had to be a test. *She takes me on as her partner after I've been in the job five minutes, and now tests me. Is she trying to help or find out if I'm any good?*

'The obvious reason being he has something to hide.'

'Such as?'

'He killed his lover's parents or is covering for his lover who did.'

'Why would either of them murder the victims?'

'Money—I guess Gavin stands to inherit the estate.'

'Or?'

This is a test. 'Revenge because the parents made Gavin's life hell over his sexual orientation.'

'But what about opportunity? Could one or both have done it?'

'Well if Dr Strange gave the correct time of death, and if the alibis Gavin and Bradley provide for one another cover that time, then they couldn't have killed the victims.'

'Be careful, Detective, you just used the naughty word twice.' Jo looked puzzled. 'If,' said Hughes and Jo understood.

She wanted to ask why she was replacing Baldwin or Payne, both of whom were more experienced, and why she was given responsible tasks and being tested. She said nothing. Then Hughes got Jo's pulse racing.

'We need to interview the cousin caught with the family jewels, so to speak.'

'Right, Sarge. Do you want me to sit in?'

'No, I want you to lead the interview.'

Bloody hell.

Benny Ross was a loser. He didn't have the ambition to make a go of anything. He had the opportunity but shunned it in favour of being selfish. When his parents finally gave up on their lazy son, he turned to petty crime. He had a record for shoplifting, drug possession and handling stolen goods. When a pawnbroker contacted police after Benny tried to sell some of his newly-acquired loot, his name loomed large in the homicide investigation. Being caught with jewels owned by his father's cousin's wife, now murdered, was par for the course for Benny, and a potential nail in his conviction coffin.

Mind you, this was a step up for the young man. Fines and suspended sentences wouldn't be on offer for a double homicide.

Jo was nervous. Leading an interview while still wet behind the ears got her blood pumping. She studied her notes and thought.

Remember what Pop told me about talking to suspects. Remember how DS Hughes operates.

'Mr Ross,' she began after the preliminaries were completed, 'you were arrested in possession of some items of jewellery. How did you obtain them?'

'I found them.'

'Where?'

'In my squat.'

'Where in your squat?'

'I can't remember. I was stoned.'

'Mr Ross, do you know David and Larissa Hall of Trent Avenue, Elsternwick?'

'Yeah.'

'How do you know them?'

'We're related. I think he's my old man's cousin.'

'Have you ever been to their home?'

'A few times.'

'When were you last at their home?'

'No idea.'

'Was it last Sunday?'

Hughes cleared her throat, and Jo hesitated. She knew it was the wrong question, and thought madly about correcting her mistake.

'Mr Ross, can you account for your movements from 8.30 pm last Sunday?' Hughes sighed, ever so slightly, and Jo knew she'd goofed again. Hughes had recently made the same mistake of using technical language.

Jo remembered. 'Where were you at 8 o'clock last Sunday night?'

'No idea. Where were you?'

Jo abandoned her notes and leaned closer to the suspect.

'A word of advice, Mr Ross. David and Larissa Hall are dead in suspicious circumstances and you were arrested trying to sell some of Mrs Hall's jewellery. I suggest you take this interview seriously. Murder is a big step up from selling weed or bent gear.' She stared at him and he stared back. 'Now where were you last Sunday at 8.30 pm?'

'I'm saying nothing without a solicitor.'

Hughes said little as they walked to the incident room. Jo thought she did okay but didn't have the courage to ask. Hughes talked about future questions, including the shoes Forensic Services found in the squat. Jo was tempted to mention her theory about the unusual footprints but backed off because Benny looked so guilty.

The incident room was filling up and Jo made sure she didn't sit next to DSC Payne.

The Gallic gendarme took control. His tailor was clearly at the top of his or her game.

'Mesdames et Messieurs,' he began.

Without thinking, Jo found herself joining in. 'S'il vous plaît.' Nobody laughed. It was a routine response.

The meeting began with Hughes reporting on her interview with Bradley Finch. Then Payne reported on his interview with TV technician, Graham James.

'James claims David Hall telephoned him complaining about his TV reception. They discussed solutions and agreed on a particular antenna and price. James performed the work when Mr Hall and his wife were away for a week. The cleaning woman let him in. Mr Hall refused to pay for the work claiming to have never ordered it. The cleaner remembered James being at the house. After three unpaid invoices, James confronted Mr Hall. The alleged incident from the police report is that James assaulted, read "pushed", Hall and threatened him physical harm—Hall's words. James has no alibi for the Sunday night and police records show he was convicted of assault many years ago—a brawl on the beach at Lorne. And that's all folks.'

Richelieu took over. 'Thank you, DSC Payne. Questions or comments, anyone?' Silence. 'Now DS Hughes, your interview with the suspect found in possession of stolen jewellery, s'il vous plaît.'

'That interview was conducted by DSC Best,' said Hughes.

A stunned silence hit the room. A babe in arms, a child, a novice detective with no experience in homicide cases led the interview of a major suspect. A soft murmur covered the sound of Payne grinding his teeth.

Jo was nervous. Every officer in the room stared at her. DI Steele slipped in just as she was about to speak. No pressure then. Jo began.

'The suspect, Benny Ross, is the son of Mr Hall's cousin, George Ross. The suspect is unemployed, lives in a Brunswick squat, and has convictions for shoplifting and drug offences. He admits to having visited the Hall house several times for family gatherings, says he found the stolen jewellery, and has refused to provide an alibi for the evening when the victims were murdered.'

'We don't know they were both murdered,' snapped Payne.

Jo hesitated. She wasn't rattled but felt increasing pressure to fail.

'Please continue, Detective,' said Richelieu, 's'il vous plaît.'

Jo could see the finishing line. 'When asked to explain his whereabouts on the night in question, the suspect refused to answer and requested a solicitor.' Jo looked at the many faces looking at her. 'The interview concluded and the suspect was returned to custody.'

'Merci, DSC Best. Questions or comments anyone?'

There was a pause and then Hughes spoke. 'Of the three suspects we have, the son and his boyfriend, the TV technician, and Benny Ross, the lead runner has to be Ross. As soon as his solicitor arrives, Ross will be further interviewed. We're waiting for a drug analysis from the male victim, and for a soil analysis from shoes found in the squat of Benny Ross.'

More silence until the head honcho spoke from the back of the room. Steele didn't stand but his tone of voice was "seen" by everyone.

'I would suggest, DS Hughes, that for such an important suspect in what appears to be a double murder, an experienced officer should lead all future interviews.'

'Sir,' said Hughes. Jo squirmed.

Other officers gave more information before the meeting ended.

Jo felt terrible. She hadn't asked to accompany Hughes or to conduct the interview with Ross. Yet she felt belittled in front of the squad simply for following orders. No comment on whether or not she did a good job, just, go back to mundane duties.

Are they testing me? Are they setting me up for a fall?

8

JO HAD AN INTERESTING FAMILY. Her older sister Caitlyn was married with two kids. Jo and Caitlyn's parents, Malcolm and Shirley, were divorced. Malcolm re-married a much younger woman, Natalie, and they had two kids so Malcolm had four children with 20 years between the two pairs. Caitlyn's two kids were about the same age as Malcolm's two youngsters and his grandkids played with his own kids. It sounded tricky and looked interesting on the family tree. Caitlyn was the same age as Natalie, her stepmother, and they were best buddies.

Shirley called Malcolm, her ex, Malcolm X. She thought it was funny and in her miserable existence, black comedy appealed. Shirley was 59, divorced, lonely and lived alone in her home in Balwyn North.

Caitlyn took advantage of Shirley's loneliness and used her mother as a regular babysitter. Grandma was unaware of Caitlyn being chummy with Malcolm X's bimbo (Shirley's words) or that Shirley's grandkids got on famously with Malcolm X's current wife's kids.

Jo knew this but was sworn to secrecy. 'Don't ever tell Mum,' said big sister Caitlyn and Jo trod on eggshells when chatting to her Ma.

So as the unhappy Shirley grew older and bitter, her first daughter and her ex-husband's child bride did the ladies-who-lunch routine in upmarket eateries in Kew, Hawthorn and Canterbury.

Jo rang her mother regularly but was not all that big on home visits. Being a cop and working shifts including the dreaded graveyard shift, made it tricky for Jo to just drop in on Mum. They were close but not that close. And when Jo followed in Shirley's father's footsteps and joined Homicide, the champagne remained corked in Balwyn North.

'Well if that's what you want, Joanna,' said her mother, 'then I hope it works out for you. Nothing new on the boyfriend front I suppose?'

'Now Mum,' replied Jo. 'I told you, you'll be the first to know.'

Jo had a day to spare and chose to visit her Pop first before her mother. Robbo was all over Jo's new job and asked questions non-stop. Jo delighted in his company and took great pleasure in seeing him so excited. You could see the pride in his eyes and in his smile.

The old man was doing it tough ever since his beloved wife was diagnosed with dementia. As fit as he was for an octogenarian, Pop simply couldn't look after his wife Ida who went into care. He visited every day and did what so many others do; he just got on with life. But a visit from his favourite granddaughter made his day. They laughed.

What a contrast then when Jo paid a visit to Pop's daughter. Jo rang her mother's doorbell.

'All right, I'm coming,' she muttered and opened the door.

'Hi Mum,' chirped Jo and closed the door following her mother into the lounge. Shirley accepted a kiss on her cheek and settled.

'How have you been, Mum?'

'The usual. I never complain because no-one ever listens.'

It was hard to believe Shirley was the daughter of the laugh-a-minute, laugh-out-loud John "Robbo" Robertson. "Misery-guts" would be a good moniker for Shirley Best.

The two women talked about everything and nothing with Jo careful to avoid any mention of her father and his second family.

It was traditional for Shirley to make tea for her daughter but this time she was reluctant to do so.

'Well, don't let me keep you, Joanna,' she said and stood to indicate the visit was over.

'What's wrong, Mum?' Her mother behaved strangely, even for her.

'I'm fine, just a little tired.' She wasn't. Blind Freddy could see that, and the promising detective spotted trouble a mile away.

'Mum, something's wrong. Now please, sit down and tell me.'

Shirley looked at Jo and for a moment thought about shouting. Then she collapsed. She dropped to her knees, scaring the life out of Jo who knelt and held her mother.

'Mum? Are you in pain? Where does it hurt?'

The only answer Shirley gave was a wail, a long continuous wail with tears as an added extra. It was pathetic with the wretchedly sad mother comforted by her confused and now terrified daughter.

Jo knew her mother suffered badly because of the divorce. Shirley hated herself. She watched Malcolm X take a young and beautiful—

49

well, quite attractive—new bride, and have children. She couldn't match that offer.

It was so unfair. She was in the First Wives' Club as a loser. There was no silver lining for Shirley. She would never be snapped up by any youthful French President. If lucky, she might grab an elderly pensioner with cataracts and an enlarged prostate.

Living alone, she suffered in silence and the misery of her loneliness built pressure by the day—by the hour. She had nobody to confide in, and her pride became a fortress. When Jo confronted her in a kind and concerned way, she crumbled.

Eventually Shirley stopped the waterworks, and managed to sit on the settee with Jo beside her.

'Now listen, Mum. Don't you ever do that again. Do you hear me?'

Shirley needed a good dressing down. Feeling sorry for herself was selfish and self-destructive. Jo decided her mother needed tough love. Sister Caitlyn would never act like this. Shirley saw a side to her younger daughter she knew existed but had rarely seen. She squeezed Jo's hand and whispered, 'Thank you.'

Jo hugged her and stood. 'I'll make the tea. Okay?' Shirley nodded.

In the kitchen, Jo saw the tray with the cups set out and the plate of biscuits all ready to go. She worried. Her mother had planned to do the usual thing but had suddenly changed her mind. Why? And what triggered that collapse and horrible wailing with waterworks?

Come on Detective Senior Constable Best, do your stuff.

Jo brought in the tray of tea and goodies and became "Mother", pouring the tea. The women sat and sipped.

Shirley found it hard to look at her daughter. She knew there would be an inquisition so chose to get in first.

'I'm sorry about before. I've been under a lot of stress of late and things just got the better of me.'

Jo knew her mother was hiding something but also knew that criticising Shirley would make her aggressive then defensive. Jo needed tact. She did what DS Hughes did with her interviewing technique. Jo said nothing.

Subtle pressure grew on Shirley. She was expecting a reprimand and none came. Instead, there was a change of subject.

'I had a really strange interview at Homicide. I told Pop and he couldn't stop laughing.'

Shirley was relieved to no longer be the focus of attention, and curious to know about Jo's interview. The full story was told including the Barbara Windsor *Carry On* costume disaster. Shirley even cracked a small smile. Jo's gentle style continued until she cut to the chase.

'Okay Mum, enough of the soft soaping. What's wrong?'

Shirley felt her anger kick in, and was about to explode when she surrendered. She wanted to surrender. She wanted to tell someone her secret. Shirley still couldn't look at her daughter but managed to speak.

'I've lost my money.'

That was it, no explanation, no histrionics, just a brief statement. Naturally, Jo wanted more.

'What do you mean? Have you made some bad investments? Oh Mum, don't tell me you've taken up gambling?'

Shirley spoke softly. 'I gave it away.'

Jo couldn't speak. Her mother was many things but never stupid or reckless. What the hell was going on?

'You gave it away? Why? Who to? When?' Jo sounded like a cop conducting an interview, only badly, and with suspect grammar.

Shirley forced herself to look at her daughter, and spoke without breaking eye contact. 'I've been scammed.'

Wow. Jo's mind went into overdrive. If she had to guess what news her mother would reveal, being scammed was not even on the list.

'Scammed?' Shirley nodded. 'You mean conned out of your money?' More nodding. 'How much, and please don't say all your money.'

Shirley's face became a wall of tears.

Jo put both their cups on the tray then gave her mother the strongest hug she could muster. Shirley sobbed. Neither spoke. The sobbing rose and fell. The length of their embrace might well have earned a mention in the *Guinness Book of Records*.

The lack of speech and the hug endured but eventually it was time to talk. Jo proved to be sensitive and supportive. Shirley found a new way to love her daughter. Once she recovered, Shirley was willing to speak but with a condition.

'I will tell you what happened, Joanna, but only after you promise you will never tell another living soul.'

'Of course, Mum.'

'No, none of this "of course, Mum" bit. I mean it. If you love me and care about me …'

'Mum,' protested Jo.

Shirley grew bolder and put some steel into her performance. 'If you love me and care about me, you will promise to tell no-one, and you will keep that promise as long as I'm alive.' There was a long pause. 'Well?' demanded Shirley.

Jo sucked in a big breath. 'I promise,' she said.

'Is that the word of a serving police officer?'

Jo sort of smiled and nodded. 'Yes, it is.'

'Your father thinks I'm a loser, and if he ever found out about this, it would prove his point.'

'Mum.'

'If ever you want to hurt me, Joanna, share my secret.'

'Why would I hurt the person I love with all my heart?'

Shirley breathed deeply, ached inside, and told all. She was brave to do so even to a trusted daughter. Her pride had taken a massive hit. Her self-esteem was in the gutter. She had fallen for the charms of a master scammer whose real name was Cornelius Kruger.

Shirley had no idea who he was and only knew that her nest egg, the money she got from her divorce, plus some savings she'd accumulated over the years, was no longer in her account. Of cash had she none.

Jo struggled with the news. Shock set in the more her mother revealed. Then Jo's police training took over.

'Right, Mum, what's your current financial situation?'

'What situation? I have no cash, and I'm too young for the pension. Selling this place is my only option.'

'Now let's not get ahead of ourselves. Okay, I'll make enquiries with Centrelink. Have you got any assets?'

'Only those shares my grandparents left me.'

'Give me the details and I'll get some financial advice for you.'

Shirley started to panic. 'I can't go back to work, I can't.'

'You won't have to.'

'I feel so ashamed.'

'Mum, you need cash right now. I can transfer a few hundred to your account.' Shirley froze. 'Have you closed it?'

She shook her head and began to weep. 'I've been too scared to do anything. They took the lot.'

'Oh God, I'm so sorry, Mum. Look, let's make a list of all the things you need to do. We'll tick them off one by one and get you sorted.'

Shirley cried even more. Having the daughter she was not always close to bending over backwards to help was a crushing yet rewarding feeling.

'Where would I be without you, Jo,' she cried.

As they hugged, Jo suddenly thought this was doubly strange. Her mother always called her Joanna but just then called her Jo.

They discussed the practicalities, and Jo drew up a list of things to do. She gave her mother all the cash she had in her wallet despite Shirley protesting. Jo promised to ring her later that day and keep her informed of what was happening.

Despite her tears and gratitude, Shirley couldn't resist a parting comment.

'Remember your promise, Joanna. Tell nobody.'

Jo gave her mother a final hug and left. At the gate, she turned and blew a kiss.

Wow! That was one hell of a visit.

9

FOR JO, IT WAS A NO-BRAINER. She would break the promise she made to her mother. Of course she wouldn't tell her father or sister or anyone connected with her family. But she would quietly tell anyone who could help her retrieve her mother's money.

Although a busy Homicide Squad detective, Jo decided to start a second job, an unpaid and secretive job as a private investigator, and find the scammer who ripped off her Mum.

How would she do it? Jo had no idea, only a determination to find the stolen money and return it to Shirley Best of Balwyn North.

First, Jo did as promised and helped her mother establish a new bank account then transferred $500 of her own money.

On the phone, Shirley said, 'I will pay you back, Joanna, every last cent.'

'Fine, Mum, but first let's get you back on your feet.'

Jo checked on the price of the shares Shirley held and helped her mother sell half of them. Now Shirley had several months of financial security to pay for food, utilities and petrol. She still cried but more from relief.

It's true that a trouble shared is a trouble halved.

Jo trusted DSC Charley Baldwin, and asked for advice.

'A friend of mine has been scammed and needs help. I know nothing about fraud and wondered if you knew anyone in the Force who might give me advice for my friend?'

'Advice to do what? Take the law into his own hands?'

'Actually he's a she and is 87 with a dodgy hip. No, I just want to explain how the police might help.' Jo was already lying.

Baldwin gave Jo the name of a detective in the Fraud and Extortion Squad. 'DS Harry Dale knows everyone in the world of computer fraud and money laundering, and is a really nice bloke.'

Jo produced her warmest smile. 'Thanks Charley, and I warn you I'm a big fan of reciprocity, so feel free to ask a favour, anytime.'

In her lunchtime, Jo went to the Fraud and Extortion Squad—in the same building as the Homicide Squad—and met DS Harry Dale. Baldwin was right. Harry did seem to know everything and everyone in the world of the illegal movement of money, and boy, did he know how to smile. Jo put her cards on the table referring to her elderly friend with the gammy leg.

'Is there someone I could chat to, from the legal side of things, who knows about hacking and scams?'

'Michael Chan's your man,' said Harry. 'He's quiet and unassuming, but don't let the shyness fool you. Mike knows more about the digital world than all the geeks in Melbourne combined.'

'He sounds brilliant.'

'His number is ...' Harry scrolled to find a number on his phone and showed it to Jo. She tapped it into her mobile.

'That's great, DS Dale.'

'Harry,' he said holding out his hand.

'Thanks Harry, and I'm Jo,' she replied as they shook. It seemed to last a second or two longer than normal. Jo wanted to mention reciprocity but felt a tad uneasy.

On the way back to her office, she rang Michael Chan. He answered after one ring.

'Michael Chan.'

Jo was thrown. 'Oh, hello. Mr Chan, my name's Jo Best, and I've been given your name and number by DS Harry Dale in the Fraud and Extortion Squad.'

'Yes?'

DS Dale was right. Michael Chan was not loquacious.

'Ah,' said Jo struggling to find the right words. 'I need some advice about tracing money online.'

'Have you been scammed?'

Jo was shocked. 'I'm not sure I wish to discuss this over the phone. Could we meet and discuss the situation in private? I'm happy to pay for your time.'

'When and where?'

'Oh,' said Jo again. 'Is tonight convenient?'

'What time?'

'Ah, 8 o'clock?'

'4 Holden Court, Northcote. Enter on the South side. Come alone.'

Jo heard a dial tone. 'Interesting,' she said, and went back to work.

That night she took 10 minutes to drive to the Northcote address, and another 10 minutes to find a park. She walked along the side of what was a converted warehouse with subtle lighting coming on as she moved. The light over the door might well have been used in the street scene outside Richard Hannay's apartment in *The 39 Steps*.

She couldn't find a knocker, bell or buzzer. She prepared to use her knuckles when the door opened.

'I'm Michael,' said the youngish geek. He looked Chinese and sounded Australian.

'Hi. I'm Jo Best.'

'Come in Detective Senior Constable Joanna Claire Best of the Victoria Police Homicide Squad.'

Jo froze. 'Right.' She peered inside. 'No metal detector then?'

Michael smiled, nothing expansive or in danger of lighting up a room, just a glimpse of his pearly whites.

The interior was huge, open-plan, sparsely furnished and spotless, and dominated by a wall of hi-tech equipment. Jo found the space and its owner welcoming, and sat on a firm settee.

'Thank you for agreeing to see me.' He nodded and remained standing. 'I was led to believe you are the best in the business but clearly you were undersold.'

There was no reaction from her host. 'I can offer you Green, Herbal or Chamomile Tea; Espresso, Mocha or Latte Coffee; or Mountain Spring or au natural Northcote tap water; or we can get straight down to business.'

'Thank you, I'll ... no, let's crack on.' He sat opposite her on a single firm chair. His body seemed as firm as the furniture.

'Before we start,' said Jo, 'may I ask how much you charge?'

'For this meeting, the initial consultation, it's gratis.'

Jo kept being shocked or surprised by what she heard. 'Wow, thank you, that's very generous.'

'Are you the victim of the scam, Detective?'

Yet again, his forthright questions or statements threw her. Talk about cutting to the chase.

'Look I'm sorry to seem uncooperative but I would like this meeting to be private.' She looked at him and waited.

'Apart from you, me and my cat, Alan, there's nobody here, and no recording will be made of our discussion. If anyone blabs about this meeting, it'll be you. And Alan no longer works for MI6.'

Jo exhaled. 'Thank you, Mr Chan. Thank you very much.'

'Please explain your situation.'

She did, telling the sorry saga of Shirley and her missing money. Michael said nothing. When she finished, he nodded and put pressure on his visitor.

'What do you want me to do?'

'Ah, perhaps I should have started with that.' He waited for her to speak. He reminded Jo of DS Hughes. 'Normally, Mr Chan, I should report the incident to my colleagues in the hope they would catch the scammers. However, a major sticking point is the victim. My mother has made me promise to never mention her loss to anyone.'

'A promise you have quickly broken.'

'Yes, so now you know I'm a person who doesn't keep her word.'

'And someone who clearly loves her mother.'

Jo stalled. That she did not expect. 'Ah, yes.'

'I repeat, what do you want me to do?'

Jo took another big breath. 'Mr Chan, I would like to engage your services to help me find the scammer who robbed my mother.'

'I can do that. But what will you do if you find the scammer?'

'I haven't quite figured that out as yet.'

'Do you have a plan?'

'I do. Well, an idea.'

'Which is?'

'Can I ask if you've read a book called *The Count of Monte Christo*?'

'By Alexander Dumas, yes, I have.'

Jo felt good. 'Great. Then you'll know that Edmund Dantès was, let's say, scammed, but got his revenge by scamming his scammers.'

'An interesting synopsis,' replied Michael. 'So rather than have the police lock up your offender, you want to become a criminal and retrieve your mother's money by stealing it back from the thief?'

Jo hesitated. He was spot on.

'I really do hope this is a private meeting.'

'Alan won't blab.'

'Alan?'

'Named after Mr Turing OBE, and who only speaks Meow.'

Jo thought she understood most of that and continued.

'So, I have two questions, Mr Chan. Will you help me with at least stage one of my project? And if so, how much do you charge?'

He looked at her. Jo's heart had been beating fast ever since she arrived. Now her pulse gave her Fit Bit a fright. He answered.

'Yes and nothing.'

Jo's brain got busy. *Say that again.*

This meeting had been full of surprises but the latest comment was jaw-dropping—literally.

'I'm sorry,' she gulped, 'but are you saying you'll help me try and find my mother's scammer, and not charge for your services?'

'That is correct, Detective Senior Constable but there is a condition.'

'Ah, the small print.' Jo regretted that comment. 'I'm sorry, that was impolite.' She thought of the Billy Hughes technique. 'Please continue.'

'We're in the same boat, so to speak. My father was defrauded in a business transaction. Unlike your mother, my father knows who is responsible but, like your mother, has ordered his son to never mention it or do anything about it.'

Jo continued to be amazed. 'I see.'

'The condition I request is that after I try and help you find your mother's scammer, you will try and help me recover my father's lost cash. Do you agree?'

Jo didn't hesitate. 'I agree, and thank you again for your generosity.'

'Thank you, Detective. I will accept your word.'

'Please do. I always keep my promises.'

'Except when dealing with your mother.'

She grimaced and nodded. 'Touché.'

A silence settled in the room. For Jo it was a brilliant result. Her optimism level shot skywards although not for long.

'You do realise, we'll require a third member of the team.' Jo was puzzled. 'I have IT skills, and you are a trained police officer, but unless you're hiding your light under a bushel, I'm guessing you have no experience in running a scam. I don't, so we'll need a scammer.'

Jo hadn't thought it through. 'Of course,' she said.

'The *Monte Christo* approach is great but Edmund Dantès was clever and created the scams. Let's say we identify the scammer. How do we get the cash? What's the scam? In short, we ain't fraudsters.'

'You're right. I have no experience with scams.' She reflected. 'Originally I thought about obtaining evidence to blackmail them.'

Michael laughed for the first time. 'And you're the police.' She looked blank. 'The men who defrauded my father, and I'm sure the scammers who tricked your mother, are not Sunday School teachers. If you try to blackmail them, they'll blow up your car, disembowel your cat, and rip off your bloody arms and *then* they'll get angry.'

Jo grimaced.

Of course. I'm a fool. Just find and arrest them.

'I really do like your *Monte Christo* solution.' Jo brightened. 'With a brilliant scam and evidence of them being sucked in, you may get your money back and scare them into hiding.'

'I don't follow.'

'A scammer being filmed being scammed will die if that goes viral, and, at the risk of blowing my own trumpet, I do a very good viral. If your idea works, plastic surgeons will do a roaring trade creating new identities for crooks who'll never show their current face in public again. It's a fantastic idea, Detective Best.' Jo buzzed with happiness. 'But you don't just need a scam. You need a brilliant one.'

Jo looked at him. She was back to being miserable. Michael was her key to success, and he was prepared to work for nothing. Okay, she would have to work for him later for nothing but …

'You need a smart criminal, Detective, a reformed scammer. Anyone spring to mind?'

Jo slumped. She was enthusiastic but ill prepared. She desperately wanted to help her mother but knew if she called in the cops and they arrested the scammers, Shirley may never get her money, and Jo would hurt, even lose her mother. No, this had to be done on the sly. But how? Without a scammer, the project was dead.

'You work with crooks,' he said. 'Find yourself a double-agent.'

He stood, indicating the meeting had ended. He spoke as she followed him to the door. 'You've got my number. Tell me when the criminal mastermind's on board.'

He opened the door for her but didn't offer his hand.

'Thanks, Mr Chan,' she said.

'Call me Michael. Not Mick, Mike or Mikey; Michael.'

'You've been kind and very helpful, Michael.'

'You're welcome, Joanna.'

'Jo's fine.'

'You're welcome, Jo's fine,' he said and produced that murmur of a smile. 'I'll look for your two-word text—*Monte Christo.*'

She liked his dry humour, and his mini smile. She stepped into the light from *The 39 Steps*. Robert Donat was nowhere to be seen.

10

BENNY ROSS WAS IN TROUBLE. His Legal Aid solicitor had never represented a client suspected of homicide, let alone two. Forensic Services had produced a report on the trainers found in Benny's squat. Soil analysis results matched the soil on the shoes with the soil in the Elsternwick garden, and Benny, silly Benny, had admitted the shoes were his.

Richelieu sat in on the interview led by Hughes. He was there to satisfy DI Steele.

Hughes began. 'Mr Ross, the trainers we found at your squat, which you have admitted belong to you, contain dirt which matches the soil found in the Hall garden. Can you explain that?'

'No comment.' Benny had a new script and was word perfect.

'We found footprints in the Hall garden which match your trainers. Can you explain that?'

'No comment.'

'The jewellery you tried to sell has been identified as belonging to Mrs Larissa Hall, who was murdered last Sunday. How did you obtain that jewellery?'

'I told you, I found it.'

The solicitor tapped Benny on the arm, and when the suspect looked at him, the solicitor shook his head.

'No comment,' said Benny.

'I haven't asked you a question yet,' said Hughes.

'No comment,' said Benny.

'Where were you last Sunday night?'

'No comment.'

The detectives looked at one another. It was time to call it a day. The recording was stopped, and the detectives prepared to leave.

'That's all for now, Mr Ross. You'll be returned to your cell. We'll need to interview you again on this matter.'

The solicitor interrupted. 'Detective Sergeant, I'd like to discuss the matter of my client's bail.'

'Would you now?' Hughes stood, which gave her a psychological advantage. 'Your client, sir, is a suspect in a homicide, possibly a double homicide, and refuses to answer reasonable questions, any questions. That's his right but these are serious matters with evidence needing an explanation. You can raise the bail issue but I'd hazard a guess your chances of success are zero or less.'

Benny scowled, and his solicitor couldn't think what to say next.

Jo quietly fumed. Her new assignment involved a visit to Dr Gabrielle Strange, the pathetic pathologist, which in itself was terrific, but alas Jo travelled in the company of her bête noir, DSC Stephen Payne.

The conversation in the car was minimal. A mutual dislike existed between the pair with Payne's feelings closer to hatred. Jo's attitude was only in response to his rudeness. She tried to clear the air.

'Look, Stephen, I'm not sure what I've done to annoy you but if we have to work together, can we at least be professional?'

'Not sure what you've done? Are you kidding?'

'No, I'm not. Please enlighten me.'

'Some of us took ten years to crack the Homicide Squad. Some of us skipped uni and went to the school of hard knocks. And some of us never had a family member running the joint. That's what pisses me off, DSC Best.' Jo said nothing. 'You got preferential treatment, Missy. They want more women and rumour is you fit the bill. It's talent and ability outscored by gender and nepotism. That's what gets right up my fucking nose.'

Again, Jo said nothing. At least she now knew his motivation.

When they arrived, Dr Strange turned on the charm.

'Ah, it's my favourite detective, and the "look what the cat's dragged in" officer. How are you Detective Payne? How's your paranoia?'

He ignored her comments. 'I understand you finally have some worthwhile information, madam.' He painted the last word with the colour of rudeness.

'Oh dear, I'm afraid you're still confusing 41 minute episodes of CSI with the real world, Stephen.' He hated her using his first name. 'Here, on planet Earth, chummy, we still can't resolve tricky scientific questions during the ad breaks. Now ...'

She looked for documents while Payne stewed, and Jo decided this mad woman was way better than wonderful. Strange spoke.

'I can tell you that Mr Hall is either a silly sausage or terribly unlucky. His blood contained significant traces of cocaine, which I suggest triggered his heart attack. The PM records his death due to a massive myocardial infarction, quote unquote.'

Payne knew everything. 'So he smothered his wife then did a line of coke to celebrate.'

'Possible. What reckon ye, O deranged detective?'

Jo smiled and Payne felt they were speaking a foreign language.

'Being a beginner, Dr Strange, I fear my opinion is of no importance and has even less truth.'

'Well said, girlie. I predict a brilliant career in Homicide.'

'Anything on the jewels?' asked Payne.

'We're still checking the DNA.' Payne sighed. 'CSI, Stephen, you're watching too much CSI.' He fumed and Jo loved the banter. 'You do know,' said the pathologist, 'you can identify the jewellery from her insurance company?'

Duh. What a fool was he? Payne had no come back. A simple check would have given the answer in minutes. Berating Forensics only made him look a bigger fool.

'From the PM,' said Strange, 'I have a feeling the person who smothered Mrs Hall is left-handed. The victim's hands were raised above her chest, like so, with her right hand in a stronger defensive position. I suggest a pillow was placed over the victim then removed after the killing. With the murderer on top, more pressure from the left. And that, folks, is about your lot. So, cuppa anyone?'

Jo was about to gleefully accept when Payne jumped in.

'We can't stay. Thank you, Doctor, we'll see ourselves out.'

He took off leaving Jo to shrug and mouth, "Next time" before trying to catch up with her colleague.

In the car he told her to follow up the Hall's insurance file, and get copies of photos of Mrs Hall's jewellery. He didn't say please. He never said please.

They continued in silence until Jo decided to have one more crack at smoking the peace pipe.

'Look, Stephen, I never asked to accompany DS Hughes, and I certainly never asked to lead the interview in the station.'

'I believe you,' replied Payne. Jo felt marginally better. 'Millions wouldn't but I do.'

Sarcastic prick.

Jo gave up.

11

COLIN GRUBB WORRIED. He was 72 and had never murdered anyone. But now with a plan to kill Larry Devine, he worried. Would it work? Would he be charged? Could he get away with it?

He shared his plan with Simone. He had to; she was his partner in crime. Could she be trusted? Would she blab? And if his plan succeeded, would she crack and spill the beans? He needed advice from the only person he felt would never blab.

Nina Waters lived up to her title of Cat Woman of the Hills. She was a vegan, never put out any garbage, and when the weather turned cold, simply added more clothes—homemade of course.

She never bought a cat because people brought them to her or else they wandered in having read about her generous terms and conditions on the *Crazy Cat Women* website.

Colin hadn't been to Nina's house for years. They occasionally bumped into one another in the main drag in Belgrave and that was about it. They knew each other through Larry Devine but with the womaniser interstate, there was no need for them to meet.

Nina's garden had returned to the wild, and the local CFA (Country Fire Authority) warned her about the risks her vegetation posed should the Dandenongs catch fire.

Colin knocked. The door opened and the aroma produced by a clowder of cats tickled his nostrils.

'Oh, it's you,' said Nina. 'Why am I not surprised?' She walked back into the house calling, 'and shut the door properly this time.'

Colin entered remembering his last visit, a while ago, when his failure to close the door properly resulted in several moggies taking up exploring the outside world. Disaster was averted but it's true; you can't herd cats.

'Sit wherever,' she said moving a large Russian Blue. Colin wasn't courageous, and sat on an ancient artefact.

'So you've heard,' she said.

'Simone told me. She's really upset.'

'Understandable now the bastard has joined the Players.'

'That's why I'm here. Can you do a spot of guard duty, and keep Chloe away from Devine?'

'It's all in hand. I've even got back-up from Jason.'

'Jason?'

Nina explained about Jason and his divorced parents.

'Okay, two guards are good.'

Both hesitated. Both had discussed the idea of murdering Larry with their respective co-conspirators but neither wanted to broach the subject with a third party.

Colin spoke first. 'So what do think we should do?'

'Not sure. You?'

'Not sure. I thought we'd seen the last of him.'

'Pity the lynch mob never got to him while he was still here.'

'True, but they would've just made threats and given him a slap.'

'I heard he's moved back permanently.'

Colin exhaled. 'I worry people'll get hurt. Chloe's the worst example. What will she say or do if she finds out Devine's her old man?' Nina fell silent. 'Simone's terrified Chloe will never speak to her again because she's never told her daughter the truth.'

'It's tricky,' said Nina. 'If I had my way, I'd kill the bastard.'

Colin blurted his response. 'Me too.'

They stared at one another. Did the other person mean that? Would they do that? Did they have a plan? Yep. Were they prepared to talk about it? Nope.

Colin changed the subject. 'I thought I'd come to rehearsals and give you a hand with protecting Chloe.'

'Fine, but how will you explain being there?'

'I'll come as a Puffing Billy person, offering to tell any new actors how the train part of the evening works.'

'But that would mean meeting Devine.'

'He met me once about 40 years ago. And it'll give me a chance to soften him up ...' Colin panicked.

'Soften him up?' Nina was more than interested. 'For what?'

Colin was about to say, 'Before I push him off the train at the Monbulk Creek bridge', but stopped just in time. He bluffed.

'I want to get close to the man, win his trust, and maybe he'll tell me something we can use to nail him.'

'To a cross, I hope.'

Colin grimaced. Nina wasn't convinced. She reckoned Colin was up to something. He thought the same about her. It was obvious they both hated Devine, and with a vengeance. They tiptoed around the topic before Colin stood to leave.

'When's the next rehearsal?'

'Sunday.'

'Okay, I'll see you then.'

'Gladstone,' called Nina, as a ginger cat tried to sneak out with the disappearing visitor. Gladstone didn't make it.

Colin arrived with the rehearsal in full swing. He watched. He immediately understood Simone's concern. Larry was standing beside Chloe and the two were laughing about a line that went wrong.

The director called, 'Take five,' and people relaxed. Larry headed off to the *Gents* and Colin, who had a waterworks issue himself, wondered if the great seducer had a prostate problem. Mother Nature might be the way to stop his sexual escapades.

Nina took Colin to meet the director, and the two men chatted. Rehearsals resumed and, when it was time for coffee, Colin was introduced, and company members who had never been involved with the train mystery were invited to meet the man from Puffing Billy.

A middle-aged woman and Larry were the only actors not previously involved with the play on the train. Colin got rid of the woman, politely, and turned on the charm with Larry.

'So how long have you been with Puffing Billy?' asked Lothario.

'Not as long as you've been acting. Watching your skills, mate; you must have been doing it forever.'

Larry lapped up the flattery. Colin kept the man he planned to kill talking throughout the coffee break. They parted as best buddies.

'Nice meeting you, Larry,' said Colin.

'Likewise,' replied Larry, who had already forgotten Colin's name.

'See you on the train next week.'

Larry gave a thumbs up and returned to the actors. He wasn't required to rehearse so sidled up to Chloe. They chatted to one side. Three "guards" watched and listened—Nina, Jason and now, Colin. They couldn't hear every word but those they did caused alarm.

'So what's your second name, Chloe,' asked Larry?

'Redmond,' she said, without a trace of suspicion.

'Redmond, Redmond,' he muttered trying to remember where he'd heard the name before. 'What's your Dad's name?'

Chloe stalled. She threw away her reply. 'Not sure. I never knew my father.'

'Really?'

'Yeah, my Mum said he was an itinerant muso, and they had a brief affair, and then he was gone.'

'That's sad.' He paused and studied her features. 'What's your Mum's name?'

'Chloe,' called Nina in an almost too loud a voice, 'can you try on this dress, please?'

Nina and the other "guards" were suffering big time. Larry's questions were getting way too close to the truth. The conversation had to be stopped, there and then. Chloe went off for a costume fitting and Larry had a flash of memory go ping in the back of his brain.

Would he get to ask Chloe any more questions? Who was her mother? And who was the itinerant musician who fathered this gorgeous girl?

Chloe survived the night.

After rehearsal, Jason drove Nina home with Chloe in the back seat. She protested that it was too far out of Jason's way but it had to be done. There was no way Simone would be dropping into rehearsals to collect her daughter with the "itinerant musician" there. Simone told her daughter she felt unwell. 'Ask that lighting guy,' she said.

So Chloe was dropped at home then Jason set off with Nina. Alone in the car, they were free to talk.

'That was a close call,' said Jason. 'I think you interrupted Larry just in time.'

'He was asking about her mother.'

'What was that Puffing Billy guy doing there?'

'Talking to the new people about the train.'

Jason reckoned Nina was not being honest with him. She held back not wanting to involve him in her murder plot in case things went pear-shaped. Her thinking was clear.

He can't lie about what he doesn't know.

They arrived at ailurophile HQ. Nina looked worried so Jason switched off the engine. They sat in silence.

Nina broke it. 'Did you tell your Mum about Devine?'

Jason spoke in a soft voice. 'Yes.'

Nina paused and dropped her volume too. 'And?'

Jason remembered the distress the news caused his beloved mother. 'She went all quiet and has hardly spoken since.'

Nina took a deep breath. 'I'm sorry.' More silence. 'I'm sure she's not angry with you.'

'If Devine remains in the Hills, I think my Mum will leave or ... die of a broken heart.'

Nina was shocked. She believed Jason was sincere and worse, speaking the truth. That last remark was the tipping point. Larry Devine had to exit stage left—permanently. She looked at Jason. Tears meandered down his cheeks.

She spoke. 'You once said you were going to help me kill him. Did you mean that?' He looked at her. 'Have you got a plan?' He nodded. 'Can I help?'

Jason recovered and explained his ideas. Plan A was to have Larry accidentally electrocuted during the play. The more he thought about it the more difficult it seemed. Plan B was to push Larry off the moving train. Jason hadn't figured how or where yet but to make sure the womaniser didn't survive the fall, someone had to perform the coup de grâce. Nina volunteered. They discussed possible dropping off points.

Poor Larry; now he had two hit squads gunning for him.

12

THE HOMICIDE INCIDENT ROOM was packed. For the two deaths in Elsternwick, many interviews had been conducted and all reports received. Jo was not confident about speaking, not even to ask questions. She just observed, sitting as far from Payne as possible.

Amazingly, she'd been right in the thick of the investigation until Steele stepped in. He wasn't having an officer still wet behind the ears, involved with important interviews, any interviews.

For God's sake, he thought, *she was even the lead interviewer of the main suspect. Ridiculous.*

So Jo was put on follow-up duties, checking statements and collecting data from the pathetic pathologist.

'Mesdames et messieurs,' began Richelieu with the well-worn automatic response from the gathering.

'S'il vous plaît.'

'I believe we 'ave all scientific reports, and interviews of suspects are now complete. Perhaps it is time to charge some dastardly villain.'

'Or villains,' called someone at the back.

'Detective Sergeant, will you kindly begin?'

Billy spoke in front of the incident board. 'Dr Strange informs us that Mrs Hall was suffocated almost certainly when she was asleep. She had a large dose of sleeping tablets in her system making her resistance weak. We don't know if she took them deliberately. We do know Mr Hall died of a major heart attack. He suffered from heart problems, and his medication was intact with no foreign prints on the container or in the bathroom. However, Dr Strange found a significant amount of cocaine in his body, and Forensics found a small amount of cocaine hidden in a bathroom cabinet. However, proving both victims were drugged could be difficult.'

'Impossible,' said a detective at the back.

'Comments or questions so far?' asked the French DI.

Payne wanted the attention. 'Do we know if they had any money or marriage problems?'

'The Halls were well off and, according to their son, friends and neighbours, were happily married,' replied Hughes. 'Everyone we spoke to said Mr Hall was the last person to take illegal drugs.'

Baldwin spoke. 'For someone with a heart condition, if cocaine is likely to cause a heart attack then the victim committed suicide or was tricked into taking the drug and thus murdered.'

Silence around the room. Baldwin's relevant comments didn't bring the detectives any closer to who killed or may have killed the couple.

Hughes indicated photos on the board and continued.

'Graham James, the TV tech, got a phone call from Mr Hall. He did the work as directed and had access to the house via the housekeeper. When James confronted the victim over non-payment, James said the man he went to see was the man he spoke to on the phone. James admitted pushing Mr Hall in a heated argument, and has no alibi for the night in question. He strongly denies any suggestion of murder.'

Payne boasted. 'He has a conviction for affray.'

'As a young tearaway, decades ago,' added Hughes.

'And Monsieur Jewel Thief?' asked Richelieu.

Hughes tapped a photo. 'Benjamin "Benny" Ross remains in custody. He was caught trying to sell jewels belonging to Mrs Hall. He's related to the victims, and been in the house several times. His trainers had traces of the soil from where we believe the break-in took place. Ross has convictions for dealing, and handling stolen goods. He's in debt and has no alibi for the night in question.'

Hughes took a breather. Baldwin commented.

'I cannot accept James is involved. You don't murder two people for a debt of $400—you take it to VCAT.'

'Which leaves the son and 'is flat mate,' said Richelieu.

Hughes explained. 'The son admits he and his parents didn't get on but both the son and his partner have given the other an alibi. On this evidence, Benny Ross alone remains in the frame.'

DI Steele, at the back of the room, gave an order. 'Charge him.'

'Sir?' Hughes was unsure.

71

'Caught with stolen property, no alibi, in debt, drug addict, his shoes with soil from the scene of crime, and has form. Open and shut.'

'I agree it looks damning, sir,' added Hughes.

Richelieu looked around the room. 'Anyone else?'

Jo spoke without thinking. 'Ross didn't do it.'

Wow. If silence can be loud, this was fortissimo. Jo felt she was living in a parallel universe.

Why did I speak? Look, I'm sorry, I didn't mean to say that.

'Senior Constable Best, you wish to elaborate?' Richelieu was afraid to ask knowing that the beginner detective had placed her head on the block, and further comment might well send the guillotine on its way.

Everyone stared at Jo. She knew she had to follow up. But in front of the entire squad, she just told the head of Homicide he was wrong.

'The footprints in the garden were not made by Ross.'

The stares continued. Steele was fuming. He did most things on the quiet and his current anger slipped into that description.

'Please explain, Detective,' said Richelieu.

'The impression is not even. It's as if a person with a smaller foot was wearing the shoes. Gavin Hall has quite small feet. I would guess a size 7. Ross has large feet about a 9 or 10.'

Hughes was impressed. She hadn't noted either men's feet. 'What about the boyfriend's feet?' asked Billy.

'Bigger,' said Jo, 'but not as large as the druggie's feet.'

Payne attacked. 'But the French windows are no longer used. The garden is overgrown and the steps not used. To force an entry, the person wearing the shoes had to stand on the balls of their feet to reach the handle; they couldn't stand flat-footed and work on the lock.'

Steele approved, again on the quiet. Payne gloated in public.

Jo thought about Payne's comment. She had a reply—*the first footprints are important*—but settled for a peace offering. 'Perhaps,' she said.

More silence broken by Richelieu. 'Well if that is all, ladies and gentlemen, we charge Monsieur Benny Ross. Merci and au revoir.'

Nobody spoke French. Nobody joked. Nobody spoke at all. Jo Best had challenged an order of the Head of the Homicide Squad and made a fool of herself. Brave woman. Or was she an idiot with a career death wish? Surely her days in Homicide were numbered.

13

THE LOCO STEAMED at the Belgrave station. It hissed, ready to pull the packed carriages of the Puffing Billy Murder Mystery Special. Period costume was encouraged and patrons posed in their 1920s finery. Hats laughed. Bowties boasted. It was a big night.

The cast and crew of the Belgrave Players looked spiffing in their costumes with Chloe a smidgeon above stunning. Jason lingered at the back, with mixed feelings. He was in love with Chloe, and in hate with Larry Devine, the man who broke his mother's heart.

The lothario considered Chloe a juicy plum, ripe for the plucking. Neither knew they were daddy and daughter.

The director gave his final pep talk. The loco's whistle pierced the night air, and with all aboard, Puffing Billy puffed into the night.

At the end of the train, in the guard's van, Colin began to sweat. He wiped his brow. Tonight would feature a pretend murder and a real murder. Colin had the lead role in the real murder. He wrote the script.

Simone Redmond, his co-conspirator, wasn't on the train. She fretted at home. Colin had gone over the murder plot many times. Simone had asked the same questions many times. Her sweating came in the form of shaky, sticky palms. She checked the train timetable for the umpteenth time.

'We leave Menzies Creek on the return leg at 2300,' said Colin. 'That means we'll cross the Monbulk Creek trestle at about 2315. Give yourself plenty of time to get into position.'

Elsewhere, Nina "Cat Woman" Waters gave her furry breed a lecture on behaving in her absence. She put her goodies in a cloth bag, threw it over her shoulder, and wheeled her ancient bicycle through the garden jungle to the road. With no light, no helmet, and no sense of direction, she started riding, well wobbling, the wrong way. She

73

realised, tried to turn, and fell off. As a possible killer's assistant, she would never have *assassin* listed on her CV. Finally, Nina began pedalling in the right direction. On the train, her partner stressed.

Jason rode in a carriage with the actors who chatted to patrons. It was all part of the play. A tasty entrée was served as the train chugged through the darkness of the Dandenongs. Could the patrons guess the murderer at this early stage of the night? None of them guessed that the audio guy was planning a real murder.

The train stopped at Menzies Creek for a pit stop and both Jason and Colin stepped out to stretch their legs. In fact, both were surveying the surrounds, going over their respective plans, due to click into gear on the return journey.

The main event kicked off in the former packing shed at Nobelius. Here the carvery meant fine fare as patrons dined in style. The actors continued to mingle, dropping hints, and answering questions, always still in character. Whodunit? What a night.

Jason handled his technician's role to perfection although his heart rate was far higher than normal.

Colin dined with the footplate crew, and made an effort to be as normal and natural as possible.

'You're a bit quiet, tonight, Grubby,' said driver Harry Styles. 'Got something on your mind?'

Murder, thought Colin but laughed off the question. 'Pass the salt, mate,' he quipped.

Then it was time. The play was a roaring success. The food and drink first-class, and patrons loved solving the murder mystery, including those who were wrong in picking whodunit. And the actors had a ball, particularly Lothario Larry. Despite his senior years, Larry was rarin' to get back into live theatre and a bit of "how's your father?"

The locomotive sounded her whistle. She was champing at the regulator, and with full bellies and bladders, the company and patrons boarded the train. On the return trip, they enjoyed tea or coffee, chocolates, and even a glass of port. What a night. What could top it? How about a *real* murder?

The train reached Menzies Creek station for the final pit stop. People headed for the facilities. Colin opened the door of the guard's van and stepped down beside the track. He looked for a particular passenger and, in looking, failed to notice someone hiding in the shadows.

People laughed, chatted and headed back to the train. Colin spotted his man. Larry was gushing over a middle-aged female patron.

Colin waved and called. 'Oi, Larry, over here.'

As Larry's chat-up charm was proving ineffective, he joined Colin. 'Did you enjoy my performance, mate?'

Colin lied with panache. He hadn't even seen the play. 'Brilliant mate, you were absolutely sensational.'

Colin worried. *Am I trying too hard?*

Larry slapped his new fan. 'Thanks, buddy.' He still couldn't remember Colin's name. 'Listen, I'd better get back on board.'

This was it. Cometh the hour, cometh the man about to commit murder. Colin popped the question.

'Fancy a ride in the guard's van?' This surprised Larry. 'We can have a wee snifter on the final leg.'

A measure of how far Larry's sex drive had diminished was the fact he accepted immediately. Once upon a time, he would have ignored Colin and been hot on the trail of a bit of skirt.

The shadowy figure in the darkness heard the conversation and took off.

'You're on,' said Larry, and Colin, now with a faster heartbeat, helped the deluded thespian into the van. Then disaster. Colin was about to close the van door when Larry spotted someone. He waved.

'Hey! Chloe, over here.'

To Colin's horror, the teenager bounced up to the van, accepted Larry's hand, and climbed aboard.

'What's happening?' she beamed.

'What's happening, my gorgeous leading lady, is that you and me is having a party right here in the guard's van.' Larry's syntax was never a patch on his lovemaking.

He gave Chloe a squeeze, and Colin entered a dark place. His sweating became a chill. The train whistle shrieked, and Colin had no choice but to shut the van door as the train chuffed towards Belgrave. The driver gave the regulator its head and the train raced along at a magnificent 9 mph.

What a fiasco. Colin's murder plot collapsed. All that planning ruined in a second. The girl he was trying to save from the wicked womaniser was now helping save the life of said villain. Was this fate? It was more like a nightmare.

Colin tried to resolve the matter. *Can I still kill the bastard? How? With Chloe here, the plan will never work.*

Puffing Billy trundled towards the Monbulk Creek trestle bridge. Beneath the bridge, Nina crouched in the bush, her bag of tricks at the ready. Fifty metres up the road, Simone sat in her car, trembling.

'Where's that drink, buddy,' demanded Larry? He hugged Chloe.

'Ah,' began Colin, 'maybe not with the young lady aboard.'

'What? The beautiful Chloe deserves a drink. Don't you, darling?'

'Well, perhaps a little one,' she replied worrying about her mother.

Colin added fear to his discombobulation. There were powerful spirits in his flask. He wanted Larry to be intoxicated before he departed the van but giving the powerful brew to Chloe, a teenager with little experience of alcohol, was plain wrong. Mind you, morality was not Colin's strong suit right now as he prepared to break the sixth of the Ten Commandments.

'Come on, give it here,' demanded Larry, and Colin reluctantly handed him the flask.

'It's powerful stuff,' said Colin, 'go easy, especially you, young Chloe.'

'We'll be fine,' grinned Mr Lascivious, as he removed the top of the flask and pushed it at Chloe. 'After you, my love.'

Chloe took a small swig and spat out the powerful liquid. 'Yuk,' she spluttered, never having tasted such a brew.

'Don't waste it, Babe,' cried Larry, who grabbed the flask and took a strong swig. He shook his head. 'Bloody hell, that's got a kick.' He offered the flask to Chloe. 'Go on, have another shot.'

Colin stepped forward reaching for the flask. 'Come on, Larry, it's too strong for the girl.'

Larry took umbrage. 'Listen, pal, you invited us to this party so don't come the wet blanket routine.'

Colin made another grab for the flask. Larry pulled back his hand spilling some of the grog which splashed on Larry's coat. He wasn't happy. 'Hey! Now look what you've done.'

Colin was pleased. The smell and presence of alcohol on Larry's clothes would support the case for the victim being drunk when he fell from the moving train. Colin suddenly became excited.

'Hey! Listen, listen to me. We're coming to the most photographed railway bridge in Victoria. You get a fantastic view of the Monbulk Creek trestle from right here in the van.'

'A bridge?' scoffed Larry.

'Is it really famous?' asked Chloe.

Colin delivered his sales pitch. 'People come from all over the world to photograph this setting, and what a view you'll get as the train crosses the bridge.'

Larry scoffed. 'It's dark, mate, pitch black.'

Colin got the flask back and did the hard sell. 'Ah, but the lights from the train plus tonight's moonlight will give you a spectacular view.' He produced his phone. 'I can take a photo of you, Larry; you and the famous bridge. You can put it on Facebook, mate.'

'Yes, Larry,' said Chloe, all excited. 'You'll be famous, it'll go viral.'

Larry wasn't sure. He didn't want publicity but he sure liked the idea of the lovely Chloe being a part of his life.

'Okay, me and Chloe.'

'No,' snapped Colin in a panic. 'The angle's too tight for two people.'

Larry wouldn't have a bar of that. 'Listen mate, I want my favourite girl with me in the photo.'

'Okay,' replied Colin. 'Let's do one of you, one of Chloe and then one of the both of you.'

Larry wavered but agreed. 'So how do we do it?'

Colin moved towards the van door. 'Move back, we don't want anyone falling out now, do we?'

Like hell we don't.

The others stepped back and Colin opened the van door. The bush came alive and waved to the passengers. Colin peered into the darkness. He knew almost every tree on this line. The majestic trestle bridge was two minutes away. He stepped towards the back of the van.

'Okay, Larry, just lean against the frame there.' Colin pointed and Larry moved then stopped.

'No,' he said, 'ladies first. Come on, Chloe.'

Colin died. He lost control. Chloe was nervous. Larry held her as she moved to the open door and stood against the frame with her back to the locomotive. The train swayed and she grabbed the leading man.

Below the bridge, Nina and Simone heard the train. Its ear-splitting whistle told the possums to stay in their trees and away from the snorting iron horse. Neither woman knew the other was there.

The women endured massive stress levels. Simone had no idea her daughter was in the middle of the murder scene. Simone's mental state would be off-the-chart if she knew Chloe was hugging the man who ruined Simone's life, and was with the would-be murder victim seconds before he was due to die. Nina checked her phone. Jason was to ring her when Larry got the push.

In the van, Colin looked at Chloe through his phone. She shivered.

'Grab the door, Chloe and turn a little towards the bridge,' he said moving closer. 'I'll get your profile as well as the famous bridge.'

Chloe turned and Colin snapped. 'Great,' he said, 'now Larry.'

Larry grabbed Chloe as she moved back into the van. 'No, I want the two of us in the photo.'

He held her tight and moved to the open doorway. The bush was close enough to touch. Ferns peeked in. The bridge drew closer. Colin panicked. He had to get Chloe out of the picture. Larry hugged her, placing the girl close to the open door. She was the one in danger.

'Go on, take it,' yelled Larry. Chloe became scared. She wanted to move back inside the van.

'Smile Babe,' cried Larry as Chloe started to struggle. She thought she was going to fall from the moving train. She *was* going to fall. As the couple teetered and the van swayed, a ferocious roar erupted.

'No!' screamed the voice. The others froze as Jason, who had sneaked aboard at Menzies Creek and crouched, hidden behind a crate, leapt out to save his girl. Well, the girl he fancied.

This was about where but not how Jason planned to dispose of Larry. Murderers must be flexible. *Carpe diem*, Jason. Once he offloaded Larry, Jason was to have Nina cycle to the spot.

Trying to save Chloe, Jason grabbed Larry. He, having almost shat himself when a lunatic stranger appeared roaring and attacking him, released Chloe to defend himself. Bugger the bird. He and Jason got stuck in. Colin, who couldn't remember his Plan B or C, froze.

Chloe scampered back into the van as the young and old guys struggled. Indiana Jones would have known what to do but Colin didn't fancy climbing on the roof of the van for a fight scene.

The train swayed, throwing the brawling blokes back inside then back towards the laughing bush. The ferns, who had never seen such entertainment, were in hysterics.

Larry chopped Jason's arms. The men separated. Larry kicked Jason's leg. As the audio man grimaced, Larry took advantage of the break in play and shoved Jason. He lost his balance, staggered towards the open door, grabbed the side of the van and just managed to stop himself from falling.

Chloe screamed in disbelief. Colin moved to save Jason but Larry got there first and kicked Jason in his privates—the 12 o'clock position. His eyes watered. His face was a smorgasbord of emotions—agony, failure, fear and unrequited love. One arm did a bird impersonation. He wanted to yell but couldn't. The others watched, hooked on his performance. What a finish as he disappeared backwards into the bracken and ferns of the Dandenongs. Chloe's screaming got louder.

The Monbulk Creek trestle bridge hove into view. Larry breathed heavily. Chloe was distraught and Colin decided to play the hero.

'You bastard,' he screamed, and went for Larry. The womaniser had up a full head of steam, just like the locomotive, as smoke poured from its chimney. The famous bridge drew closer.

Larry had knocked off one attacker tonight, a young buck, so fancied his chance of a brace with his latest opponent, a pensioner. Colin stumbled and fell. Larry bent and shoved him towards the van door. Colin, on his knees, scrambled to recover. He couldn't stand. Colin grabbed the frame of the van but then had no free hands to fight Larry. The momentum edged him towards an early departure.

Chloe couldn't believe her eyes. Larry aimed a kick at Colin's face. It missed but crashed into Colin's shoulder. He started to lose his grip.

The sound made by the wheels changed. The train was on the bridge. Colin clung to the van for dear life. His feet were over the edge.

Terrified to let go of the frame, Colin was at Larry's mercy. The lothario wound up a final kick. Colin flattened himself to minimize the blow. Larry's leg started its journey. Chloe screamed and launched herself. Larry was on one leg in mid-kick when she pushed him. Chloe pushed well. Larry staggered towards the open van door, clutched at the frame, and got a grip. He was safe—just. Then the van swayed as it crossed the bridge and Leaping Larry flapped his arms like those magnificent men in their flying machines and screamed—this time in a deeper pitch—and Lover Boy got off without paying.

Chloe dragged Colin back inside the van. He lay on the floor, his heart pleading for a drinks' break. She knelt beside him gasping the fresh air of the hills.

What had happened in the van? Half the partygoers had gone home early. Jason left without having his ticket stamped, and just now, Larry did the same. Devine had been dispatched as planned but not by either of the nominated assassins.

Was Chloe Redmond guilty of patricide?

14

IT WAS TRAGIC with a touch of black comedy. Jason was lucky because he landed in a forest of ferns and bracken, and sustained scratches, bruises and an artistic green stain on his new jacket. Larry was not so lucky. He had further to fall.

Now had Larry landed on the road, he would have suffered crippling injuries, and probably instant death. Had he landed in the creek, he would have suffered crippling injuries, probably death, and wet clothes. He would've struggled to drown as it wasn't called a creek for nothing. Unluckily he landed on the grassy bank area—unluckily because instant death would have been preferable to what followed.

He had broken and dislocated bones, and a thumping headache as his head clipped the bridge on the way down. He was not drunk but tipsy, and maybe the grog relaxed him during his Wright Brothers' experience covering all of 14 metres.

He lay still, trying to think. *What happened? How can I get help?*

Larry could see the road, and figured if he could drag himself to it, a passing motorist would call an ambulance or take him to hospital.

He began the journey. It was agony clawing at the grass and reeds, dragging himself to the road. He made it and felt proud of his never-say-die attitude. Miraculously his bravery was rewarded. An angel of mercy appeared on cue. Larry was saved.

'Hello Larry,' said the angel and knelt beside him.

How does she know my name?

'Help me, please,' he croaked.

'With pleasure,' she said removing the goodies from her bag. Nina had raided the costume department at the Belgrave Players, and Larry was in for a game of dress-ups.

'I'm in terrible pain,' he moaned. 'I fell out of the train.'

'What a silly-billy you are,' said the angel.

'Call an ambulance,' he begged.

'I'll call a hearse, arsehole,' she spat, removing his shoes and replacing them with stilettoes. Foot size perfect. 'Pucker up, you prick,' sneered Nina.

Larry coughed and dribbled then cried as bright red lipstick was generously smeared over his lips. He sounded and looked pathetic.

Nina struggled to put the frilly nightie and bra on the almost comatose victim, and finished just as some car headlights lit up the scene. Nina swore and scurried back into the bush. Larry found religion and gave thanks to the deity of his choice. Alas God wasn't driving the car. It was the mother of his daughter.

Simone saw him fall, tried to set off straightaway, flooded the engine, and took ages to get going. Once the car was good to go, there was no stopping her. Larry rolled his head towards the oncoming vehicle, at last being grateful for help from someone who cared.

Wrong again, Larry. Face it, mate, when your luck's out, it's out.

Simone decided that a fast death was far too good an end for the man who caused her so much pain. She braked and drove at a snail's pace. Larry felt joy.

But wait. The car was not slowing to stop and help him; it was slowing so as to be sure not to miss him. His scream was part strangled. The car kept coming. He screamed louder. The car crept forward; no deviation. He could see the tread of the approaching rubber. Larry lost control of his bodily functions.

'Stop!' he scurgled (half scream/half gurgle), and wept. The pain from his injuries was horrendous but forgotten as the automobile crawled ever closer. Simone didn't want his face to suffer. She wanted his death face to be seen by the world. She drove over his lower abdomen, the area he once put to frequent use for his gratification, the area that caused such misery to his conquests. Crunch. The front wheel squashed him, the back wheel became the free steak knives.

Larry Devine died—slowly and in agony.

Billie Joe MacAllister got an ode for jumping off the Tallahatchie Bridge, and that was only half as high as the National Trust endorsed trestle over the Monbulk Creek. Larry Oswald Devine didn't jump, he was pushed and, instead of an ode, scored a cossie from *No Sex Please, We're British*.

Simone stopped the car and got out. She inspected the lifeless body of the man she'd hated for the last 19 years.

'How did you ever get a licence?'

Chloe's mother spun around, and in the spooky darkness saw the Cat Woman of the hills holding a pantomime plastic knife.

'I knew you were here as soon as I saw his outfit,' said Simone. The women stood over the corpse. 'What was your plan?'

'Who cares? Great minds think alike.' They paused. It was over. 'How do you feel?' asked Nina.

'I'm not sure,' replied Simone. 'I worry that in killing him, he'll make my life even more miserable than it was before.'

'I think we should move the body.'

'What?' Simone had been told to leave it where it lay.

'In the bush, it may not be found for a day or two.'

'So?'

'Hide it well and the animals will have a feed.'

Simone turned away in disgust. She looked again at the lifeless body of the man who fathered her child. Would the police reckon it was murder? Of course they would. Would she and the others be charged?

'And we should pinch his wallet,' said Nina who bent and found it.

'No! I draw the line at theft.'

'I don't want his damn money,' hissed Nina. 'If there's no ID on him, the cops will take longer to start asking questions.'

Simone shuddered again at the thought of being investigated. She grabbed the arms of the dead man and ordered Nina to help.

'Okay, let's move him. Over there in the bush.'

They did. He was "laid to rest" under ferns and bracken, and the women looked at one another then hugged. Nina added a final touch. She placed a rubber knife where his heart, if he had one, might have been. Sweet.

And so Larry Lothario Devine died at the oft-photographed Monbulk Creek trestle bridge. He was accidentally shoved out of the guard's van of the Puffing Billy train by his daughter.

Bring on Homicide and a certain Detective Senior Constable.

15

HAL FRENCH RETIRED and loved his new freedom. One of the benefits was taking his beloved Labrador for long walks. Lucy was chocolate brown and super friendly. Hal took her through the bush near his home in Melbourne's picturesque Dandenong Ranges. Lucy was usually off lead and, if missing, a whistle quickly brought her to heel. Not so on this crisp autumnal morning.

'Lucy, here girl,' called her lord and master. No dog. A whistle would do the trick. It didn't. Another whistle. Still no Lucy. Hal worried because they were close to a road and if she wandered that way, a car could wreak havoc. He called again and, in the midst of his panic, heard a bark. He headed in that direction.

Is she injured or trapped?

'Lucy, where are you, girl? Lucy?' She barked again and Hal changed direction. He spotted her, tail wagging and looking especially pleased with herself. Hal beckoned and called her again. She wouldn't move. Hal approached, preparing to put Lucy's lead on her collar, and that's when he saw the body.

It's often the case in murder mysteries that the body is found by a person walking their dog, which is what happened with Larry Devine.

Hal had been a public servant, and finding a dead body was never part of his job. He pulled Lucy back a bit, spoke to Larry, then using his foot, gently tried to wake the stiff. Larry was a brilliant actor and played the role of a corpse to perfection.

Hal called the cops.

The sergeant at Belgrave Police Station was patched through to Hal who was trying to keep a lid on his excitement. Lucy couldn't control her tail wagging.

'And you're sure the person's dead, Mr French?'

'Well he's not moving or breathing and he won't reply when I speak to him.'

'Have you touched anything?'

'No sir.'

'What about your dog?'

'She's on her lead and under control.'

'Well done.'

Hal was told to touch nothing, keep his dog under control and remain at the scene until police arrived. Hal explained his location, and tingled knowing he was part of a possible murder investigation. Lucy believed she was Ms Smarty Pooch.

Soon Hal heard a car door slam, and a voice calling.

'Hello?'

It was Constable Thomas Jones, police officer of this parish, who came second last in his graduation class at the Police Academy. You don't want to know about the officer who came last.

Jones found Hal and Lucy, inspected the body, and agreed with the dog-walker. The victim was definitely deceased. The constable took Hal's details, and Lucy's, (the officer was thorough), thanked them both for their good work, and watched them depart into the bush.

As per his instructions, Jones rang his sergeant.

'It's me, Sarge. I've found the body.'

'Congratulations. And?'

'And I'm guarding it like you said.'

'I gathered that, Constable but is it a suspicious death?'

'That's a maybe, Sarge.'

At the station, the sergeant's blood pressure started jogging.

'Did you say, "That's a maybe"?'

'That's an affirmative, Sarge.'

'Jones, what have I told you about mimicking the cops on American TV shows?'

'Oh yeah, sorry Sarge. Correctomundo.'

The superior officer shook his head in despair and took a deep breath. 'Now Jones, I want you to listen very carefully to what I'm about to say.'

'Yes, Sarge.'

'Don't speak.' Pause. Being unable to think of a reply, the constable fell silent. 'Now if I send the CIB up there for a bloke—is it a bloke?'

'Yes, Sarge but ...'

'For a bloke who's tripped over 'cos he's drunk, or for a local lad who's had a heart attack, I will cop it big time and, in return, I will give you shifts and duties that will make you cry for your mother. You will hate me forever. Do you get my drift?'

'Yes, Sarge.'

'Good man, so I'm going to ask you again, and I want a crystal clear yes or no answer. Okay?

'Okay, Sarge. What's the question?'

The sergeant's blood pressure explored new territory. He spoke slowly, softly, and with emphasis. 'Is it a suspicious death?'

'In a way, yes.'

That was it. The sergeant began searching for his sanity. 'In a way? What the hell does that mean?'

'Well the deceased person is a bloke wearing lipstick, a bra, high heels, and some sort of nightie.' The sergeant became speechless. 'It's a frilly nightie, Sarge, and so I ask you, is that suspicious?'

The "Sarge" felt a headache coming on. If he called the local CIB and they called the Homicide heavies, and the victim was a cross-dresser who'd had a stroke, or a stag night victim who'd been dressed up by his mates, and then suffocated on his own vomit, the sergeant would look a complete tit, and be the butt of jokes from here till Christmas. On the other hand, if this *was* a homicide, and the big boys from the big end of town were not called immediately, the sergeant from Belgrave would be in deep doo-doos.

However, right now the problem was that said sergeant was dealing with a constable who could win Prat-of-the-Year without trying. So a new tack was tried, one which went specific.

'Tell me, Constable, is there any blood on the body?'

'Very little, Sarge.'

'Excellent. Are there any missing or obvious broken limbs?'

'No, Sarge.'

'What about protruding daggers, bullet holes, or other suspicious features?'

'Just the one, Sarge.'

'Oh?' he asked with a mixture of hope and dread.

'There's a knife in his chest.'

'Ah, brilliant.' Suddenly the sergeant panicked. 'Hang on. There's a knife in his chest but no blood stains? Was he stabbed post-mortem?'

'Sorry, Sarge, whereabouts is his post-mortem?'

'Never mind.'

'Maybe there's no blood because the knife's not real, Sarge.'

The sergeant now understood why some officers took stress leave.

'So he's been stabbed but there's no blood. Is it a store dummy, Dummy?'

'No, he's real, Sarge.'

Under his breath, the sergeant muttered. 'Unlike others I know.'

'Sorry, I missed that, Sarge.'

He spoke freely. 'So tell me about the knife.'

'It's one of those rubber ones they use in plays.'

Apoplexy encircled the Sergeant. 'If you're on drugs, Constable, so help me I'll ...'

'They stab the victim under his arm and the audience think he's been stabbed when really he's just pretending. I've seen it in a panto, Sarge. Right now it's been shoved into the dead man's bra.'

Right now the sergeant would dearly have loved to shove a real knife into Constable Jones. The senior officer made a decision.

'Okay, listen. I'll inform CIB we have a suspicious death. If it turns out to be an accident, a death by natural causes, or a mysterious murder by Martians, you'd better emigrate. Do you hear me?'

'When do I emigrate, Sarge?'

More heavy breathing in the Belgrave cop shop.

'Just stay there till CIB arrive. Understood?'

'Will do, Sarge.'

'Over and out.'

The sergeant thumped his fist on his desk. He could not believe he just said "Over and out". He was about to break the connection when the Constable remembered something.

'Oh Sarge?'

'What now?'

'Don't know if it's relevant but the lipstick, bra, high heels and frilly nightie are all the same colour.'

'Red?'

The constable was surprised. 'How did you know that, Sarge?'

The sergeant suddenly had a brainwave. 'Jones, can you take a picture of the deceased and send it to me right now?'

'On my phone, you mean?'

'Yes, on your phone. You do know how to take a picture?'

'No problemo, Sarge. I'm good on the selfies. Hang on.'

Time ticked by and the sergeant had the dreaded thought that his colleague was taking a selfie with the corpse.

Jones spoke. 'All done, Sarge. I've just emailed it to you.'

'Good man.' The sergeant opened the attachment and looked at a picture of Jones taken at the football last week. It was a selfie with Jones wearing his Collingwood beanie and a ridiculous grin.

'Stay there, Constable,' muttered the defeated sergeant. 'I'll send the CIB boys and they can decide if Homicide is required.'

'Roger that,' said Jones.

He didn't hear his sergeant groan then mutter. 'What's the number of the Assassination Squad?'

Two local CIB detectives joined Constable Jones and quickly decided. This was a suspicious death. They contacted Homicide.

Jo Best was on call. She didn't have to be in the office but had to be ready to go anywhere within the state if a homicide occurred. She was enjoying a leisurely Saturday breakfast when her phone rang. It was Billy Hughes.

'Good morning, Sarge.'

'Sorry to break into your weekend, Senior, but we've got a possible homicide.'

'Possible, Sarge?'

'CIB and Uniform in Belgrave have a body in the bush they reckon is suspicious.'

'Meaning?'

'Apparently the body's dressed in unusual clothes but is unlikely to be a natural death. It needs checking.'

'You want me to come with you?'

'Not me, I've got a stabbing in Craigieburn. I think you can tackle this on your own.'

'By myself?' Jo was surprised, delighted and scared.

'Relax, you're not the OIC. Liaise with the local CIB, and if you agree with them, call me.'

'Right. Thanks, Sarge.'

'We'll probably need the mad woman but there's no way we can drag Dr Strange away from her *Saturday Age* crossword to discover a local pervert's had a heart attack.'

'Okay.'

'If it's a homicide, call me and I'll send a team and Strange and you can support them.'

Jo noted the location details, jumped under the shower then dressed. She had an idea. Now this was one of Jo's bad habits—having ideas. Worse still was her acting on them. She rang Dr Strange.

Speaking in a supposedly ghostly voice, the pathologist answered. 'Hello, I'm Strange.' Her sense of humour was weird.

'Good morning pathetic pathologist, it's ...'

'Senior Constable Best,' sparkled the medico, 'how lovely to hear your dulcet detective tones. What news, pray tell?'

Jo explained the body in the bush without mentioning that Billy Hughes would decide whether to call the pathologist.

'The Dandenongs,' enthused Strange. 'What a brilliant idea. You can drive and I can drink.'

Jo hesitated. 'Doctor?'

'Luncheon, my dear. There are some wonderful eateries in the hills, and I'm paying. Do you have my address?'

Jo drove to collect her travelling companion in the adjoining suburb, and pondered the situation.

I've disobeyed DS Hughes's orders. She warned me about the eccentric pathologist who now wants a day out in the hills. What if the death is a homicide and Strange insists on going to the pub? What will I do? What have I done?

Dr Gabrielle Strange owned a charming brick cottage in North Fitzroy. Jo knocked and the door flew open.

'Detective Senior Constable, the top of the morning to you.'

Before Jo could reply, her companion, complete with bag of goodies, took off calling as she went, 'Close the door, my dear, and let's be having you.'

It was a fair drive to Belgrave, a good hour and then some. Strange was a talker. 'How clever you are to be heading the case. I knew from the moment we met, great things lay ahead.' Jo wanted to correct her but chickened out. 'So tell me your life story, dear girl, leaving in all the salacious bits.'

Jo now regretted not following DS Hughes' orders.

'Well,' began Jo, 'my uncle's a former senior sergeant in Traffic, and my maternal grandfather used to be the boss of Homicide.'

'What? Who?'

'DCI Robertson.'

'Robbo Robertson?'

'That's him.'

'Damn good man. I was only starting when he retired. So, being a cop runs in the family?'

'I guess it does.'

'Tell me more.'

'I've always wanted to be a cop. I went to uni then joined the Force.'

'You went to uni? Where and to study what?'

'I did Law at Melbourne.'

'You have a law degree and became a cop on the beat?'

'Indeed. I was Constable Best for years catching shoplifters, sorting domestics and even directing traffic.'

Strange fell silent, which was rare for her.

'I can see why they grabbed you at Homicide.'

Jo was defensive, too quick and too loud. 'Why?'

'Settle down. I'm sure it's your talent and potential.' They joined the Eastern Freeway and literally headed for the hills. 'And now the personal stuff, my girl, but make it interesting, I want the *whole* truth.'

Jo laughed. 'If you want interesting, I'll have to make it up.'

'What, no boyfriend, girlfriend, or both? Come on, we won't be there for ages, tell the good Doctor—patient confidentiality of course.'

'I'm not your patient!'

'You will be if you don't start talking.'

Jo laughed. 'Okay, I'm currently single, if you must know.'

'Is that by choice or misfortune?'

'Dr Strange, why is it when I'm with you, I keep thinking of the phrase, "Too much information"?'

Strange laughed and changed topics. 'I went to this divine little restaurant in Selby, or was it Olinda? Can't remember. We'll find it. Nice wine list too. Are you a red or white girl?'

Jo was feeling uneasy. 'I'm really not much of a drinker.'

'Well that won't last if you stay in Homicide.' They drove in silence. 'Don't you want to know about me?'

'I think I already do.'

Strange made a strange sound. 'So, checking up on me, hey?'

'You've been a pathologist working with the Victorian Institute of Forensic Medicine and assisting Victoria Police for seventeen years.'

'Eighteen,' corrected Strange.

'You have an outstanding record of achievement, and are held in high regard by all who work with you.'

'Well you learn something new every day. I never had you down as a bullshit-artist and soft-soaper.'

'And you don't mind a tipple.'

'That's me,' she cried, miming raising a glass. 'Cheers!'

They laughed and drove to the Dandenongs.

16

SURROUNDED BY TOWERING GUMS, bracken and tree ferns, Jo parked beside the Monbulk Creek trestle bridge. Getting out of the car, Strange grumbled. Sitting for long periods didn't suit her and she struggled with her protective clothing. Jo wandered into the bush.

'Hello, police,' she called.

'Over here,' came the reply from Constable Jones.

'Where?' called Jo.

'Here,' yelled Jones.

'Where's here?'

Strange sang a la Nelson Eddy. 'I'll be calling you-ooo-ooo-ooo-....'

Jones appeared from the bush. 'Are you from Homicide?'

Jo produced her ID. 'Detective Senior Constable Best and this is Dr Strange, the pathologist.'

'Hello,' he said, 'PC Thomas Jones. The CIB detectives got called away but ...'

'Shouldn't you be guarding the body, Constable?' asked Jo.

His face dropped. 'Ah yes.' He set off, calling. 'This way, please.'

The women followed and got their first look at the deceased. Jo perused the area, and with more groans, Strange knelt to examine the body. She didn't look up when she spoke.

'Have you called the Fashion Police, Constable?'

Jones didn't do satire. 'No, Doctor. Should I do that now?'

Strange and Best exchanged glances.

'Never mind, Constable,' said Strange, still examining the body.

He took out a notebook. 'For the record, Doctor, can you please confirm the deceased is ... deceased?'

'I may need a second opinion and run some more tests, young man, but after my preliminary examination I am prepared to stick my neck out and declare that at 1029 life is now extinct.'

'Thank you,' said Jones scribbling. The man was sincere.

Strange examined poor dead Larry while Jo took details from Jones including Lucy the dog's registration number.

'Technically it was Lucy who found the body and not Mr English.'

'French,' said Jo.

'I'm sorry?'

'You said Mr English.'

Jones looked confused, something he did quite often. 'Oh right, I can see what's wrong. The man speaks English but his name is French.'

Jo was hoping Jones would not have any role in the investigation.

Strange had an opinion. 'I think you should inform your superiors, Detective. This is a suspicious death and a most interesting case.'

'Not an accidental death, Doctor?' asked Jones.

'Not in a million years, Constable.'

Jo spoke to Jones. 'Perhaps you should contact your station, Constable, and advise them of recent events.'

'Oh right,' he said and moved to make a call.

'Not there, Constable,' Jo exclaimed as the inexperienced officer disturbed possible evidence. Jo pointed. 'There.'

Jo knelt beside Strange.

'Don't quote me, Jo Best, in fact *never* quote me, but the deceased has suffered a variety of injuries including broken limbs, road trauma, fight marks, and been subject to unusual transport.' Jo looked blank. 'The body's been moved, my dear.'

Jo nodded then looked sheepish. 'Dr Strange?'

The pathologist examined. 'Why do I feel a confession coming on?'

'I wasn't supposed to contact you today, just confirm the case was a homicide, and then advise DS Hughes of my assessment.'

'Because she didn't want the pathetic pathologist dragged out on a Saturday for some drunk who tripped and broke his neck.'

Jo nodded. 'You should have been a detective, Doctor.' The pathologist laughed. 'So I'm in a bit of trouble, Detective Strange.'

'Nonsense. You rang me concerned about the body's injuries.'

'No I didn't.'

Strange looked at Jo. 'Keep up, darling. I made my own way here, examined the body, declared the death to be suspicious, and left. Just ring your boss and tell her she needs Forensics and an OIC. Too easy.'

Jo's smile was large. 'Thank you, Dr Strange. I owe you.' She stopped. 'Ah, where's your car?'

Strange waved her away speaking with a Big Apple (the Bronx) accent. 'Don't bring me problems, bring me solutions.'

Jo rang Hughes and told her it was a suspicious death. The phone call from Hughes to Strange was strange. The pathologist lied about her locale. Jo got away with it—for now.

Finally a new uniformed officer arrived. Jones was relieved and Jo and Strange were glad. Jo told the new watchdog to call her the moment other Homicide detectives arrived. She drove Strange to the main Belgrave station. There are two. One is for the suburban rail network in Melbourne, and the other for the narrow gauge tourist train, Puffing Billy. The pathologist was not a big public transport user.

'We'll do lunch another day,' she called, waving and boarding the train.

Heading back to the crime scene, Jo stopped at the Puffing Billy HQ where she met the Stationmaster.

'A dead body?' he exclaimed.

'It was located near the railway line, and I wondered if you've had any reports of people going missing, accidents and the like?'

'No, nothing.'

'Did you have a train running last night?'

'We did.' He explained the murder mystery train, and the time it returned to Belgrave.

'What about people on that train?'

'Apart from the passengers, there were catering staff and the crew.'

'Could I have their details please?'

'Of course.' He found the information, made copies and gave them to her. 'Oh and we had the actors from the Belgrave Players. Here's a programme from their show.'

'Thank you. How might I contact them?'

The SM gave Jo more details and she left. She thought about starting interviews then reckoned it might be better to be on the plot when the big boys arrived. Wise move. She drove back to the bridge wondering who the OIC might be.

Wouldn't it be wonderful if DI Richelieu was my boss? DSC Baldwin I could work with but DSC Payne, my God no, please no.

Her hopes were shattered when two cars arrived with the Forensic Services crew in one and, in the other, DSC Payne and worse, far worse, the Officer in Charge, the big boss, DI Steele.

'Sir, DSC Payne,' she said, trying to disguise her disappointment. She showed them the body, and then Steele took her aside with Payne in tow. Payne's perpetual smirk seemed bigger than ever.

Steele was blunt. 'And Dr Strange declared it a homicide?'

'She did, sir. The estimated time of death was midnight last night, and the cause of death involved multiple injuries.'

'What's that in English?'

'Dr Strange believed the victim had been in a fight, a fall, probably from that bridge, in a hit and run, and the body had been moved.'

Steele sniffed. 'And what have you been doing in the mean time?'

'A train crossed the bridge last night at about 2300 hours. I've interviewed the Stationmaster at Puffing Billy HQ in Belgrave. There are no reports of accidents or missing persons. I have a list of all who were on board including the actors who performed a play.'

She impressed not only because she had useful details but because she rattled them off without pausing. Payne's smirk retreated.

Steele was in a bind. Surely he wouldn't offer any praise.

'Thank you, Senior Constable,' he said in a muted tone.

'Sir,' she replied. She paused. 'Sir?'

'What?'

'Am I to return to normal duties?'

'No, you will work on this case answering to DSC Payne.'

'Sir,' she said.

Payne's smirk resurfaced.

'Make a start using those on your list. Divide up the names and get cracking. Priority of course is to identify the victim. Take both cars and be back here by 1200 hours. If I need you, I'll call.'

He turned his back and returned to the Forensic officers.

'Show me the list,' demanded Payne. He had never learnt the words *please* and *thank you*. He studied the names. 'I'll take the railway staff, you can have the actors.' He thrust the pages he didn't need back at her. 'If you get lucky and find something, notify me immediately.'

'And does the same ruling apply to you?'

He glared at her then strode to his car and sped away. His licence plates might well have been *Macho Male*. Payne chose to interview the driver, fireman and guard on last night's train. Jo looked at her list of actors and chose Nina Waters.

In her car, she saw the theatre programme on the passenger seat. She opened it and froze. In the cast photos was a man who looked like the body of the man in the bush. She checked the photo on her phone, the one she took with Dr Strange. No doubt. The deceased was a Mr Larry Devine. Should she ring Payne and inform Steele? A professional cop would but she allowed their rudeness to cloud her judgement.

Payne began with the locomotive driver on last night's train. Harry Styles loved steam and, for him, driving at Puffing Billy was a joy. He lived in the hills and Payne found him chatting to his runner beans.

News about the body spread like wildfire on the local grape vine, and Harry already knew the basics when Payne arrived.

'Did you see anything unusual, Mr Styles?'

Harry gave new meaning to *laconic*. 'Not a sausage,' he said.

'Did you hear any sounds of a fight or screams?'

Harry thought about telling Payne that the steam locomotive is the closest thing to a living being, about the sounds it makes and the volume of those sounds for those on the shifting footplate. He reckoned he'd be wasting his breath.

'It's a bit noisy on the footplate.'

'What about people on the track? Might you have hit someone and not seen them in the dark?'

Harry again tried to educate the cop. 'Did you know Puffing Billy has a race each year with people running to beat the train? Many do. I think you're confusing us with the Tokyo Bullet Train.'

Payne got nowhere and left to find the fireman. Had Payne known that shovelling coal or controlling oil made the fireman unlikely to see or hear anything other than his shovel, the firebox door, and the engine, he wouldn't have bothered. Payne got nowhere fast.

Elsewhere, Jo started with the Cat Woman of the Hills.

17

'GOOD MORNING,' said Jo showing her ID and introducing herself. 'Are you Nina Walters?' She nodded. 'I understand you're associated with the Belgrave Players.'

'Go away, go away,' yelled Nina and Jo thought the woman loopy or anti-police. Actually she was both but in this case happened to be preventing a black and white moggie called Houdini escaping to the jungle outside. 'Come in,' said Nina now using her foot to block a naughty tortie.

Jo liked cats but found the number in this house a challenge.

Nina was blunt. 'Have you come to arrest me?'

'Not unless you've murdered someone.'

Nina seemed to shrink. 'It's usually the council who come about my cats. They've never sent the police before.'

'I've not come about your cats. I understand the Belgrave Players were part of the Puffing Billy train last night.'

'Yes, they staged their murder mystery play in the packing shed.'

'It's just that we've found a body by the railway and would like to speak to company members who were involved.'

'I wasn't.'

'No?'

'I was here all night and I've got all these witnesses to prove it.' Nina gestured to the rooms of sleeping cats.

'Right,' said Jo mentally ticking the box marked Loopy. 'And you've not heard from anyone in the theatre group about a missing member?'

'I'm not in the plays.'

'That wasn't what I asked.'

'I do the costumes.'

'Costumes?' Nina nodded. 'Do you have a costume store?' More nodding. 'And is there a list of what you have, an inventory?' Jo wondered if Nodding Nina would ever speak. 'Would it be possible to see this list?'

'What are you looking for?'

'High heels, bra and frilly nightie, all red.'

Nina shrunk even more. 'I'd have to look.'

Jo wanted to improve her detective skills, and tried to read Nina's body language. Something didn't nag Jo about Nina's behaviour; it grabbed her in a headlock.

'Do you have the list with you?'

'No.'

'Do you know where it is?'

'At the store.'

'Could we go to the store?'

'I haven't got a car.'

'I can drive you and bring you back.'

Nina snapped. 'I can't leave the house. Bernard's got a cold, Lucrecia's recovering from her op, and Sally and Harry always fight on the weekend.'

That's not what happened when Harry met Sally.

Jo didn't know what to say to the last comment. Making a note to peruse the costume inventory, she produced her phone.

'May I show you a photo? It's not gory but it is a deceased person.'

Again Nina nodded. Jo scrolled, looking for the face of Larry Devine. Yes he was dead but apart from a garish splurge of ruby red lipstick, his face was almost pristine. He could have been sleeping. His murderer had respected his features. Larry looked quite peaceful, remarkable given the pain he suffered at the end. Jo turned her camera to Nina. She lifted her glasses, looked at Larry and dropped a cat.

'You should know, Nina, you can be arrested for wasting police time.'

She nodded again then changed her plea to guilty. Jo cautioned her. Nina waved away her rights and made a full confession about how she lured Larry into the guard's van with a promise of sex, rejected his advances, and when he opened the van door and attempted to throw her from the moving train, he slipped and fell himself. She then cycled back from Belgrave to find Larry had been the victim of a hit and run.

She dressed him to make it look like a bizarre sex crime, and dragged his body into the bushes. Nina was adamant. She acted alone.

Jo found Nina's story to be improbable, impossible or ridiculous. *Nina, a sex goddess? Nina in the Tour de France?*

'You say all this took place in the guard's van?'

It was back to the nodding from Nina.

'So where was the guard when all this happened?'

This wasn't a question to which a nod would suffice. She scrambled for an answer.

'I knocked him out.'

'How?'

'With his lantern. He wasn't looking and I whacked him. I think he's okay. Colin saw nothing, and did nothing. I acted alone.'

Jo paused. Should she arrest someone clearly lying? If she didn't arrest someone who confessed to a major crime, what would happen to Jo? She rang the local nick and asked for officers to collect a suspect. She cautioned Nina again then arrested her on suspicion of the murder of Larry Devine.

Jo asked for Colin's address which Nina gave then began to cry.

'What will happen to my cats?' She looked pathetic and several cats looked up, concerned about these latest developments.

Jo knew the train guard was on Payne's list, and he'd ordered Jo to tell him about any development. She rang him.

'What?' was all he said.

'I've arrested a suspect who's admitted to murder. The victim's name is Larry Devine.'

Payne fumed. He had nothing, and that bitch Best had identified the body and made an arrest.

'How?' So far his entire vocabulary consisted of *what* and *how.*

'The suspect identified the victim and then confessed.'

'She identified the victim?'

'Yes, I showed her a photo.'

'You have a photo?' Payne's voice got louder and more frantic.

Jo kept calm. 'The thing is, Detective, the guard on last night's train can verify the statement made by the woman I've arrested. He lives here in the hills. You need to interview the guard as soon as possible.'

'Don't tell me what to do.'

There was a pause. It smouldered.

'Detective?'

'I'm with the fireman in bloody Boronia. It'll take me half an hour.'

'I'm close to the guard's place. Should I interview him?'

The smouldering silence continued. 'Yes,' he spat, 'and keep me informed.' He rang off hurting his finger as he stabbed his phone.

Jo grinned but saw the predicament Nina faced. She howled.

'Who will look after my cats?' Her crying got serious.

Jo guessed and hoped. 'What about a neighbour, a friend or relative?' Nina shook her head and sobbed.

'They hate me. They think I'm mad.'

So do I.

'What about an animal shelter?'

Nina came alive. 'Yes,' she shouted and went looking. She returned with a business card. Nina's eyes went from blurry to begging.

Jo dialled the number. 'Is that the cat rescue centre?' It was. 'I'm a police officer, Detective Senior Constable Best, and I'm with a lady who has several cats and ...'

'Indoor cats,' yelled Nina.

'... several indoor cats, but the lady has to go away and has nobody to care for the animals.'

The conversation continued with Nina placing her front door key under the mat on the verandah, (Jo shook her head at the stupidity of that decision), and the cat rescue centre promised to care for the cats.

Nina continued to cry but this time from happiness. She didn't have a care in the world about the demise of Larry Devine.

The police car arrived and Nina farewelled her family.

Jo drove the short distance to the guard's home, and knocked on Colin Grubb's door. Brunel was super excited but when Jo introduced herself, Colin immediately sensed trouble.

She began with the obvious question. 'How's your head, Mr Grubb?'

'A bit sore. I fell getting out of the van last night.'

'You fell?'

'Yeah, I'm not as young as I used to be.'

'We have a witness who said they hit you on the head with your lantern.'

Colin tried to move up Shit Creek but couldn't find his paddle.

'Ah no, no, I think I would have remembered that.'

'So the witness is lying?'

'Possibly.'

'Possibly?'

'I could be sure if I knew the name of the witness.'

'I'd like to show you a photo, Mr Grubb,' said Jo, preparing her phone. 'Can you tell me if you know this person?'

She showed Colin the photo of Larry, and found his lack of reaction pretty darn good.

'Nope, never seen him before.'

'Do you know a man called Larry Devine?'

Colin opened his mouth and left it open. He was thinking.

They've got me so what's the best course of action from here?

'Right officer, you've got me. I'm the guilty party.'

Jo paused then recovered. 'Guilty of what, sir?'

'Fighting that prick who unfortunately fell out of the guard's van.'

'Before we go any further, Mr Grubb, I have to caution you and ...'

'Yes, yes, I know all about that. Look, I want to confess.'

'Okay, please go ahead,' said Jo flipping the page on her notebook.

'On the return journey, I invited Larry into my van at Menzies Creek. We had a bit to drink, and got into a fight. I tried to escape so opened the door of my van and, during the fight, Larry accidentally fell just when we crossed the Monbulk Creek trestle bridge.'

'And then what did you do?'

'After we got to Belgrave, I drove back to the bridge and saw his body lying on the road. I saw he was dead so drove my car over the body to make it look like an accident.'

'Then what did you do?'

'Ah, then I went home.'

'Did you move the body?'

'No.'

'Did you dress the body in other clothes?'

Colin was in trouble, well deeper trouble. He and Simone had agreed not to communicate in case their phone or email accounts were tracked. *What had Simone done?* He guessed.

'Ah, come to think of it, I may have done.'

'You may have done what?'

'Ah, what you said.'

'Do passengers often fall out of your van, Mr Grubb?'

'Look, I may have grabbed a few things and put them on the body.'

'What sort of things?'

'Oh God, I can't remember.'

'Why?'

'Why what?'

'Why grab a few things and put them on the body?'

'Ah, to confuse the police.'

'What colour were these things?'

Colin was now a very long way up Shit Creek and still without his paddle. 'I don't know. It was one o'clock in the morning.'

'Mr Grubb, I'm sure you know murder is a serious crime.'

'Of course, but it wasn't murder.'

'As is making a false statement and wasting police time.'

Colin went for his final speech. 'Look, I've told you what happened. Larry and I had a fight and he fell out of the train. I drove over him, on my own. He was not a nice man and I'm glad he's dead.'

She cautioned him, arrested him on suspicion of murder, and called the cops at Belgrave for yet another car to collect a suspect.

'Another one?' said the sergeant. 'Do you lot get frequent flyer points when you make arrests?'

Jo laughed and waited with Colin. Brunel was doing his best to make Jo fall in love with him. She felt terrible.

Why do all these possible murderers have to be animal lovers?

'What's your dog's name?'

'Brunel.'

'What will you do with him?'

'I have friends who'll take him. I won't be away for long will I?'

'Not my department,' said Jo, 'sorry.'

They waited. Jo made conversation. 'Why is he called Brunel?'

Colin beamed. 'I named him after Isambard Kingdom Brunel, one of the world's greatest engineers.' Jo nodded and almost nodded off as Colin let fly. 'He built ships, railways, bridges, tunnels, you name it. You know the Puffing Billy runs on a narrow gauge line?'

Jo felt a kind of haze settling over her while Colin was on fire.

'It's two foot six. Here in Victoria we have a mix of gauges including Standard gauge which is four foot eight and a half, and Broad gauge which is five foot three.'

Jo struggled. *Where is that police car?*

'Brunel designed and built a line called the Wide gauge; seven foot and a quarter of an inch. Can you imagine that?'

Jo couldn't but having won Colin's attention and trust by not falling asleep she gently turned him around to discuss Larry Devine. Colin was generous with his facts. Jo discovered pretty much everything there was to know about Larry, the leaping lothario. He sounded like a right royal bastard.

The cop car arrived and Colin was led away to face the music.

'What about Brunel?' asked Jo.

'Oh God,' said Colin.

'Where are your friends?'

'A few minutes away.'

'I can take him,' offered Jo, and she did. She stood at the front door of Simone and Chloe's house with the tail-wagging Brunel. She thought about phoning Payne then decided she'd had enough of his bullying and rudeness for one day.

Simone opened the door with red eyes and trembling hands, and that was before Jo introduced herself.

Chloe was sitting on the settee with her legs up against her chest. She looked worse than her mother.

'Have I come at a bad time?' asked Jo.

'No, we've just had some sad news,' replied Simone. Now that bit was true. They'd been up most of the night. Chloe told her mother about the incident in Colin's van, and tears aplenty were shed. Simone didn't mention her involvement. Their tough time was about to get tougher. Simone questioned Jo. 'I'm sorry, but why are you here?'

'To ask you to look after this wonderful dog.'

Brunel thought it was Christmas as all three women gave him pats and fondled his ears. Jo explained.

'I'm sorry to have to add to your misery, ladies, but Brunel is here because your friend, Colin, has just been arrested for murder.'

Wow. Talk about a slap in the face. Simone was hoping Larry's demise wouldn't be discovered for weeks or even months. Chloe was still living last night's nightmare. She couldn't help telling her mother what happened. Her mother couldn't help being relieved Chloe's father was no more. Simone was now super determined to never tell Chloe the truth. The poor child had been involved in the death of her father. She must never know.

What a mess.

Now, a few hours later, the police were in town and had arrested Colin. What a disaster. Simone couldn't bear the strain. She cracked.

'Officer, I wish to confess.'

Jo thought she was dreaming. She'd called on three people associated with the Belgrave Players, and all had admitted to killing Larry Devine. *Payne will self-combust.* Jo saw inconsistencies in the statements made by the people she'd arrested or would arrest, but was convinced all had some connection to the crime.

Now a third person confessed to the murder, and as Jo struggled with Simone about to explain her role, her daughter joined the circus.

'No, Mum, I won't let you.'

Simone screamed. 'Chloe, no!'

The daughter confessed and Jo was impressed with Chloe's version. It had a ring of truth. Simone despaired. But four murderers!

'I was there,' said Chloe. I saw everything, and I was the one who accidentally pushed Larry out of the van.'

For a while, Jo wished she'd stayed in uniform. For the one murder, she had four people confess to the same crime. Her phone rang. She moved to the kitchen and identified herself.

'Detective, it's Sergeant Consolides from Belgrave.'

'Oh, hi Sergeant. I was just about to call.'

'You were?' said a now worried sergeant.

'You might need to sit down, Sergeant, because I'm about to arrest two more for the Puffing Billy murder.'

'Really? Well, I'll see your two, and raise you one.'

'Pardon?'

'A local resident has just walked into the station claiming to have killed your Mr Larry Devine. I reckon that makes him murderer number five. Your real name's not Agatha Christie by any chance?'

Jo, who rarely swore, uttered a softly spoken oath.

'What's the name please, Sergeant?'

'Jason Bartholomew.'

Jo re-entered the lounge, covered her phone and spoke to the red-eyed women. 'Do either of you know a Jason Bartholomew?'

'Is he okay?' shouted Chloe.

'I assume so. He's just confessed to murder.'

Chloe exploded. 'It wasn't Jason. He tried to save me. Larry pushed him off the train. I'm the one who killed Larry.'

Now Jo was really struggling. That's two passengers pushed off the train, one dead and five confessions. Imagine how the cops at Belgrave were coping. Jo felt like she was ordering a pizza.

'So that's a car with the lot, please Sergeant, to 24 Houghton Road.'

'Would you like extra cheese, Detective?'

'Ha, ha.'

'And any chance you could make this the last one? We're getting close to lighting up the *No Vacancy* sign.'

Jo's mind was spinning. So far, for the death (possible murder) of Larry Devine on the Puffing Billy night train, she'd arrested four suspects while a fifth had handed himself in.

Where the hell is Hercules Poirot when you need him?

Mother and daughter were arrested and left in tears. Jo had seen the two uniformed officers from Belgrave so much that day she thought they should be on her Christmas card list.

As the officers led the weeping women away, the female constable pointed to the wagging canine. 'Is anyone looking after the pooch?'

Jo nearly died. She walked back to the house, put Brunel's lead on his collar, and led him to her car. He was having the Best of days. With her new friend beside her, Jo sat in the vehicle and rang Payne. She wasn't looking forward to the call.

To date he'd discovered zip. When Jo told him she'd arrested four people, and a fifth had handed himself in, her fellow detective was lucky to be alone at the time. Had anyone been with him, Payne might well have been up on an assault charge.

'I'm heading to the station at Belgrave, Detective,' said Jo.

'Do nothing till I get there. And I'll inform DI Steele,' he snapped before the line went dead.

Jo walked into the Belgrave police station with Brunel in tow. 'Can I help you, madam,' asked the constable on the front desk.

Jo raised her ID. 'I'm Senior Constable Jo Best from Homicide.'

The constable called. 'Hey Sarge, Super Cop is here.' Jo wasn't sure if that was sarcasm or praise. The sergeant appeared.

'Detective Senior Constable Best,' he said offering his hand. 'Sergeant Consolides. It's a pleasure to finally meet you.'

'Sergeant.'

He patted the canine. 'And don't tell me you've arrested Brunel?'

Jo realised she was in a community where people and their pets were well-known. Brunel thought it was Christmas.

'No, Sergeant, I took the dog to be cared for by friends of Mr Grubb but then I had cause to arrest the Redmond mother and daughter so I've brought the animal with me.'

'You've had a busy day, Detective.'

'It was actually my first homicide arrest, sir.'

'First arrest! And you've nabbed four!' He turned to the officer on the desk. 'Constable, take Brunel and see he has water and a feed. Oh and a walk. No peeing in the cells.'

'Yes, Sarge,' he said, and Brunel left with his tail in full voice.

'So, what are we to do with your merry band of outlaws?'

'Not my decision, Sergeant. DI Steele and DSC Payne from Homicide are in the area, and they'll make the call on your prisoners.'

'You do the hard work and they get the glory.' Jo half smiled. 'Coffee?'

She relaxed for the first time in hours. Sadly not for long as certain voices were heard. Steele entered looking angry. Payne entered looking furious. Jo stood.

Steele spotted her. 'Detective Senior Constable Best.'

'Sir,' she replied and felt like she needed to salute.

'DSC Payne has told me some tale about multiple arrests. I hope you followed protocol and this is not some giant cock-up.'

'I did everything by the book, sir. People confessed and I arrested them.'

'Why did they confess? Did you trick them or force them?'

'Not at all, sir. I conducted proper interviews and each person willingly admitted their involvement in the death of the victim.'

'DSC Payne tells me you chose people you wanted to interview.'

'That's not how I remember it, sir.

Payne raged. He chose the targets he wanted to interview and chose badly; his choice, his error. Jo's thoughts turned to despair.

Did I ever think Homicide would be like this?

'And is it true you withheld a photo of the victim from DSC Payne?'

'No sir. I assumed an experienced detective would have taken one.'

Jo would have been more subtle had she kicked Payne in his privates. Payne melted. Steele stared at her. He knew Payne was a plodder and that Best was intelligent and a quick learner. He knew Payne would support him no matter what but suspected Best was a free thinker. He was right.

'DSC Payne and I will interview those arrested. If they walk because of your interview technique or because they're innocent, you're on dangerous ground. We go by the book, Senior Constable, and I will not tolerate detectives trying to make a name for themselves.' He spoke softly but his eyes were shouting. 'Do you understand?'

'Sir.'

'Now return to the scene of crime, and once Forensics finish, arrange for the body to be removed. Then return to Melbourne and resume normal duties. Dismissed.'

'Sir,' she said for the umpteenth time and as she left the bowels of the station, caught a glimpse of liar Payne and his supersized smirk.

In the front office, Brunel lay on the floor watching the world go by. He saw Jo, and increased his tail wagging from standard to deluxe. She patted him wanting to cry at the rude injustice she'd just received.

'He likes you,' said the constable on the front desk.

Jo had an idea. 'Look, I have to return to the scene of crime. Could I take Brunel with me and drop him back on my way home?'

'Sounds good to me.'

So Brunel hopped into Jo's car, and the two chatted about railway gauges all the way back to the trestle bridge. Brunel was a brilliant listener. Emily Bronte was spot on when she said she preferred dogs to people. Working with Brunel or DSC Payne? No contest.

The Crime Scene Officers (CSOs) were just finishing and poor old Larry was carted away for a more invasive investigation.

'Come on, Brunel, it's time I took you home.' The dog looked at her with his talkative eyes. 'I wouldn't mind taking you back to my home in Melbourne, old boy. You could come on my runs around Clifton Hill.'

Brunel barked with delight. Sadly, for both, he was returned to the Belgrave police station, and Jo headed home.

En route, she rang her mother. 'It's Jo, Mum. How are you going?' Jo immediately regretted asking that question.

Shirley sounded terrible. 'What do you think?'

'I'm on the road, Mum, and thought I'd drop in.'

Shirley took a deep breath. 'If you must.'

Wow. Talk about an enthusiastic response.

'I'll see you soon,' said Jo and worried.

She rang the doorbell, the door opened, and her mother disappeared. Jo followed her into the lounge.

'Big news, Mum; I've just made my first arrest.'

'Oh?' she said.

'And would you believe it was four.'

'Four what?'

'Four arrests, Mum, not one, four. I should've rung Pop but he's probably with Nan. He's usually there until about three isn't he?'

'Usually,' mumbled a lethargic and miserable Shirley.

Jo was troubled. Her mother was much worse than last time.

How long before this scam disaster causes permanent damage? Will she ever recover? Will she do something terrible?

Shirley broke the silence. 'I know about your sister and Malcom X's trophy wife.'

Jo had long known about Caitlyn and Natalie and their "ladies who lunch" routine. Caitlyn had sworn her sister to secrecy.

So that's why Mum's so wretched. What the hell do I say?

Jo spoke quietly. The nasty secret was out. It was like there'd been a death in the family. 'How did you find out?'

'Not from you, that's obvious. My daughters stick together keeping secrets from their mother.'

'Look, Mum, I'm ...'

'Don't you "Look, Mum" me. How long have you known?' Jo honestly couldn't remember but it was a fair time. 'Typical.'

'I'm glad you found out, Mum. I've hated knowing and not saying anything.'

'I'll bet Malcolm X knew. I bet you two laughed behind my back.'

'Not true, Mum. I've haven't seen Dad for months, and he's stopped calling me because I often don't return his calls.'

Shirley looked surprised. 'Is that true?'

'I told you I wouldn't take sides and I never have.'

The distraught mother sighed and whispered. 'Thank you.'

Jo went for a change of topic. 'I'll make us a cuppa.'

Shirley stood. 'No you won't. I'll do it.'

Shirley headed for the kitchen and Jo called, 'I'll just use your loo.'

She headed into her mother's bedroom and searched. The laptop was on her desk. Jo opened the top and hit the *On* button. The machine whirred into life and played three notes. They seemed very loud. Jo froze. From the kitchen came sounds of crockery and cutlery.

Jo hit the email icon and up came a host of emails all of which were boring stuff, some from Caitlyn and the inevitable spam. Jo flicked down the list. Nothing.

Of course, she thought. *Send*. Jo clicked on *Send* and scrolled. Gold. There were emails to the scammer, replies to his emails. Jo felt ashamed, invading her mother's privacy. Meet the daughter who spies on her mother. The emails she read were pathetic. "Where are you?" "Please, please reply" and worse. It was heartbreaking.

'Where are you?' called Shirley.

Jo panicked and turned off the laptop. It took forever.

Oh, please, don't play those damn musical notes.

It did and to cover the sound, Jo yelled, 'Coming,' trying to sound relaxed. She headed back to the lounge then remembered the loo. She darted into the en suite and hit the flush button.

They shared a cuppa and some upmarket biscuits. Jo was pleased. Her mother was almost broke but maintained her standards. Upmarket biscuits had long been her style. *Good on you, Shirl.*

'I've made some progress with Centrelink, Mum. No promises, but you might be able to get something due to your changed situation.'

'My changed situation? That's one way of putting it.'

'Trained by my mother,' said Jo, but Shirley remained Mrs Glum. Jo decided to go for the jugular. 'Mum, have you considered talking to someone about your experience?'

'No.' The reply had *definite* written all over it.

'A professional perhaps?'

'No.' That reply was even more definite.

'It's just that I'm worried about you being worried.'

'You promised you would never speak about that business.'

'No Mum, I promised I would never speak to anyone else about that business.'

Shirley pulled back. Jo of course had broken her promise but only because she wanted her mother to regain her money. Because of her goal, Jo told herself that lying to her mother was justified.

'How about I find an experienced female counsellor or therapist?'

'No, I want to forget the whole thing.'

'I'll pay for a session and you can see if it helps.'

Shirley went into her shell. She was deeply grateful her daughter showed such concern and was offering to help.

'I'll think about it.'

Jo was pleased. Bit by bit she would wear down her mother's resistance. Bit by bit she would find a way to retrieve the money.

18

THAT NIGHT JO LOUNGED on her settee with a coffee. She imagined Brunel curled up in his bed beside her. She thought about her trip to the Dandenongs, her first arrests, and the unbelievable rudeness she copped from Steel and Payne. She thought about her mother, and her misery and financial nightmare.

Her phone rang. It was her father. She thought about sending it to Voicemail then answered it.

'Hi Dad. How are you?'

'I could be dead for all you know. How come you haven't returned my calls?'

'Sorry, I've been flat out at work.'

'With a lie like that you could be an estate agent,' said Malcom X the estate agent.

'Ha ha. So how are the kids and ...' Jo pretended not to remember the trophy bride's name.

'Ha ha, yourself. Natalie and the kids are fine. When are you coming to see us? And when are we going to meet your fabulous boyfriend?'

'Never I'm afraid.'

'What? You've dumped *another* one? Stop being so bloody picky. You wanna be careful my girl or you could end up on the shelf.'

'On the shelf! Oh Dad, you're showing your age—again.'

'So how's your mother? I heard she was doing it hard of late.'

Jo stalled. *What has he heard? Is Mum's secret a secret no more? Has Michael Chan leaked the facts? Surely not.*

'She's fine. I had a cuppa with her this afternoon.'

'Oh, so you visit your mother but not your old man. Listen, I'm the wealthy one. You need to be nice to me, my girl.'

'Not even remotely funny, Dad. Listen, I've gotta go. I'll give you a call and we can have coffee. Bye.' She hit *End*.

What a situation. Her love life, her family and job were all the pits. Her phone rang again and she answered in a huff.

'Dad, I'm sorry but ...'

'Dad?'

Jo recognised the voice and looked at the Caller ID.

'Oh God, Sarge, sorry, I thought you were my father.'

'Biologically impossible, Detective. So how are you?'

'Fine,' lied Jo.

'I'm ringing to reprimand you.'

Terrific, thought Jo. *Everyone else hates me, why not you?*

'Sarge?'

'I know about you ignoring my instructions, and taking Dr Strange to the crime scene.'

'Yeah, sorry, Sarge. I just thought ...'

'And I also know you made your first arrest as a Homicide detective and I'm ringing to congratulate you.'

Jo felt a warm feeling wash over her body. Something good was happening—at last.

'Thanks, Sarge, I appreciate it.'

'And I now know you're a bloody show off.'

Jo lost that loving feeling in an instant. 'Sarge?'

'Four arrests, Senior Constable Best—four! What are you, greedy, or just trying to show up your colleagues?'

Jo was back to feeling warm. 'I just got lucky I guess.'

'Bloody marvellous, Jo. I'll be working under you pretty soon.'

'Hardly.' Jo wanted to say thanks but also to ask questions. 'Sarge?'

'I'm still here.'

'Why are DI Steele and DSC Payne giving me such a hard time?'

Billy went quiet. 'Don't copy me.'

Jo didn't follow. 'Sorry?'

'Don't make the mistake I made and try to be one of them.'

'I'm not sure I follow, Sarge.'

'You're intelligent, capable, and have a law degree. You're moving *up* the greasy pole. Payne is Mr Plod. He peaked before he joined the Squad. He hates you because you're so much better than he ever will be. And DI Steele squashes anyone who threatens his career. He

112

sidelines officers who might stand in his way five, even ten years down the track.'

'But surely I'm not a threat to the boss of Homicide.'

'Not today but for a career-planner like Steele, trust me, you're a future threat.' Jo was shocked. Hughes continued. 'I made the big mistake of trying to join the club. They despise me for that. Some male cops hate women full stop, and particularly a woman who has balls. Never develop balls, DSC Best.' Hughes took a breather. Jo waited for more. It didn't come. 'Anyway, bloody well done on your first arrests. Good night, Jo.'

The phone went dead.

Well, that's a nightcap and a half, she thought. 'Thanks Sarge. I'll remember that.'

Back at work, Jo entered the incident room. Things were happening. There was the double murder in Elsternwick, the murder on Puffing Billy in the Dandenongs, and now a stabbing death in Frankston. Jo sat as far from Payne as possible. Richelieu entered and called the meeting to order.

'Mesdames et messieurs.'

'S'il vous plaît,' replied the detectives in an almost bored fashion.

'Sergeant, where are we on the double 'omicide in Elsternwick?'

Hughes reported that the Squad had agreed to prepare a brief to charge Benny Ross with both murders. Jo had serious doubts about that decision but said nothing. Sticking her neck out, and in front of the entire squad, was definitely not appealing. If the bullies wanted to silence her, they were winning.

'Thank you Sergeant. Now, DSC Payne, what's 'appening with our Murder on the Orient Express?'

Payne had no idea of the relevance of the question. He last read a novel in Year 11 at Glen Waverley High School, failed to grasp any of its themes, and was lucky to earn a D. Whether the D stood for Drongo or Dickhead, probably both, was unknown. He reported.

'We had a number of suspects and interviewing them with DI Steele proved tricky. Some were directly involved in the murder, some were accessories after the fact, and some were innocent bystanders.'

Jo choked.

'The main suspect is a young man who came into the station voluntarily and confessed to his part in the crime.'

Jo couldn't believe the way Payne belittled her work, let alone failed to even mention her arrests. According to Payne, the main suspect was the only suspect *not* arrested by Jo.

'We believe a number of charges will be laid including murder, conspiracy to murder, concealing a dead body and providing a false statement.'

'Thank you, DSC Payne. Is that all?'

'Sir,' said the smug detective.

'I think you forgot one minor matter, Detective.' Payne looked uncertain. 'You neglected to mention that your colleague, DSC Best, arrested four of the five suspects through excellent police work.'

Richelieu looked straight at Jo and applauded. She blushed. The room followed Richelieu's lead and joined the acclamation. Two non-congratulatory detectives were Payne and Steele, with the boss again slipping in at the back. Steele was good at slipping in quietly. Hughes grinned. The applause and stirring died and Richelieu continued.

'Now we move to the stabbing in Frankston. Sergeant, where are we with that, s'il vous plaît?'

'We have two suspects in custody who will be interviewed this morning. I will be leading and DSC Best will assist.' Billy refused to bow to Steele's pressure tactics.

He wanted to object but thought better of it. The granddaughter of a former popular head of the Homicide Squad had just received a warm round of applause from her colleagues, having arrested four suspects in a murder investigation. Steele knew all four arrests were sound but said nothing to Jo about her success.

She was good was Jo Best. Steele knew she needed watching, and chose to bide his time.

'Merci, ladies and gentlemen,' called Richelieu and the meeting broke up only to suddenly stop when a voice called.

'Have you finished?'

It was Beryl from Reception. She stood in the doorway with the biggest bunch of flowers ever seen in Homicide. Many officers stirred.

'Now, now,' said Beryl, 'a bit of respect please.' Silence settled. 'These are for Detective Senior Constable Best.'

More stirring. Jo nearly died. Richelieu took the flowers from Beryl and moved to the stunned and embarrassed young detective.

'Belles fleurs pour une belle dame,' he said, handing the blooms to Jo. The final touch saw him lean in and kiss Jo's cheek.

Wow. Magnificent flowers and a kiss from the French movie star.

Ribald comments flowed and finally the meeting broke up. Payne's teeth suffered due to his grinding. Hughes approached Jo.

'A secret admirer?'

Jo read the card. 'Yes, from the man I love.'

Hughes raised her eyebrows. The card read *Congratulations on your first arrest. Go girl! Love Pop.*

Hughes gave Jo the details of the stabbing murder in Frankston. They escorted the first prisoner to the interview room and, once formalities were over, Hughes began.

'Mr Hatton, you were arrested in possession of a knife we believe was used in the stabbing of your late brother-in-law, Robert Gregson. What can you tell us about the incident?'

Hatton was forty-five, surly, and shaved every third day or so. He could have shaved every third hour but would still look like the grandson of the late President Nixon. Hatton did a nice line in jowls.

'It wasn't me. I came into the room and there was Bob on the floor, and Ponzi had the knife and said, "I've done it, mate. I've killed him".'

'According to forensics, Mr Hatton, the only fingerprints found on the knife are yours. Can you explain that?'

The prisoner answered immediately. 'Ponzi had gloves.'

'How would you describe your relationship with your late brother-in-law?'

'Okay. We wasn't mates, like, but we was okay.'

'We have statements from neighbours, your brother-in-law's wife and your sister who all say the two of you were always quarrelling and last Christmas even came to blows.'

Hatton remained silent.

'Mr Hatton?'

He paused. 'It was Ponzi.'

Hughes looked at Hatton. The man was not for moving. She ended the recording and the interview. Hatton looked relieved.

'Can I go now?'

'Not yet, Mr Hatton,' said Hughes. He scowled. 'In fact, unless you come up with some truthful answers, I'd say not for quite some time.'

Hatton's jowls got a serious workout, and he left for his cell.

Hughes turned to Jo. 'Your thoughts, Detective?'

Jo loved these moments. She loved being treated with respect by a fellow officer, and the challenge of trying to solve a case. The difference in attitude between Hughes and Strange as opposed to Steele and Payne was like chocolate and concrete.

Jo opined. 'Well, on the surface it's an open and shut case. Hatton killed Gregson, and is trying, pathetically, to shift the blame to someone else. Who is this other prisoner, Ponzi?'

'Real name David Baggio, a friend of the family and fellow criminal. Hatton, Baggio and the deceased are all, as they say, known to police. Nothing major but all have a string of convictions.'

Jo wondered why they called it a "string" of convictions.

Hughes offered advice. 'One thing I've learnt is to never accept "caught red-handed" as necessarily true.'

'Are you saying this Baggio guy isn't the killer?'

'I'm saying let's have him in and hear his story.'

David Baggio, nicknamed Ponzi, was a weasel. He was cunning, deceitful, clever and bad. He sat opposite the detectives with a look that screamed innocence. Butter wouldn't melt.

'Why am I here? I had nothing to do with Bob's death.'

'Thank you, Mr Baggio,' said Hughes. 'I'm sure you know the routine. We ask the questions and you get to say things like, *I didn't do it, I've been framed* and *No comment.*'

The interview began with Baggio denying everything, maintaining his innocence, and demanding to be released. It was like the previous interview where again the police failed to score.

Before ending the interview, Hughes turned to Jo. 'Any questions, Senior Constable?'

Jo had been studying Baggio's history. She smiled at the prisoner, coming across as the good cop.

'You have Italian ancestry, Mr Baggio?'

He nodded. 'A long way back.'

'Then I guess you've heard of Al Capone?'

He was confused and even Hughes didn't see the relevance.

'Possibly.'

'The cops couldn't get the gangster for murder but he got eleven years for tax evasion—eleven years for a lousy tax crime.'

Baggio was cagey and interested.

'So?'

'If you tell us what really happened with the stabbing, we might, just might be able to have another look at those tax matters Fraud Squad is investigating. No promises mind, but a bit of mutual back scratching here could be in your best interests.'

Baggio concentrated hard. Even Hughes was hooked.

'How do I know I can trust you?'

'You can't. But what are your options? Life for murder, two for a tax fiddle or maybe, maybe nothing—if you tell us what really happened.'

Baggio worked through his options. 'If I tell you what happened, you'll forget the other stuff?'

Jo stood. 'Okay, Mr Baggio, the interview's over. You've blown it.'

Hughes was pleasantly shocked at Jo's acting. Baggio believed her.

'No wait, wait, please.' Jo stopped and looked at him. 'Don't mess me around, Mr Baggio.' She paused then sat. Hughes was impressed.

He twitched and started to sweat. He came clean. 'Ola did it.'

The detectives looked at one another. Hughes was about to take over then stopped and nodded to Jo.

'Ola being Mr Gregson's sister, Mr Hatton's wife?'

Baggio nodded.

'For the tape, please Mr Baggio.'

'Yes.'

'What happened?' asked Jo.

'I got there to talk about ... I went there to have a meal with my friends. When I arrived, they were panicking. Gregson was dead. Hatton and Ola were arguing something crazy like.'

Jo went to ask a question but stopped when Hughes put a hand on her arm. The message was clear. "Let him speak". Baggio did.

'Ola's son told his mother that Gregson had ... had been touching him. She went ape shit and challenged her brother. Gregson said it was a pack of lies. Hatton and Ola didn't believe him. Hatton and Gregson started fighting. Ola grabbed the knife and stabbed her brother.'

There was a long pause. Jo looked at her colleague who nodded.

'What happened next, Mr Baggio?'

'I arrived and they told me everything. Hatton wiped Ola's prints. He said they'd claim it was self-defence, and that Hatton called Gregson a paedophile. He went mad and attacked Hatton who grabbed a knife and defended himself.'

'They claim it was you who stabbed Mr Gregson.'

Baggio shook his head. 'Hatton is protecting his wife.'

Baggio felt good having told his story. The police were glad they had another theory. Hughes was doubly glad with the brilliant piece of detective work by her colleague.

'Please,' said Baggio, 'I had nothing to do with this. I'll put me hand up for the tax stuff but murder, no way.'

'Will you sign a statement detailing what you've just said?' asked Jo.

Baggio nodded.

They took his statement. He signed it.

'Can I go now?'

'Not yet, Mr Baggio,' said Hughes. 'We need to check a number of things you've told us.'

He looked miserable. 'It's true,' he whispered.

'What's true?' asked Hughes.

'Gregson interfered with kids.'

With Baggio back in a cell, the detectives walked back to their office.

'Thanks for the opportunity, Sarge. I really appreciate it,' said Jo.

'And I really appreciate having a clever detective on my team.'

They stopped and looked at one another. Jo smiled.

From his office, DI Steele watched the two women and noted their friendship and respect. *Those two are trouble*, he thought.

19

PATTERSON LAKES is a suburb in Melbourne's vast sprawl. The "Lakes" offer residents a mini alternative to Florida or the Gold Coast in Queensland. After work, Jo used her Sat Nav to find the address. It was a basic home with no water frontage, a sort of nice try but no cigar.

She parked, walked along the drive and rang the doorbell. The person who opened the door got one hell of a fright. Fear was the immediate reaction; the fear of being arrested and going to jail. Then hate came into it. Hate for the cops who tricked people.

'Mr Baggio,' said Jo, 'remember me?'

He nodded. He wanted to say, "You bitch" but restrained himself.

'What do you want?'

'A little chat.'

A woman called from inside the house. 'Who is it?'

He looked at the detective. 'Not here,' he said.

'Suits me.'

He called to the woman. 'It's business. I'll be five minutes.'

'Ten,' said Jo.

They walked to her car and got in.

This time he did say it. 'You bitch. We made a deal.'

'Easy, Mr Baggio, I'm not here to arrest you.'

That took some of the wind out of his sails but he was still angry.

'What then?'

'I've been looking at your record, David. May I call you David?' He didn't reply. 'I'm working for a secret task force trying to catch people who scam their victims. I have to admit we know very little about the schemes criminals invent, which is why I've come to see you.'

'I don't follow.'

He did follow and didn't like what he thought was coming.

119

'We need advice from someone who knows about scams, and I reckon you might be the man.'

The more he heard, the more nervous he became.

'You want me to work for the cops?'

'Not as such. True, I'm a cop, but this task force is unofficial. It's police and IT experts working privately, under the radar.'

'You've lost me.'

'We're a small team dedicated to retrieving money stolen by scammers. We get the scammer to invest in a scam then we return the money to the person who was stung. It's a type of Robin Hood deal.'

'But running a scam is illegal.'

'Perhaps, but what if you're righting a wrong?'

Baggio thought about it. 'What if I refuse?'

'Da-vid,' oozed Jo.

'You'll treat me like Al Capone and find some tax fiddle in my past.'

'Let's face facts, Mr Baggio.' He was back to being a client. 'Yes, this involves crime. But as a cop, how much greater will my punishment be if we're caught? They'll throw away the key.'

More think music for Baggio. 'How much do I get?'

'You're on 5%.'

'Of what?'

'The first scam is 200 grand.'

'The *first* scam?'

'There are at least two and who knows, this could be a nice little earner for you, David. It's 5% of 200K, ten grand, cash, tax-free, in your pocket and no questions asked. It's a no-brainer.'

Another pause. 'Let me think about it.'

'Dave, come on, we both know you're in. What choice do you have?'

'If you rat on me, so help me I'll do what Ola did to Gregson.'

'And a Merry Christmas to you too,' said Jo, starting her car. Baggio got the point and hopped out. 'I'll be in touch. Bye.'

She drove off leaving the crook wondering what the hell he'd agreed to do. Jo drove around the corner and pulled over. She took out her phone and sent a text to Michael Chan of Northcote.

Monte Christo.

Michael Chan thought long and hard about Detective Joanna Best. He liked her and her proposal. He liked it even more because he saw it as a way to help his father recover his money.

Within parts of the Chinese community, there was great pride in behaving a certain way, in being honourable. There was shame in failure. Michael's father would never mention his folly, his disgrace in being defrauded. He believed he was at least partly to blame and therefore would bear the financial consequences.

Michael knew he must never tell his father about the Jo Best partnership, and scammers must never know about him or his Dad.

But all that was in the future. First, Michael had to help the police officer get back the money her mother had lost. How?

Find the scammer and create the scam was Michael's job. Dodge the cops and stay out of jail was Jo's job.

Simple.

Ha.

Michael sent a text to Jo. *Northcote 2100 hours.*

She replied *RT.*

He had to think about that then figured it meant *Roger that.*

They sat in Michael's warehouse, and this time Jo accepted his hospitality, enjoying a latte from Michael the barista.

'So tell me about the scammer,' he said as they sipped.

Jo described Baggio, his background, and their meeting at Patterson Lakes. She didn't mention how she persuaded him to join Team Monte Christo other than to say he was known to the police, and when offered 2% of the takings he jumped at the chance. Jo lied to Michael about Ponzi's attitude and cut—her lies were mounting.

'His nickname's Ponzi.' Michael laughed. 'What's funny?'

'Charles Ponzi was an Italian who moved to the States where he conned people out of their savings. Today's get-rich-quick schemes are named after Mr Ponzi.'

'Baggio's got Italian blood.'

'Well let's hope he's smarter than his namesake.'

Jo turned serious. 'Michael, I've got questions.'

'Shoot.'

'What if we can't find the scammer?'

'No scammer, no scam. Jo, this entire project is like any Ponzi scheme. It could collapse in an instant.' She looked glum. 'If we can't find the scammer, or if we can and he won't take the bait, we're done. There are no guarantees. And here's the kicker; if we make a mistake, we could be killed or worse, go to jail.'

'Going to jail is worse than being killed?'

'If you're a cop it is.'

Jo felt a chill and whispered, 'Ouch.'

He spoke softly. 'It's not too late to pull out.' He paused. 'Want to?'

She paused and looked into his eyes. 'No'.

Jo knew her idea was now a goer. This was no longer a wish, a hope or a dream. This was a project with a goal, and with Ponzi on board, it was all systems go. But OMG it was scary, and making it work seemed enormously difficult or more likely, impossible.

'So how do we find the scammer?'

'We set a trap, and play him at his own game.'

'How?'

'We do what your Mum did. Her profile was real but we invent a middle-aged, lonely woman, put her photo and details online, and hope like hell he takes the bait.'

Jo filtered this information. 'Okay, so a scammer responds, maybe more than one. How do we know he or she's the right one?'

'There are ways.'

'And what about lonely blokes who genuinely want love? What if they respond?'

'We politely tell them we've found our one true love.'

He looked at Jo. She thought. *Speaking of love, is he flirting?*

'Yes but the Count of Monte Christo knew his enemies, we don't. I only want to scam the bastard who ripped off my Mum.'

'Understood, and unless we're sure it's him, we don't call in Ponzi.'

Jo liked Michael's thinking. His answers were sound—so far.

'So how can we tell?'

'Has your Mum kept any of his emails?'

'They're on her laptop.'

'Does she know you've seen them?'

'No.'

'Keep it that way. But I need to see those emails yesterday. Can you get me copies?'

'I think so.'

'You'd better know so.' He gave her a USB stick. 'Use this.'

She took the device. 'I'll get them tomorrow.'

'From his emails, we study his language, writing style and background story. We might get lucky if he uses the same one.'

'Will he do that?'

'It worked for him before, and the chances of him being sprung are reduced because most victims say nothing.'

'The perfect example being Mrs Shirley Best.'

'Obviously the name and photo he uses will change but I reckon his speech pattern and sales pitch will be like a fingerprint.'

Jo trusted Michael. She thought he'd make a good scammer. She reckoned he was capable and honest, but she had more questions.

'So we create and post the profile, the scammer replies, and we reckon it's him. What then?'

'Come on down, Ponzi.'

'What, straightaway?'

'Immediately. The timing is everything. The longer we chat with the scammer, the easier it is for him to discover our lady doesn't exist. Once we're chatting, we introduce the scam.'

'How do we do that?'

'That's a question for Signor Ponzi. My idea is to have the woman tell the scammer she's been offered this deal and ask him for advice. He checks it out and tells her it's a scam while believing it's not.'

'What deal?'

'I'm still working on that.'

'Okay, but will he bite? Surely the best person to spot a scam is someone who runs a scam.'

'True, these guys are pros, but I reckon they run several victims at any one time. If Ponzi's scam is good and we tell the scammer we've invested and it's paid off, maybe, just maybe he'll nibble.'

'God, there are so many ifs and maybes.'

'And if the scammer gets serious, he'll check out our woman.'

'Who doesn't exist.'

'Which is why we need to scam first.'

Jo sighed. This was exciting but she didn't feel excited. This was risky and she did feel bilious. More questions.

'So we get the money. How easy is it for him to find us?'

'Difficult. His emails to your Mum may exist on her laptop but I'm sure nowhere else. His copies, his ID, and ISP details are all gone. Ours will be too. And if we can get vision of him being scammed and post that online, he'll be ropeable, and hugely embarrassed. How can he show his face? He'll be busy looking for cosmetic surgery.'

Jo expelled air. So many thoughts told her to quit. This could end her career, devastate her family, even send her to jail. In her head she screamed, "Don't do it, girl". But the thought of her mother's misery and empty bank account, the sheer bloody injustice of the situation spurred her on. She looked at Michael.

'So what now?'

'Let's invent a lonely woman.'

Cornelius Kruger went on holiday. He wanted to return to his native South Africa, to his beloved Joburg but no chance. It was far too dangerous. Too many law-abiding citizens, not to mention fellow crims, were keen to stretch his neck, remove his testicles or do something far worse. He went to Noumea for an affair with the Sun.

Now let's clear up any misunderstanding. Scammers do not necessarily live the life of Reilly. It ain't all beer and skittles for Kruger and his ilk.

He could spend weeks, even months trying to scam a victim and finish up getting peanuts, even nothing. All that graft for zero return. And if he did crack the jackpot, as he did with AUD $203,048 and 29 cents from Shirley Best of Balwyn North, don't forget that type of return doesn't happen every week. And remember that was his gross return. You have to consider his expenses.

Computer experts cost money. Private investigators aren't cheap, and muscle, I mean good protection costs a bundle.

Then there are operating costs such as overseas bank accounts, fake IDs, money laundering and the like. They all cost money. And money is what Connie lived for—the more the better. His conscience, if he ever had one, died a long time ago. The pain he provided free to his victims never bothered him for a nanosecond.

He returned from holiday and to work, trawling the Net for wealthy women looking for love. Sometimes all they wanted was affection or companionship. Some would settle for an online pen friend.

He clicked on his favourite web site and checked out the talent. He thought there was not much on offer until ... Bingo.

Helen Varigos grabbed him. She was in Melbourne, handy for a personal check, looked 45, and her background seemed Southern European. Maybe she married a Greek. Then he grew suspicious.

The victim's appearance didn't matter to Connie. The size of her bank balance did; in fact, the more plain the patsy, the better. But this bird was nudging attractive. Not stunning but better than most women on this site. Why is a good-looking woman lonely?

Because of this red flag, Connie checked Helen's picture using photo recognition software. Michael Chan anticipated this. He'd used a photo of a deceased woman he found in a family photo sent by a former neighbour. Michael checked her visibility online and found nothing. So Connie kept reading. He noted she posted late last night.

She's online at all hours. I think she's worth a reply.

Connie typed.

Hello Helen.

What a fantastic smile you have. Are you an actress or a model? My name's Marco. I was born in Greece but moved to Sydney as a child. I still dream about those sundrenched islands in the sparkling Aegean Sea. I work for an international bank, boring financial stuff, and have done so for far too long. I'm thinking of settling down. My photo's attached, and if you'd like to chat, I'd love to hear from you. Marco.

He polished his post. He was taking a punt running with the Greek angle but experience taught him that playing safe rarely produced results. If you're going to lie, make it a biggie.

He read his post aloud, smiled and congratulated himself.

'Bloody marvellous, Kruger—subtle flattery, an appeal to her possible roots, and here's me, a successful international businessman. God you're good, my son.' He hit *Send*.

It was mid-morning when Helen's incoming post went ping on a computer in Northcote, and Michael Chan got excited. He immediately sent a text to Jo.

She looked at her phone and read the text. It was that code.

Monte Christo.

She read it and started to shake.

On Michael's advice, Jo chose not to talk to him by phone unless for an emergency. She wasn't free until that night and sent him a text.

Tonight sans Al?

Al was short for *Al Capone* and the name they agreed to use to identify Ponzi. Michael confirmed the meeting and sent, *sans Al.*

The game was afoot. But before tonight's meeting, Jo needed data.

She headed to Balwyn North. Shirley was worse than ever. Jo was tempted to tell her the plan to reclaim her money.

A ridiculous idea, particularly as it may never work.

'Mum, I need to set up your new account. We can do it online.'

Shirley grumbled but led Jo into the bedroom and to her laptop. 'A new account for someone else to steal my money,' she moaned.

'Let me, Mum,' said Jo and took the seat. 'I'll do it. You make us a cuppa. Go on.'

Shirley did as told and Jo immediately opened her mother's email account, found the scam emails and copied them. She had started on Shirley's bank account changes when her mother called.

'Tea's ready.'

'I'll be right there.'

Jo finished entering the new account details, closed the laptop, pocketed the USB stick, and joined her mother.

'All done, and I've left the details beside the laptop. Put them somewhere safe and ...'

Shirley joined in. '... never give your banking details to anyone.'

They drank their tea with Jo thinking about Michael and Ponzi.

Gentlemen, can you please help my desperately sad mother?

Jo drove to work. In her bag was one USB stick with data for her partner in crime that night.

20

JO STARED AT THE PHOTO on the incident board. 'I know that woman,' she said, 'but from where?'

Baldwin joined her. 'That's Dora Madigan, the cleaning lady who found the bodies in the Elsternwick double homicide.'

'Where have I seen her? Did you interview her?'

'I did.'

'And?'

'She's a quiet woman who suffered a massive shock when she discovered her employers dead in bed. Wouldn't you?'

'Isn't the killer often the person who finds the body?'

'I think you're confused. It's actually the butler what done it, guv.'

Jo laughed. She liked Baldwin. His manners were impeccable even if he seemed to be guilty of tunnel vision. To her, he couldn't think outside the box, and his next statement seemed to justify that.

'The last person to see the couple alive was Benny Ross, the man who killed them—the man we charged with two counts of murder.'

'How do we know he was the last person?'

'Okay, I know you made four arrests from confessions, and this case has no confessions, and these charges are based on incriminating, not circumstantial evidence but there's a lot of incriminating evidence.'

She couldn't argue. 'Fair enough.' Still her curiosity kept nagging as she stared at the photo.

Hughes entered carrying files. 'That stuff on the incident board can come down. And when you've finished that vitally important task, Detective, I've got something really exciting for you.'

'Sarge?' asked Jo in hope.

'Read these notes.' She plonked the files on Jo's desk.

'What am I looking for, Sarge?'

'There was a sudden death in Ballarat earlier this year. The coroner declared it an accident.'

'You think otherwise?'

'Possibly a suicide but the victim's family reckon it's a homicide.'

'So what am I looking for, Sarge?'

'If I knew that, Senior Constable, I wouldn't ask you to look. Give me your findings in the morning. I'm off. See you tomorrow.'

Hughes departed and Jo started removing the double murder material. She kept staring at the photo of the cleaning lady.

'Dora Madigan ... where have I seen you before?'

Baldwin explained. 'She said the Halls were wonderful employers.'

'People or employers? There's a difference.'

'Her neighbours gave her a glowing reference.'

'How did she get the job?'

He shrugged. 'No idea.'

'It might be interesting to know that.'

Baldwin stopped work. 'Jo, if I may speak bluntly.'

'Please do. I like bluntly.'

'Boring homicide detectives like me tend to rely on evidence. If you keep chasing hunches, you might get lucky, or you might get bitten.'

Jo looked at the colleague she liked and respected. 'Thanks. And I've already been bitten—several times.'

She continued removing material and then it hit her.

She buzzed. 'Yes! Now I remember where I've seen her photo.

'Where?'

'In Bradley and Gavin's flat. The photo's in the bookshelf.'

Baldwin was shocked. 'Are you sure?'

'It's a group photo with the boys and this woman's in the middle. It's Dora Madigan. The cleaner knows the son of the murdered couple.'

'And his boyfriend.' Jo looked at a worried Baldwin. 'Shit.'

'What's wrong?'

'You.'

'Me?'

'You're dangerous, Jo Best.'

'Sorry?'

'If I don't follow this up and you're right, I'm in trouble.

Jo was confused. 'Why wouldn't you follow it up?'

'Because the case is closed. Because we've charged Benny Ross with two counts of murder.'

'So?'

'Jo, the evidence is very strong. Steele has signed off on it.'

'Who's the OIC?'

'Richelieu.'

'Run it past him.'

'He's on leave; not back till next week.'

'And DI Steele?'

'At some meeting in Geelong.'

'And Billy's just gone.'

The conversation stalled. Jo was sure she was right about the photo. Baldwin dreaded having to tell Steele there might be a complication in a case, which, from the Homicide POV, was wrapped up nice and tight.

'Your call, Detective Baldwin.'

'If I follow it up and you're wrong, I'm in trouble.

'What, for doing your job?'

'No, for investigating a case when a suspect's already been charged.'

'But he might be the *wrong* suspect. He might be innocent.'

'That's not a reason.'

Despite his serious face, she knew he was joking. Baldwin respected Jo, even liked her but he was no leader. He could follow orders but grabbing the bull by the horns was not his style.

Jo switched tactics. 'Charley, if you follow this up and find that Dora is involved with the son or his boyfriend ...'

'Or both.'

'Or both, then doesn't that create a question?'

He was being sarcastic. 'One or two.'

'So what are you waiting for? If it helps, I'll come with you and tell the bosses it was all my idea.'

'It *is* all your idea.'

'But I'm happy for you to take the glory.'

He paused then grabbed his jacket. 'Come on, Sadie the cleaning lady awaits.'

In the car, they discussed tactics. Jo had ideas. 'We need to catch her denying something we know or can later prove is true.'

Baldwin admired her insight. 'Such as?'

129

'What's her relationship to the boys? Why is she in that photo?'

'*If* she's in that photo.'

'She is, I'm sure.'

'In one way, I hope you're hopelessly wrong.' She looked at him. 'You must know you've made enemies here.'

'Not deliberately.'

'The Pope himself has blessed this case.'

'The Pope?'

'DI Steele.'

'Oh.'

'I thought you knew.'

'Knew what?'

'Steele's the Pope, and Richelieu's the Cardinal.'

Damn. Cardinals have taken a vow of chastity.

'So if we, meaning you, Jo Best, find an alternative killer and, horror of horrors, prove they're guilty, His Holiness will not be happy.'

'But why? Surely making the right arrest is all that counts?'

'True but embarrassing His Holiness is playing with fire.'

'Meaning?'

'There are some officers you do not want to cross.'

'Understood, but I meant what I said. If this turns out a winner, it's your case and you'll get the gold star.'

Baldwin thought about the suggestion. 'Nah, I can't handle praise whereas you can handle bullying.'

She agreed with that and liked it. 'You're not my enemy, Charley.'

He laughed. 'I haven't got any enemies. That's my weakness.'

She had to think about that.

Dora Madigan was surprised, and invited the detectives into her small home. Jo was introduced, and all three sat in the lounge-room.

Baldwin began. 'Thank you for seeing us, Mrs Madigan. There are a couple of things we'd like to clear up.'

'I'll help if I can,' she said. 'But I thought you'd found the man who killed Mr and Mrs Hall.'

'Can you tell us how it was you came to be employed by them?'

She thought about that. 'Oh, let me think. It might have been an advertisement in the local paper. Yes, I think that's how I got the job.'

'And is it true you had a key to the property and could come and go when necessary?'

'Yes, that's correct. But I gave the key to their son, Gavin.'

Jo jumped in. 'Not to Bradley?'

A change of questioner unsettled her. There was a flicker of panic. 'Who?'

'Gavin's boyfriend, Bradley Finch. Do you know him?'

She had to think. 'I may have met him once or twice.'

Jo switched topics. 'What size shoe do you take, Mrs Madigan?'

This threw Dora. 'What size shoe? Why do you want to know that?'

'Our forensic people have found some footprints, and we need to eliminate everyone who's been in the house.'

'Oh.'

'And the garden.'

'The garden?'

'Have you ever been in the Hall garden, Mrs Madigan?'

'Of course, many times, and I'm a size 6.'

Jo took notes then handed Dora the notebook and pen. 'And might I have your date of birth please?'

She was flustered. 'Whatever for? Is this really necessary?'

'Just for the record … please.' Jo produced her winning smile.

Dora shook her head, wrote her DOB then handed back the items. 'Many thanks, Mrs M. Now just a couple more things, please.'

Baldwin watched this with growing wonderment. He could never have thought of these questions. And what did the answers mean?

'Do you know a man called George Moss?'

Dora needed think music. She looked worried. 'The name sounds familiar.'

'He came to the Hall house on several occasions.'

'Well a lot of people did that. Mr and Mrs Hall were very sociable.'

'And did you perform domestic tasks such as food preparation and serving food?'

'For dinner parties I helped prepare food but never served it.'

'Well, thank you, Mrs Madigan. You've been very helpful.' Jo looked at Baldwin. He got the message and stood.

'Yes, thank you, Mrs Madigan. We're sorry to intrude and let's hope this whole tragic business can be resolved without us needing to trouble you again.'

'Please God,' she said.

The detectives left and sat in their car.

'I hope you know what you're doing, Jo Best, because I haven't got a bloody clue.'

'We need to get to Gavin and Bradley's flat in Carlton.'

'What? Why?'

'Come on, I'll explain on the way.'

En route, Baldwin heard all of Jo's thoughts and theories from Dora's interview. He was not convinced.

'But why didn't you just ask her if she knew the son and his boyfriend?'

'Come on, Charlie. Cops are allowed to be clever you know.'

'I cannot believe that old woman was involved in the murder. What, you think she helped the son or his boyfriend?'

'Or both. Or worked alone.'

'Alone? She's tiny. Jo, please don't say any of this in front of Steele.'

'Dora had the means and opportunity. All we need is her motive.'

'What motive? Jo, you're doing what I warned you about, following a hunch. Evidence is what cracks a case.'

They continued arguing, which Jo considered a discussion, until they arrived at Gavin and Bradley's flat.

Gavin opened the door and wasn't pleased. They showed their ID.

'You people make me sick,' he said.

'We're terribly sorry, sir,' said Baldwin, who was as unhappy as Gavin. When, not if, Steele heard about this visit, Baldwin dreaded the consequences.

Jo didn't care. She smiled. 'May we come in for a minute, please?'

Bradley came from the kitchen and was equally miffed. 'What now?'

'I promise this will only take a minute,' said Jo.

The occupants stepped back, and the police entered. Jo made straight for the bookshelf to pick up the photo. Disaster. It wasn't there. She looked around the room.

'I'm looking for the photo which was here in your bookshelf.'

Bradley was confused. 'What photo?'

'The one with you gentlemen and an older lady. It was right there when I interviewed you on my previous visit.'

Bradley looked at Gavin. 'What's she talking about?'

'No idea,' replied his flat mate.

'Gentlemen, I saw the photo in this room. I know what I saw.' The occupants remained mute. Jo persisted. 'Gentlemen, I'm not lying.'

Oh dear. Grab a shovel, Jo, and this way to your grave.

Baldwin took up religion. Right now, he'd take help from anyone. 'Detective Best,' is all he could say.

Gavin gave her both barrels. 'I'm not calling you a lair, officer, but I am calling your superiors and complaining about this harassment and bullying at a time when my partner and I are trying to grieve. Have you forgotten? I'm the son whose parents have just been murdered. Their funerals are next Monday.'

Jo was stumped. She knew it. A grovelling retreat was her only option. 'Gentlemen, I apologise for the intrusion.'

'Yes, we're very sorry,' added Baldwin ushering Jo outside.

At the door, Bradley called after the detectives. 'Sorry won't cut it. You people make us sick.'

The sound of a door receiving a harsh punishment followed the detectives as they returned to their car. To say Baldwin was furious would be an understatement. Jo was angry and frustrated, but ignorant about her colleague's state of mind. She raged.

They got in their car and Jo let fly. 'They moved it. They were expecting us. Dora rang and warned them and they hid the photo.'

If she was angry, Baldwin was fuming. He was a boiler expelling steam ready to explode. 'Jesus Christ, Jo, will you listen to yourself?'

She was shocked at her well-mannered and polite colleague blaspheming with ease.

She still didn't get it. 'But it's true. I saw the photo and they've moved it.'

'What is wrong with you? Will you never learn? What is true, and what you can prove is true are not necessarily the same.'

In despair he slapped his hands on the steering wheel. Jo now knew she was in trouble.

The only sound was Baldwin's breathing. It was savage. After a while, who knows how long, she plucked up the courage to speak.

'I'm sorry, Charlie. I'll take all the blame.'

'Well thank you very much, Detective Best, how mightily magnanimous of you. And who's the senior officer in this totally shambolic shambles? Hey?' She dared not answer. 'Just do me one more favour, if you please, madam.'

'Of course.' She'd do almost anything to help him right now.

'Remind me to never trust you again.'

He started the engine. The return journey took place in silence. The only saving grace being Steele was out of town. It was at best for Best, a stay of execution.

Jo's worries about the bollocking she would receive in the morning were softened a smidgeon by news from Michael. She left work early and headed to Northcote.

21

'HAVE YOU HEARD FROM MARCO?' Jo forgot to greet Michael or enquire about his health. After her horrible day at Homicide, she was off her game and failed good manners.

'And hello to you too,' he replied.

'Sorry, I've had a bad day.'

Michael quickly shifted to business. 'I think we've heard from Marco. Have you got your mother's emails?' She gave him the USB stick. 'We've had a few replies but I reckon only one's a possibility.'

He brought up a split screen with Shirley's scammer's emails on one side and the message from Marco on the other. They stared at the text. Michael was excited, Jo confused.

'I'm not sure. Are they the same?'

'I thought you were the detective.'

I am, but today was not my best day.

Michael was convinced. He indicated the similarities in sentence structure, vocabulary and flattery. 'See here how he compliments her with the bit about being an actress or a model. To your mother it's "once a glamourous woman, always a glamourous woman" malarkey.'

'But it's so false,' said Jo. 'Why can't women see that?'

Michael stared at Jo who felt a tad uncomfortable. 'Your hair looks different. I like that casual style.'

She stared back. *Is this a joke or a sincere compliment?*

'Thanks,' she said.

'I rest my case. If you receive a compliment, and especially from someone you can't see, a part of you is excited, happy even grateful.'

She nodded. 'So you're a psychologist too.'

'And I *do* like your hair. It suits you.'

She smiled. *I think he's serious.* 'Okay, Mr Scammer, what now?'

'I've had second thoughts about Ponzi.'

Jo worried. 'Oh?'

'I think we need him but I never want him to come here. In fact, I never want to meet him. Have you told him about me?'

'No, and I won't,' she replied not knowing where this was going.

'I think he's better as the checker of scams. We come up with the scam then have him check it for possible flaws.'

'Michael, we don't have a clue when it comes to creating a scam.'

'I know but I've had a chat with a stockbroker friend. He told me about scams in the investment world.'

Jo was interested and concerned. 'Okay, I'm listening.'

'One scam has two friends who pick their victim. The friends buy a lot of low-priced shares in a failing company. They make sure the victim hears them talking about a massive windfall the company is about to receive. The victim buys up big, sending the shares higher and the two friends cash in before the price collapses.'

'Which it does.'

'Exactly. They make a killing but the victim owns useless shares.'

'So we buy useless shares, then what?'

'Not literally.'

'You've lost me.'

Michael gestured to his wall of equipment. 'Welcome to my magical kingdom where shares are created at the flick of a switch.'

'You create shares?'

'In our favourite novel, remember the message sent by telegraph, and paid for by the Count of Monte Christo?'

'It was a fake news message.'

'Good old fake news was around way back then.'

Jo started to understand. 'Ah, so we send a fake message.'

'Lots of them. I set up phony web sites with articles, reports, and fake op-ed pieces which all relate to the shares. And we have a manned phone line in case Marco rings to check.'

'Who mans the phone?'

He was surprised. 'Jo, there are such places as answering services. They answer on behalf of the out-of-town CEO.'

'Okay. So where does Ponzi fit into all this?'

'Maybe not at all.'

'But you insisted we find a scammer.'

'Jo, if we create a brilliant scam we could still come unstuck if someone leaks. *We* won't but Ponzi's a crook. Do you trust him?'

'So we drop him?'

'No. We use him to vet what we create.'

Jo saw Michael's logic. 'Can you tell me more about the scam?'

He did. To Jo it sounded plausible but she still had difficulty believing a scammer would fall for a scam.

Then they wrote their first reply to Marco.

Dear Marco

I'm delighted to hear from you. As you've guessed, I'm a single, middle-aged woman looking for friendship and companionship. If I found love, that would be a bonus.

I am a woman of independent means as my former husband was ordered to provide for me after our divorce.

My interests are reading, travel, and caring for my baby. He's a Shih Tzu called Aleksy. I have attached a photo of my darling.

So if you wish to write back, I'll be delighted to hear from you.

In friendship,

Helen

Jo was impressed with Michael's sensitivity.

'Michael, you're an Agony Aunt. And I love the dog.'

He produced his tiny smile. 'The tricky part is to sound sincere. We have to get to the heart of the criminal.'

'Criminals don't have hearts.'

He grimaced and stared at her. 'So, do I send it?'

She stared back. 'Send it.'

He did.

Then Michael typed an email with details of the share scam. He printed a copy and Jo read it.

'It looks fine to me. What now?'

'We wait to hear from Marco then send this latest email once we get the okay from Ponzi.'

'We send this to Ponzi?'

'Not send; hand deliver.'

They stared at one another.

'What, now?'

Michael shrugged. 'The sooner he approves it, the sooner we send it and the sooner we get to scam Marco.'

Jo grimaced. 'I'm scared, Michael.'

'Join the club.'

'I'm scared we've both made a seriously bad mistake.'

He looked confused then understood. 'Oh, fingerprints?'

She held up the page he'd printed for Ponzi. 'Both our fingerprints are now on this page. If Ponzi turns snitch, this'll kill us.'

'That's why a nerd needs a streetwise cop. Any suggestions?'

She opened her bag and took out a folder. Inside was a piece of paper. She removed some latex gloves. 'Please put these on.'

Michael did and she held out the folder. He removed the piece of paper, turned it over and saw a letterhead.

'Victoria Police? Are you crazy?'

'I thought we might need to give Ponzi some paperwork. If he gets a screed on official letterhead, he'll be impressed.'

'Forget Ponzi, *I'm* impressed.'

Michael printed the scam details on the police letterhead.

'Fold it in half,' said Jo, 'and half again.'

Michael did then placed the folded document back inside the folder. Jo placed the folder in her bag. They looked at one another.

'Michael, I worry that by consorting with a criminal, my life as a police officer will be over.'

He knew she was under pressure. He didn't know she was under even more pressure in her job.

'You'll be fine,' he said. 'Think of the cause.'

'Thanks. Okay, I'm off to see the wizard.'

It was late afternoon as Jo drove to Patterson Lakes, and worried about their scammer.

Is Ponzi a risk? Can we do this without him?

She parked and knocked on his door. Mrs Ponzi answered. Jo thought on her feet, and pretended to be surprised.

'Oh, hello, are you Natalie?'

'Who do you want?'

'I'm looking for Natalie, the dressmaker.'

Suddenly Ponzi appeared in the hallway and made eye contact with the visitor. He shook his head.

'What's her address?' asked the wife.

Jo had studied the geography before her first visit. She looked at her phone. '27 Waterview Drive.'

'This is 27 Hilton. Go back to the roundabout, left and left again.'

'Thanks, sorry to trouble you.'

She turned to leave when Ponzi came towards her.

'That's not the best way. I'll show you.'

He pushed past his wife and walked out with Jo. They headed down the drive where he spoke softly but with fury.

'What the hell are you doing? You wanna wreck my marriage?'

'We have a scam and need your input.'

'So send it to me.'

'We're not happy with phone calls and texts hence my visit.'

'Well I'm not happy with visits. My wife is a problem.'

'Look, I've got a document in my bag. We need you to read it and tell us if it can be improved.'

'Don't hand it to me in the open.'

Jo realised that being a good cop didn't necessarily make you a good crook. She didn't know what to do.

'Drop your bag,' said Ponzi as he pointed up the road.

'What?'

'Drop your bag,' he hissed. 'We'll both bend to pick it up and then hand me the folder.'

'It's too big.'

'Just drop the bag.'

Jo got the message and dropped her bag. She pretended to fumble. Ponzi knelt to help. She held her bag open revealing the open folder. Ponzi grabbed the folded screed, and stuffed it in his pocket. They looked up the street as he continued to give directions.

'I need your email,' she said.

'That's traceable too.' She fluttered her eyes and got his email.

'I'll email you from a public computer. In the meantime, read our scam and be ready to tell us how it can be improved.'

She did the big smiling act, thanking him for advice and drove away. Only as she left did she notice her shaking hands. Only now did it dawn on her. A serving police officer consorting with criminals was not a good look. Not good? It was dynamite. Were they seen? Would he double cross her? Getting caught did not bear thinking about.

Ponzi made a show of looking in his letterbox, before returning to his nosy Missus. Jo and Michael's scam was about to be studied.

Next morning she was not looking forward to work. Baldwin hadn't spoken to her and memories of her major stuff-up were fresh. There was no one in the office so she resumed looking through the case notes as requested by DS Hughes.

See, she had a hunch. Some detectives do follow their feelings.

Baldwin arrived looking worried. They made eye contact.

'Good morning,' said Jo.

'What's good about it?'

'I meant it, Charley, when I said I'd take all the blame.'

'Ah no, you've done enough damage already. I will handle this.'

'Sure,' said a chastened junior officer. 'You're the boss.'

'Is that supposed to be funny?'

Jo said nothing. Whatever she said would be wrong.

His body language spoke volumes. He spoke facing a window. 'I hope you realise, Detective Best, you're about to ruin my career.'

What could she say? Plenty, but she remained silent as Hughes arrived.

'Well then, who is the bigger moron? Three complaints for bullying and harassment, and from witnesses in a case which is closed. What part of "Move on" and "Leave it alone" don't you two understand?'

Baldwin jumped in. 'It was my call, Sarge.'

'Bullshit,' snapped Hughes. 'Charley, you haven't the bottle to bully anyone, including a junior who thinks she's God's gift to policing.'

That hurt.

Jo had to speak. 'It was my idea, Sarge.'

Hughes went for her. 'You were given fair warning, Best. If you choose to ignore advice, and stuff up, be it on your own head. In here, we go by the book, and I hope you're on a fantastic diet, Missy, because the probation ice you're skating on right now is wafer thin.'

The conversation stopped abruptly when Payne entered. His work in the gym at building up his smirk had paid dividends.

'Oooh,' he said at the sudden silence,' somebody die?'

Steele appeared. 'Baldwin, Best, my office, now.'

It was a short reprimand. Steele did really well to maintain a sense of calm. His words, however, were lethal.

'Detective Senior Constable Baldwin, I've made a note on your file which you will not want to show your mother. Questions?'

'No sir.'

'Dismissed.'

Jo was alone, standing in front of Steele's desk. He sat forward with hands clasped. Surprisingly, for someone who was enraged because of the complaints made against his officers, and the zero gain from their visits, Steele spoke in a reasonable voice. Perhaps it was because he took great pleasure from his utterance.

'Detective Senior Constable Best, I've spoken to you before about the need to follow procedure, and the orders from senior officers. Yet again, you've failed to do both. Do you know what besmirched means?'

'I think so, sir.'

'Tell me.'

'I think it means to damage a reputation, sir.'

'It does, Detective, and you have besmirched the good name of the Homicide Squad. You've offended innocent people who are grieving, and you've produced nothing to overturn or even challenge the decision of your colleagues re the charges laid—nothing.'

This wasn't going well and Jo fought to stop shaking.

'Your behaviour is unacceptable, and if I had a say in the matter, I'd have you thrown out of the Force. I do, however, have a say in the staffing of this squad. Your probation is over. Clear your desk and return to uniform at your previous station. Now get out.'

Jo froze. This could not, was not happening.'

'Sir,' she began but got no further.

The real DI Steele popped out from hiding. His voice caused pictures on the walls to cringe, paint to blister, and the potted palm, which wasn't well anyway, to wilt. Half the floor heard him.

'Get out of my fucking office!'

22

JO WENT TO SEE MICHAEL. She wanted to tell him her news in person. When he opened his warehouse door, he immediately sensed trouble. His concern took over, and she saw another example of his kindness and sensitivity.

'What's happened?'

'I've been sacked from Homicide. I'm back in uniform,' she said.

'God, I'm sorry. Do you want to talk about it?'

She did and she didn't. 'I've done nothing wrong. Yes, I should have gone about things another way but I know there's more to a case where the wrong man may have been charged.'

He didn't rush his reply. 'Coffee, tea or cyanide?'

She tried not to cry. He smiled a little and she smiled less.

'I want you to know, Michael; this business of me being sacked will not stop me trying to scam Marco.'

'Are you sure?'

'I'm sure.'

'I'll understand if you want to drop the whole thing.'

'No, please, we have to do this.'

'Okay. Well Senior Constable, I have good news.' Jo brightened and followed him to his work area. 'Confirmation that Marco is our man.'

He showed Jo the sentences from Shirley's emails where her scammer asked to switch from the dating site to private email. Then he showed Marco's latest reply. Jo was stunned.

'But he's used exactly the same words.'

'Verbatim, and that shows he's either overconfident, lazy or has so many lines in the water, he hasn't got time to create some new patter.'

'Then he's our man,' said Jo with confidence.

'Indeed,' said Michael, 'although he could be a she.'

Jo forgot Homicide and thought about Marco. 'Right, what's next?'

'We move to email and accept his request to leave the dating site.'

'And then what?'

'What did Ponzi say about the proposed scam?'

'I left the document with him and got his email address. Can we contact him without leaving a trail?'

'We can email him via Russia. If it's good enough for the President of the free world then it's good enough for us.'

Jo had no idea how Michael did what he did but thought him brilliant. They sent an email asking if Ponzi had read the scam.

He replied promptly. He'd read it and made a suggestion.

'He wants this to work,' said Michael. 'Look what he says.'

Jo read. 'Put the share business in the middle of the letter as if it's just another bit of ordinary news.'

'Good man, Ponzi,' said Michael, re-writing the Marco reply. He showed it to Jo. She was pleased.

'Looks good. Send it and please Marco, please believe every word.'

Michael sent the reply, made coffee then showed Jo the two phony company web sites he created. To Jo they looked like multinational companies with all the trappings that come with success.

'They're brilliant, but what if someone finds them by chance?'

'Difficult as the URLs are not listed on any search engine. So now Detective Senior Constable ...' He stopped mid-sentence. He called her Detective. 'I'm sorry, Jo. I wasn't thinking.'

Once again, her sacking danced in her brain. She tried to put it behind her. Her major regret would be telling her grandfather. She was tempted to lie but knew (a) he probably knew already, and (b) she'd always been told by him to tell the truth.

'Michael, looking at all the work you've done, I feel guilty.'

'Don't.'

'It's my mother we're working for, and I've done next to nothing.'

'You can do the work when we try to help my father.'

'I'm sorry, I've forgotten to ask. How is he?'

'Struggling but nothing the return of his savings won't fix.'

'Wouldn't it be great if we could pull off both these scams? Did you say you know the scammers who ripped off your Dad?'

'I did, I do.' He stopped.

'Do you want to tell me?'

'Let's finish this scam first.'

'Sure. Listen, my shifts will be strange now I'm back in uniform.'

'No problem. I'll keep sending you texts whenever Marco replies.'

She thanked him again and left.

It would be a long day. She had to face her uniform colleagues and explain why her probation at Homicide finished early. She had to tell her grandfather the same thing. She had to pray her mad quest to recover her mother's money wouldn't send her straight to jail. She had two choices. Feel sorry for herself or get stuck into her job.

Can I still work for Homicide when I'm back on the beat?

She felt dreadful as her sacking hangover kicked in. She rang her grandfather and lied. 'I'm fine, Pop, how are you?' He was fine. 'Can I come over?' He couldn't think of anything nicer.

His life was dominated by the health of Ida, his wife of almost sixty years. She had dementia and lived in care. Pop visited every day, and sometimes she didn't know him or even thought he was her father.

Jo arrived at Pop's place. They hugged and sat in his sunroom.

'How's Nan?'

'Not too bad.'

She looked at him. 'You know, don't you?'

He nodded. 'The old grapevine, my darling, it still works.'

'I only lied on the phone, Pop, so I could tell you to your face.'

'I know that. So, what are doing about being reinstated?'

She was shocked. 'I'm finished, Pop. I blew it.'

'Oh so you didn't tick all the right boxes or whatever it is they say these days. Tell me about the case.'

She did and as she did, her excitement returned. She wanted to solve that double homicide. Pop suggested new lines of enquiry. He wanted her back on the case. *She* wanted her back on the case.

'Pop, if they catch me anywhere near this case, I won't just be sacked from Homicide, I'll be thrown off the Force.'

'Then don't get caught.'

She hugged him, kissed him and started to cry. 'Give Nan my love.'

'I will.'

'And thanks, Pop. I want to make you proud.'

'And help your poor, old mother. She's got real problems that girl.'

Jo looked at him. Surely, he didn't know. He couldn't know. Mum would never tell him. And she and Michael had been super secretive.

When she left Pop, she was refreshed and enthusiastic. Now she wanted answers. If she was wrong, so be it, but at least she would try.

Driving home, she made a detour to Elsternwick, to the street of the double homicide. No sign of police. The case was closed, awaiting trial. She parked, hopped out and stood looking at the house and garden.

Don't go on the property, Joanna. If spotted, you'll be shot.

She began to retrace her steps when someone called.

'Hello love. Fancy a cuppa?'

Jo looked at the smiling woman. 'It's Winnie, the nosy neighbour.'

'I can see why you're a detective, young girl. Come in.'

Jo remembered the nose-twitching baking smells, and compared her mother's misery with Winnie's joie de vivre.

The old woman busied herself making tea. 'So how goes the murder solving? Have you arrested that horrible cleaning lady yet?'

Jo froze, gobsmacked. 'Sorry?'

'Mrs Madigan, the hypocrite from Hell.' She looked at Jo's stunned expression. 'I told you she was a nasty piece of work.'

'No you didn't.' That sounded rude. 'I mean, I'm sorry, Winnie, but you told me no such thing.'

She looked confused. 'Well I thought I did.'

'Have you been interviewed, Winnie?'

'Yes, by you.'

'No-one else?'

'A nice young constable asked me some questions—nothing like your questions. Oh and a reporter came. I saw him on TV.'

Winnie poured the tea but Jo lost all interest in refreshments.

'What do you mean by the "hypocrite from Hell"?'

'Oh she's the world's greatest gossip is Mrs Madigan. In the Village, in Glen Huntly Road, she's always yapping away. We go to the same hairdresser and she spreads gossip like confetti. From my bedroom window I'd watch her bowing and scraping to Mr and Mrs Hall then, to her friends, she'd run the Halls down behind their backs.'

'Do you know how she got the job?'

'Through her godson, Bradley.'

'Bradley Finch?'

'Don't know his second name but he's the boyfriend of the Hall's son, Gavin.' Jo's pulse accelerated. 'I guess Gavin told Bradley his parents wanted a cleaner and Dora only lives a couple of streets away.'

Jo tried to stay calm. All she had was interesting information. There was nothing linking Dora or the boys to the murder. There was a heap of physical evidence pinning the crimes on Benny Ross.

'Have another biscuit, Detective,' said Winnie.

Not Detective, Winnie, I'm plain old Senior Constable.

'What do you know about Bradley and Gavin?'

'They're an item. Is that what you say?' Jo nodded. 'I guess the Halls knew that but I never saw Bradley go in the house. He'd drive up and park outside my place, Gavin would get out and visit his parents, and Bradley would wait in the car.'

'For how long?'

'Not long, maybe half an hour.'

'And that happened often?'

'Whenever Gavin visited. Sometimes Dora came out, got in the car with her godson, they waited for Gavin, and I guess they gave her a lift home.'

Jo pondered her next move.

'Winnie, I need to tell you I'm no longer in the Homicide Squad.'

'You've quit the police?'

'No, I'm still a police officer but working on other duties.'

'Well that's a shame. I told that uniformed officer a few things but you're the only detective who asked the right questions.'

Jo smiled. 'Winnie, may I come back and have another chat?'

'Of course, I'd love it.'

Jo wondered if Winnie was lonely and would invite Jack the Ripper in for a cuppa such was her desire for company.

'But can I ask a favour?'

'Of course you can, my dear.'

'If a police officer asks you about the murder, can you please not mention I've been here? Please?'

Winnie tapped her nose. 'Mum's the word.'

She walked with Jo to the door and waved goodbye. At the gate, Jo blew a kiss, and Winnie's heart beat that little bit faster.

23

BACK IN UNIFORM, Jo became a cop on the beat. Her toughest task was not to cry. Her colleagues were sympathetic and most talked about other things. She was back testing drivers for alcohol and drugs.

'Bit different from chasing murderers,' said her insensitive partner.

'I thought we agreed not to talk about it.'

A car pulled in. 'Good evening, sir,' said Jo. 'Have you had anything to drink today?'

The driver replied but Jo was distracted. Her mobile pinged as a text message arrived. She finished testing the driver—whose reading was negative—and reached for her phone.

Big news.

That was it, two words. It was another example of the text being mightier than the firearm. The sender was the computer guru from Northcote. Jo knew Michael well enough to know he didn't overplay anything. He was Mr Cool. So if he sent a text with the message *Big news*, it meant just that. *So what could it be?*

She still had two hours before the end of her shift. Bugger. She might get a chance to make a call but not if the line of cars stretched out in front of her was any guide.

The roadside testing was full on. It was a Friday night and people often had a drink before heading home. Jo found herself asking a number of drivers to "please step out of the vehicle, sir (or madam)".

Finally, the equipment was put away, the witches' hats collected and Jo and her partner headed back to the station. She was driving so still couldn't ring Michael, and knew he was never keen on having her calling him anyway. Why texting was okay had her confused.

She sent a text, *On way*. Michael was a night owl, and if he had "big news", he would expect Jo to visit.

He opened his door and raised his eyebrows.

'Come in.'

She did. 'Your text got me salivating. What's happened?'

'Sit.' She sat. 'Come on, Michael, please.'

'I may have another way of getting your Mum's money.'

Jo was speechless. She recovered. 'Another scam?'

'Rather than have Marco invest in our phony shares, which was always going to be tricky, we simply steal back the money.'

'We steal it? How?'

'I hack his account.'

Whatever else Jo was thinking, this definitely qualified as big news.

'Okay. I need more details.'

'Marco has replied and mentioned the share deal. He's interested. With luck, we could pursue this line, go through the stages, use the fake web sites and fake office, and hope like hell he buys it.'

'Or what?'

'Or I hack his account, and, if he's got 200 grand, we simply move it to a new account, and from there back to your mother.'

Jo found it hard to breathe.

'Can you do that?'

'Can I hack into web sites?'

'Ah, perhaps you shouldn't answer that.'

'I can but only if he gives me his banking details.'

'And why would he do that?'

'Because he's greedy.'

'No, why would he give you his banking details?'

'Because Helen tells him she needs help investing her money. She doesn't understand shares and wants him to invest on her behalf.'

The jigsaw pieces started to slip into place. Jo tingled.

'That sounds too good to be true.' She corrected herself. 'Please, I'm not doubting your hacking skills, but surely the last person to hand over their banking details is a scammer.'

'True but not if he only has 50 bucks in his account. I mean we'll offer him two, even five grand.'

Jo slipped into mock indignation. 'Oh really? That sounds like a scam, Mr Chan. I give you five grand and you help yourself.'

He released his smidgeon of a smile. 'We pay him nothing. We can't until he gives us the code.'

'The Monte Christo code?'

They laughed.

'If he only has a few bucks in the account, obviously we won't get our nest egg. But once I'm into his bank, I may be able to find his other account or accounts.'

'If they exist.'

'If they exist.'

They stopped speaking. Michael was excited about his idea, and Jo was doubly excited they had another option to retrieve her Mum's money. Jo's already high opinion of Michael headed north.

He flattened her excitement. 'There is a possible problem.'

'Here we go.'

'If we get the money, Marco will be mad. But if he coughs up through the sting with the shares, and is recorded and exposed online, he'll be ashamed, humiliated and desperate for a new image.'

'And mad.'

'Of course, but if he's hacked, only he will know. We can't film him. So he'll try to get his money back, or smash the robbers, or both.'

'And here I was thinking this was all good news.'

'But now we have two options. And if we go for the hacking option, we have no need for Ponzi.'

'But I promised him 5%.' She cringed.

'You said 2. You *are* a liar.'

She fessed up. 'I'm sorry. I didn't want you mad at a criminal being rewarded with ten grand.'

Michael moved on. He wasn't one to dwell on mistakes or failures.

'If we hack Marco, you should give Ponzi a decent tip. I think it's called a bung. He'll have done almost nothing and you can promise him work in the future.'

'Okay. Now you said Marco's sent a new reply.'

'He has.' They looked at the new email.

'You're right,' said Jo. 'He is interested. Maybe Ponzi's tip about placing the share idea in the middle helped swing the response.'

'So you're happy for me to get Helen to ask Marco if he'll help with her investment plans?'

'More than happy.'

'If we tell him she'll probably go for fifty grand later if the shares look solid, you'd think he'll be super keen to take the five grand.'

'I would.'

'I'll write the email now.'

Jo looked at Michael. She was pleased to have met such a smart and decent person. He accepted her despite her faults. He had a pretty high opinion of her as well. They would make a good team—*Best and Chan, the Scambusters.*

'Michael?'

He kept typing the email. 'You rang?'

'Can you hack a phone conversation?'

That stopped him. He turned to look at her. 'You are one dangerous hombre, Senior Constable Joanna Claire Best.' She smiled. He liked her smile. 'What have you got in mind?'

Jo told him about the double homicide, her opinion that the police had charged an innocent man, and about her hunch involving the son of the murdered couple, his boyfriend and the boyfriend's godmother.

'But I have no evidence. In fact, all the evidence points to the guy who's been charged. And he may be guilty. But something is nagging me about this case.'

'Such as?'

'Well for starters, it's too perfect. It's as if the evidence, the jewels, and his shoes, were planted on someone who has a drug problem, a police record and who knows the house where the murders took place.'

'You know most criminals get caught because they're thick?'

'Sure but the guy they've charged had his shoes at home with dirt from the garden of the house where the homicides occurred.'

'I told you, crims are thick.'

'But the footprints weren't even. It was like someone with smaller feet stood in the shoes.'

Michael paused. 'This means a lot to you.'

'Only because in trying to solve it, I got sacked.'

'Right, let's do it. Which law would you like me to break tonight?'

She told him the name and address of her three suspects. She explained how, if she could record them confessing to the crime, that might get the right murderer arrested, the wrongly arrested man set free, and might just save her bacon.

It was time to go.

'I'll let you know,' said Michael as he opened the door, 'on Marco's emails and a spot of phone hacking.'

'Thanks,' she said and stopped. They looked at one another. He wasn't going to make a move so she did. She leant in and kissed his lips, briefly, then turned and walked away.

She felt good. He felt fantastic.

Michael got cracking. He replied to Marco gently raising the topic of investing in shares using her money. Marco replied with a warning that there are sharks out there who want to take the money of beautiful and lonely women.

Marco didn't do irony.

Within minutes, Helen replied asking ever so politely for Marco to do some small investing for her.

Hello Marco
Now that I've met you and can see what a successful and honest high-flyer you are, would you help me? Do you trust me enough to take a small amount of my money and invest it in the companies you think will offer the safest and best returns? I was thinking of $5,000.
I have quite a bit put aside for investing but would like to see some success first before I try for a bigger portfolio.
Your new friend,
Helen

Marco's happiness was tempered by his rat cunning. Women gave him their banking details and never the other way round. But who cares about the horse's choppers if the nag's a freebie? He agreed to her request. He did think about Helen being a possible fraud so covered his back by sending her his banking details with his account holding the princely sum of $20 and 56 cents.

Michael thought about going to bed. He didn't want to. The scheme could break in the next few hours. If he got lucky, he could literally steal hundreds of thousands of dollars at any moment.

He was right to stay awake. It started. Michael got Marco's latest missive. Michael rubbed his eyes. Is this true? Has he really sent me his banking details? He had.

Michael set to work. He had no intention of making a deposit. He wanted to hack. Using Marco's details, he hacked into the account, and smiled at his $20.56 balance.

No surprise there then.

The young computer whiz tried this way and that to discover if Marco had another account. Unless Michael could find the pot of gold, the whole project was dead in the water.

Midnight came and went. The longer Michael (or Helen) failed to hand over the promised money, the greater the chance Marco's suspicions would take over and he'd walk away.

In his home in nearby Kew, Connie checked his accounts. Neither had been touched. It was late and he went to bed.

Michael made coffee. He came back and thought his equipment had suffered a meltdown. No, someone was trying to hack his system.

He forgot the coffee and stared in astonishment. He knew he could stop the attack in an instant but kept watching. Suddenly he saw what they were doing in trying to break into his set-up.

'So that's how they do it.'

He got busy. He killed the hacker attack but used their method on Marco's bank site. Yes. It worked. He was in. A list of accounts popped up on his screen. But which was Marco's?

Michael had no reference, no name or number. Marco wasn't his real name. The list of accounts meant nothing. He scrolled in vain.

I've hacked into his bank and am stuck in Reception. I can't find his other account, assuming he has one.

He'd failed. He felt lousy, having failed Jo Best. Then inspiration.

Why not give the bank a call?

He looked at the bank's site. He wanted security or emergency or some link to report a theft—anything. He found a number. It was in Zurich. Michael's breathing became irregular. He dialled.

Someone answered in English. 'Security, how may I help?'

Michael went for a South African accent. He switched to panic mode. 'Oh thank God I've found you. You got to help me, man. I'm being hacked right now. I can see it on the screen right in front of me.'

'Thank you, sir. If I could have your name and date of birth, please.'

Michael whipped up his hysteria. 'Are you not listening to me?' He shouted the number of Marco's account.

'Just a moment, sir.'

'Oh for God's sake, look at your screen. It's happening right now.'

The bank official came under pressure. Marco's account had a flashing light. This meant trouble. The man on the phone was right, his account was being hacked—yes, by the man on the phone!

Michael tried a new form of hacking. The guy in Zurich saw new activity. Pressure. Michael shouted.

'Oh come on, man, do something, stop them!'

'Stay calm, sir, we will close your account and stop the hacker.'

'But what about my other account?' Michael went flat out with his hysterical acting. 'If my other account is hacked and you've had a chance to prevent it, I will sue your arse from here to Botswana.'

Botswana?

'What is your other account ...'

'Oh come on, you imbecile. Look at your list. My accounts are listed together. Just hurry.'

The official needed a toilet break. He had a flashing screen, a customer in meltdown, a possible lawsuit, and likely dismissal if he didn't fix this problem. He found Marco's other account.

'Ah is that 1123 9603 3359, sir?

'No it finishes with 3359.'

'Yes, that's correct, sir.'

'Come on, come on man.'

'I'm working on it, sir.'

Michael scribbled like mad. He stopped the hacking on Marco's account with its huge balance of $20. The security guy found the second account. It was dormant."

'It's all quiet on your second account, sir.'

'Are you sure? Check again.'

'I have and there's no sign of any hacking.'

'Thank God for that. But what about my first account?'

The security guy was sweating. He clicked back to the first account and saw nothing. No warning light, no sign of any attack. Michael ramped up the hysteria.

'What's happened? Are they in?'

'No sir. All attacks have stopped. Our security has done its job.'

'Really?'

'Absolutely, sir. Your accounts are safe.'

'All of them?'

'Well we don't have any record of a third account, sir.'

'That's fantastic, brilliant news. You, young man, are my saviour.'

'Just doing my job Mr Kruger.' Michael scribbled.

'Oh no, I won't have any of that false modesty. What's your name young man?'

'Rodger Greyling, sir.'

'Well, Rodger Greyling, sir, I am going to contact the Chairman of your Bank and tell him how you saved my accounts from ruin. You, sir, are a hero.'

Rodger felt all warm and fuzzy. 'Thank you, Mr Kruger, you're most kind.'

'Now, now, none of this Mr Kruger business. After what you just did, I want you to call me by my first name.'

'Oh that wouldn't be appropriate, sir.'

'Listen, Rodger, anyone who does me a huge favour, I consider a friend. Please, call me by my first name.'

Rodger hesitated. 'Well, if you insist, Cornelius.' Michael scribbled. He remembered a politician called Cornelius who had a nickname.

'Everyone calls me Connie.'

'Okay ... Connie.'

'You, young man, are a credit to your family and employer. I promise you, Rodger, you will get your reward. Thank you again, and goodnight.'

'Goodnight Mr Kruger ... Connie.'

The line went dead and Michael came alive. The main event was about to begin. Later that day, Rodger's main event would begin. The whole conversation with Mr Kruger had been recorded and Rodger the Todger would face the full wrath of his employer.

Sorry Rodger.

Go Michael.

24

MICHAEL STARTED HACKING and got into Kruger's second account. Mama mia! Hooley Dooley! Oh my lordy lord! It was big. It was like the real Count of Monte Christo's discovery with treasure beyond his wildest dreams. Michael saw a cash balance north of two million and concentrated on the job in hand. More than two million!

How much should I take? If the exact amount was stolen then all roads would lead to Shirley then Jo and then him. He didn't want to take less because Mrs Best was surely entitled to the full amount.

So he settled for $210,000 with the extra going to pay Ponzi, and cover Michael and Jo's expenses. Mr Kruger could afford a small tip.

Now it was time. Michael had established a holding account into which he would place the 210 grand. From there, he would transfer the money to Shirley's new account. Hacking time drew nigh.

Michael knew what he was doing but didn't know if it would work. He keyed in the banking details then the transfer request. He wondered if Kruger used the same password for both accounts. He did—Joburg007. Even clever people sometimes do dumb things.

The hacking moment got closer. Michael's heart took up playing the drums. He couldn't swallow. His clothes felt too tight. He typed in the amount he wanted to pinch. He double-checked every step. D-Day arrived. He took a deep breath then pressed *Enter*.

He shut his eyes. He dared not look. He heard nothing. *What am I expecting?* He opened his eyes and saw a box of text. There was no mention of the money. He panicked—unnecessarily as it turned out. It asked if he wanted to complete the transfer. Silly question. Dumb, very dumb question. He hit *Yes*. Nothing. The screen remained unchanged. Michael clenched his fists.

'Come on, come on.'

He couldn't believe that all his expertise, research, planning and effort, including his ham acting, meant the deal wouldn't go through.

Michael froze because his screen blinked and text appeared.

You have successfully transferred $210,000 to account #41098MC. Do you wish to make another transfer?

Michael stared at the screen. He laughed. His laugh got louder and longer. 'Yes!' he yelled. 'Yeeeees!' Alan woke up.

Michael's brain struggled to believe the information. But there it was in black and white. Well, in grey and black and white.

He reprimanded himself with the job not yet complete. He hit *No* to the Bank's question and opened the temporary account he created last week with a balance of $100. Right now, it had a balance of $256,688 and 43 cents

'What? What the hell? That can't be right.' Then he twigged. Kruger's account was in US dollars and Michael's in Australian dollars. The Oz dollar was currently worth about US 78 cents. He'd taken too much, almost AUD $50,000 too much. Shit. Now he really was a thief. He thought about putting some back. That meant more transactions, and the more transactions, the greater the chance of being discovered.

He told himself it was a genuine, a stupid but honest mistake.

Did I just say honest?

He got stuck into finishing the job. He transferred the full amount from his temporary account to Shirley Best's new account and then began to destroy everything: his Marco dating site account, his emails, his hacking information, and his temporary bank account, everything related to the quest to help Shirley Best was wiped. He kept a note of Marco's email address in case of the need for one last flutter. His heart rate kept accelerating. Has Kruger discovered the scam?

Michael couldn't erase the conversation he had with Kruger's bank. He didn't care. Voice recognition was sophisticated today. But was Michael's voice on any database? And anyway, who was Kruger going to tell? He got scammed. He was robbed of money he'd robbed from a vulnerable woman. No way would he complain to authorities. He'd want to kill the thieves but would never complain to police.

It was Kruger's bad luck to rob a woman with a daughter who didn't take kindly to criminals, especially cowardly fraudsters.

Job done, Michael hopped up and danced. He was hopeless, and made Dad dancing look good. He didn't care. He cried. He was so happy, even his tears started dancing.

He thought of Jo and how happy she would be. He thought of Jo's Mum—he'd never met her—and how happy she would be. He thought of his father, and madly wanted to do for him what he'd just done for Jo and Shirley.

'You're next, Dad.'

Michael was tempted to send Jo a text with the great news but knew if he did, they'd both be up all night celebrating.

It was late. Michael came back down to planet Earth. He fought hard to not contact Jo there and then. He fought extra hard to not have any more contact with Marco. *Job done, walk away.* Perhaps foolishly, he couldn't resist a parting shot. He penned a final email.

Hello Marco

I am so sorry. All hell has broken loose here. My darling Aleksy was attacked by a horrible dog in the park and I've spent ages at the all-night vet, hoping and praying. I think he's going to be okay. That's Aleksy, not the vet. Touch wood.

Silly me, I don't have pet insurance and the operation is going to cost almost $4000. Can you wait a little while for the money I want you to invest? It shouldn't be long as I need to give notice to take money off term deposit.

That's wonderful news about you coming back home. As you know I'm in Melbourne, and if you could come down south, I'd be thrilled to finally meet you. You're more than welcome to stay here as it's just Aleksy (I hope) and me.

Love

Helen

xo

Michael read the email. 'Wow, a kiss and a hug for Marco. This relationship is hot to trot.' He hit *Send* then wiped every trace of his dealings with Cornelius Kruger. Michael never wanted to hear from, speak to or in any way deal with that person again.

Connie got up for a pee and read the latest from Helen and swore. He was hoping for the five grand but never mind, it should come soon enough.

Another email had arrived. It was from his bank. He felt puzzled. He opened the email and felt more than puzzled. It was confirmation of his transfer of $210 grand to a bank account he'd never heard of.

His stomach muscles tightened. His teeth started to ache. This wasn't right. Connie caused pain, he didn't receive it. WTF?

Connie tried to stay calm. He was the fraudster. He was the conman. He was the one who received the ill-gotten gains. He was not the one who gave it away. His brain struggled. It seemed unbelievable. It *was* unbelievable but as the seconds ticked by, his brain slowly began to convince him of the truth. He'd been robbed. Once his brain won the argument, he went off—right off.

'I've been hacked,' he screamed. He lost it.

Connie and DI Steele were ideal candidates to attend anger-management classes but sadly both never had or would.

Connie assaulted a wall then turned a coffee mug into an impossible-to-solve jigsaw puzzle. His blood pressure exploded. He tried to think. Amid the fog of his fury, he dialled a number.

'Hello,' answered a fellow South African.

'It's Kruger.'

'You owe me money.'

'How much? I'll pay you now.'

'Jesus, Kruger, are you about to die?'

'I've been hacked.'

The person started to laugh. He couldn't stop.

Kruger growled. 'It's not fucking funny, man.'

'Ja, man, that is beautiful. The fraudster gets defrauded. How much did they take, you doos?'

'That doesn't matter.'

'Yes it does. That's your first clue, man.'

'What do you mean?'

'First I want my money. Then I want payment up front for what I know you want me to do.'

Kruger had been hacked and now had to pay to get back "his" money. The former Joburg crook was close to frothing.

'How much do I owe you?'

'Wow, you really are in the shit. Only a nuclear explosion under your bed would make you pay a debt, and even then you'd still try some of your bullshit haggling.'

Kruger was angry. 'How much, man?'

The contact told him a figure and Kruger sent it.

'It's gone,' snapped Kruger.

The man looked at his bank account. 'Amazing.'

Kruger was agitated. 'How soon before you can find him?'

'Whoa, easy man, it may take ages and it may be never.'

'What?'

'If the hacker's smart enough to get inside your bank, he's smart enough to hide his tracks.'

'So what now?'

'We start with the obvious. Is your machine switched on?'

Kruger screamed. 'What are you talking about?'

'The obvious, man. Did you give your banking details to anyone?'

Kruger fell silent. The frothing continued but he stayed silent. He now knew he'd shot himself in the foot.

'Hello? Kruger, are you there?'

He was and in pain. His guts churned. He spoke softly. 'Ja.'

'Well who's the biggest doos in Joburg?'

'I gave him details of an account which had a lousy 20 bucks.'

'And do you have another account with that bank?'

Kruger felt an involuntary puke. He spoke softly. 'Ja.'

'And does that one contain megabucks?'

Kruger spat his answer. 'Ja, all right man, so how can I get it back?'

'Well more fool you, Kruger. You let him in, he hacked your other account, and helped himself.'

'But how? My other account has a different name, different number and password.'

'I bet you use the same password for both accounts, and I bet your password is *password*.'

That was pretty close.

'Enough of the smart arse remarks. I want my money back, man.'

'You mean you want back the money you stole in the first place.'

Kruger wanted to swear and slam down the phone but couldn't. He needed this expert to help him find "his" money.

The man took pity. 'All right, man, how much did they take?'

'Two ten.'

'Is that two dollars 10, two hundred and ten dollars, two ...'

'All right, two hundred and ten grand.'

'And how much was in the account?'

'That's none of your fucking business.'

'Listen, Kruger, I can't help you if you won't help me. Now how much was in your account?'

'About 2.5 mill.'

'US dollars?'

'Ja.'

'So there's your first clue. Why would a hacker break into a high security bank, and steal less than 10% of the money? Would you?'

'No.'

'Three more keystrokes and he gets the lot. You're looking for an honest criminal, man.'

'Cut the jokes. What do I do?'

'Well the person you gave your banking details to—I still can't believe you did that—is your target. How did you get their details? Kruger paused. 'Kruger?'

'It's a woman who posted on a web site.'

Uproarious laughter drifted across the world from Cape Town. 'Oh man. The hunter got hunted. So now we know for certain your woman doesn't exist, and is probably a geek who could even live next door.'

'Can you find him?'

'I can try.'

'What can I do?'

'Make a list of possible enemies, people you've ripped off and who might want revenge.'

'That's a big list.'

'Just for the last, say, three months.'

'Then?'

'Do your Sherlock Holmes thing.'

'Which is?'

'Eliminate the impossible.'

'Are you taking the piss?'

'Cross off your list anyone who no way could've scammed you.'

'What else?'

'Where are you living these days?'

'None of your business.'

'Well wherever you are, find a local geek. Only the best, a geek who knows hacking. Find someone you can work with, face to face.'

Kruger fumed. He'd paid this guy in South Africa thinking he would snap his fingers and solve the problem. But there was no magic wand.

The contact wound up the conversation. 'Okay man, I'll do some searching, and let you know when I've got something.'

The call ended.

What else could Kruger do? He became the defrauded fraudster.

Michael took a deep breath. What a night. What a fantastic result. He felt proud and happy and wondered what Jo would say when he told her first thing in the morning. He started to shut down the equipment then froze when his phone started ringing. He panicked.

Who the hell is ringing at this hour? Oh no! It's the bank in Zurich.

Michael's skin went all prickly and his face flushed with fear. Suddenly his digital recorder came alive. The phone kept ringing.

This had to be the first step in his downfall; the phone call, then the cops, then the trial. Michael could run but knew he couldn't hide. The phone stopped ringing.

'Hello.'

'Gavin, it's Dora.'

'Dora. Do you know what time it is?'

'Yes, I'm sorry, but I've just found a letter which had been pushed under my door.'

'A letter?'

'My neighbour sometimes gets my mail and shoves it under my door.'

'What letter?'

'It went under my mat and I just saw it when I was locking up and going to bed.'

'Dora, tell me about the letter.'

'Oh, right, and it's wonderful news.'

'Tell me.'

'Remember you asked me to contact your father's solicitor to see if I was a beneficiary.'

'Yes, yes, and?'

161

'Well they've replied.'

'I gathered that. What do they say?'

'Do you want me to read you the letter?'

'No, just tell me … (softer) for Christ's sake

'Well they won't say if I'm a beneficiary because we have to wait for probate to be declared.'

'Okay. What else?'

'And that new will your father threatened you with …'

'Yes?'

'The solicitor knows nothing about it.'

'Are you sure?'

'The solicitor says the current will was made almost four years ago which is before you met Bradley.'

'That's fantastic news, Dora.'

'I thought you'd be happy.'

'And our deal still stands. Your share will be honoured.'

'Thank you. Will you tell Bradley?'

'I sure will, he's right here.'

'Okay. Bye.'

'Bye. (louder) Yes!'

The line went dead and the device stopped recording.

'Well, Ms Best,' said Michael to himself, 'that's two for the price of one. You are in for one heck of a day, Senior Constable.'

25

MICHAEL SENT A TEXT at 0630 hours. *Monte Christo triumphs.* Jo saw it and went numb. Her brain refused to believe it. Then she panicked, flew out of her flat, leapt in her car and sped to Northcote. Forget breakfast, forget make-up, and forget ... *what the hell am I wearing?* She should have been booked for speeding.

That message can only mean one thing. What else could it mean?

She could call Michael but wanted to see him when she heard his news. She parked and raced to his front door. Michael's warning system announced her arrival. He opened the door and smiled a smile Jo had never seen before.

'Michael, please don't send messages like that unless it's important.'

'I like your outfit,' he said cheekily.

Jo was almost angry. 'Michael.'

'Walk this way,' he said leading her to his workstation, performing a terrible John Cleese silly walk. She wanted to laugh but her excitement level was at fever pitch.

Michael stopped beside his largest monitor in standby mode. Pointing to a button on his keyboard, he said, 'Press that.'

Jo looked at him. 'Michael, I'm scared.'

'Scared? I've been terrified all night.' He looked her in the eye. 'Go on, it's good news.'

She hit the keyboard and the monitor sprang to life. Jo looked at a screenshot from Kruger's bank in Switzerland. It was a mass of figures and her mind was racing. There was a box of text in the middle.

'What? Where?'

'Box of text,' he said.

She focused on that part of the screen, and did what Kruger and Michael did. She saw the figure but her brain kept dragging its feet.

Jo gasped. 'What is that?'

'Let's call it interest. I forgot it was in US dollars.'

She looked at him with eyes blazing. 'You did it.'

'We did it.'

He opened Shirley's new account and showed Jo the new balance. She stared at the screen, then at Michael, then threw herself at him, hugged like crazy and couldn't stop the tears.

Once she settled, he explained the saga. She listened with an array of gasps, headshakes, smiles and more tears.

'Michael, I don't know what to say.'

'I suggest you tell your mother as soon as possible. If she logs on and sees her new balance, she might have a heart attack.'

'You're right. I'll go there now. God, what time is it?'

He moved to another part of his workstation. 'Before you go, Detective, there's something else you need to see, or rather hear.'

He hit *Play* and the clear phone call between Dora and Gavin boomed out from his speakers. Jo was stunned. Stunned at his technical wizardry and stunned at the damning evidence. When it finished, she was speechless—literally. He asked a question.

'Interesting?'

'Interesting? Are you kidding? What can't you do? Retrieve a lonely woman's life savings, entrap murderers who were never charged, leap tall buildings in a single bound. I mean, Michael Chan, you are, as the lingo goes, a legend.'

He gave a polite but mock bow. 'At your service, ma'am.'

'I could never have done any of this. Your need rewarding. I have to pay you. How about the interest on my Mum's account?'

'You've already paid me.' She didn't understand. 'You agreed to help me recover my father's life savings.'

'Right,' she said pointing at him. 'We start tonight.'

'Aren't you on night shift?'

'Okay, tomorrow.'

He laughed. 'There's no hurry. And you've still got some loose ends to tidy up first.'

'Loose ends?' She worried again.

'Tell your mother the good news, pay off Ponzi, and arrest the real murderers in your double homicide.'

164

She grimaced. 'If only.' She snapped out of her momentary gloom. 'First things first, it's good news for Shirley.'

'Oh and that screenshot you saw and that phone call you heard never existed and are about to disappear.'

She pointed at him. 'Gotcha. Please, wipe the lot.'

She headed for the door. He followed. Both remembered that brief encounter involving osculation on this very spot a few hours ago.

I think it's his turn to make the move this time.

Maybe it was the lack of film noir lighting or the fantastic financial news, or something else, but the second kiss didn't eventuate.

'You're a star, Michael Chan, and I'll be back to fulfil my part of the bargain.'

She headed for her childhood home and its only resident.

Jo didn't ring her mother. She arrived and rang the doorbell. Shirley shuffled towards the door wearing nightie, dressing-gown and slippers.

My God, thought Jo. *My mother's become an old woman.*

Jo called. 'It's me, Mum, your law-abiding daughter.' That was an untruthful statement if ever there was one.

The door opened and Shirley even looked old.

'What's wrong? Why are you here, and why at this time, so early? And why are you dressed like that?'

'How are you, Mum?' Jo followed Shirley inside.

'You know I prefer you to ring first. I don't like answering the door unless I know who's there.'

'I thought I'd drop in on my beautiful and young-at-heart mother.'

Shirley felt a flicker of love which was immediately squashed by her now permanent state of misery. 'You're being silly.' She sat. Both cushion and person wheezed.

'Mum, I don't want to add to your woes but I was wondering if you could possibly repay some of the $500 I gave you?'

Shirley's face changed instantly from unhappiness to shame. She put her head in her hands.'

'Oh God, I completely forgot. Joanna, I am so sorry.'

Jo was by her side, one arm around her and the other hand rubbing her arm. Her mother had put on weight. No exercise, living alone and seldom going out.'

'Come on, Mum. It's no big deal.'

'Yes it is.' She struggled to stand. 'I'll do it now.'

Shirley headed for the bedroom and her computer. Jo followed. She stood by her mother's shoulder as Shirley turned on her laptop. They waited for the unit to warm up.

'I'll give you the whole amount and whatever other costs you've had. I know there are things you did for me.'

'Mum, it's not necessary.'

'Necessary or not, I'll do it. Now, what is my new account number?' Shirley typed in her details.

Jo's heartbeat took off. 'Don't forget your new password. We had that changed too, remember?'

'I know, I know. And never give your banking details to any tall, dark stranger.'

At least my mother hasn't lost her sense of humour.

'I hope you've got my new banking details,' said Shirley. 'If I drop dead, you'll be able to access my meagre funds.'

'Stop talking like that, Mum, please.'

Shirley finished typing in the required information then hit *Enter*. The seconds ticked by and Jo found it hard to breath. She was sure her goosebumps were excited.

The screen changed and Shirley casually looked at it then at the keyboard. 'Let's say $600, and I need your banking details.'

'Mum,' said Jo, trying to interrupt her mother.

'Please Joanna, don't try and stop me. I insist you let me pay you back. Now, what are your details?'

'Look at the screen, Mum.'

Shirley stopped typing, looked at her daughter then looked at the screen. Her eyes went from one column to another.

'What?'

'There,' Jo pointed.

Shirley saw the current balance. She blinked, thinking her eyes were playing tricks. The figures didn't change.

'What's happened?' She looked up at Jo. Shirley had a kind of fear in her voice. 'What's happened?'

Jo wanted to cry. 'Your money's been returned, Mum, with interest.' Then she did cry. So did Shirley.

They hugged and wept then Shirley barely managed to speak. 'But how? Why? Oh my darling girl, what have you done?'

It took a while to explain. No, it took longer than a while. Jo gave details but no details. It was a "no names have been mentioned in the telling of this tale" explanation.

'I had some people trace the criminal and retrieve your money.'

'But how did you do it?'

'Mum, all that matters is your money's back where it belongs.'

'And with interest, so much interest.' She went back to the laptop. 'Now it's time to repay my wonderful daughter.'

She did and left a generous tip. She could afford to. Jo wondered what the tax department would think of this nice, little earner.

Shirley recovered to have a decent conversation. 'I can never thank you enough, Jo, never.'

There she goes again, calling me Jo.

'Now I want to see changes, Mum. No more shutting yourself away. No more bad eating. I want you back to your walking group and U3A classes, and you have to start seeing your grandchildren again.'

Shirley nodded. 'I will. I promise.'

'And remember, this is our little secret. What happened with your money, never happened. Okay?'

Shirley nodded. Jo stood and Shirley followed her to the front door. Gone was the shuffling, replaced with an almost jaunty gait.

'You're my guardian angel, Jo,' she said hugging her girl. 'And I promise to never ask about your boyfriends again.'

They laughed. Jo waved from the gate, and Shirley went inside and cried with happiness. Jo drove away thinking about Michael, her Mum's bank balance and the double homicide in Elsternwick.

She stopped at a local internet shop, went in and used one of the computers. She sent an email to Ponzi saying they needed to meet and she was free right now. She asked him to name a time and meeting place and send those details to the library computer.

His text came through almost immediately.

Patterson Lakes Library carpark 10 am.

It was now 0910. The traffic was normal—horrendous.

She stopped at an ATM and was late when she arrived at the half empty car park. She couldn't see Ponzi. He'd parked elsewhere and loitered beneath trees. He approached. She released the lock and he climbed in.

167

'This had better be good.'

'And a very good morning to you too.'

'Nice to see you've dressed for the occasion.'

'I've got good and bad news. Which would you like first?'

'Just tell me what's happened.'

'We've decided to go without your services this time.'

What?'

'We're not using the scam we told you about.'

'You've blown it. The job's off.'

She ran with that story. 'Okay, we screwed up. But we want to keep you on the team. There's another job and your skills might be perfect.'

'You promised me ten grand.'

'I'm not sure promised is correct, but there's some good news.' She opened her bag allowing him to see a wad of notes. Using gloves, this was the money she'd recently collected from a hole in the wall.

'What's this,' he asked peering inside.

'Your retainer.'

He took out the notes. She put her hand on his arm.

'Don't wave it around.' He lowered the money. 'It's a little thank you for being ready to help if and when required.'

He looked at Jo. He wanted to abuse her but reckoned slagging off a cop would not be in his best interests.

'Take your wife out for a fancy meal,' she suggested.

He scowled and got out of the car. As he was about to slam the door, she called. 'Take care, Ponzi, I'll be in touch.'

The door was closed with too much force, and Jo drove home to change.

Will I ever see that man again?

26

CONNIE NEVER THOUGHT ABOUT THE LOCATION of his victims. He cared about their bank balance and vulnerability. Having fled South Africa, he settled in Melbourne, and carried on as before. His scams were all online. The victim could live across the road or across the world. It made no difference to Connie the criminal.

He pondered the advice from his acquaintance back in South Africa. Find a good geek. He didn't know where to look. He needed advice. Then he figured, why not?

He rang the Victoria Police Fraud and Extortion Squad and spoke to the same officer who sent Jo Best to Michael Chan.

'Fraud Squad, DS Harry Dale speaking.'

'Oh officer, hello,' said Kruger. 'My name is Tobias Smith. I know this sounds a little crazy but I am having trouble with the security of my computer system.'

'Have you been defrauded, sir?'

'Quite possibly.'

'Possibly?'

'Yes, you see my system does not have the latest software protection and I need an expert in that area and here I am thinking, I bet the police know the best security firms in the business. Can you recommend a geek?'

'That's funny. You're the second person to ask me that this week.'

'Oh, and who was the first?'

'Now that would be telling, Mr Smith.'

'Of course, forgive me.'

'But I can give you the same name I gave the other caller.'

'Please.'

'Mr Michael Chan is the best when it comes to digital know-how. Would you like his number?'

'That would be most kind,' said Kruger, feeling excited.

And so Kruger took Michael's details and began the campaign to reclaim his money.

Michael's phone rang and was answered after a single ring.

'Michael Chan speaking.'

'Ah, Mr Chan, just the man I want.'

Kruger's South African accent thundered down the line reminding Michael of his recent acting role when hacking a bank in Zurich.

'The Victoria Police Fraud Squad gave me your details, Mr Chan, and you come highly recommended.'

Now Michael would never claim the detective skills of one Senior Constable Joanna Best, but he found this phone call suspicious. A man with a South African accent, and a recommendation from the Fraud Squad, had his phone number. Michael thought about co-incidences.

Hours ago, he "reclaimed" about a quarter of a million dollars from a criminal named Cornelius Kruger, a name with a strong South African flavour. Michael didn't like this type of coincidence.

Oh shit. They've found me already.

'What do you want?'

'Ah, I like a man of few words.'

'I'm sorry; I'm very busy and am not taking any new clients.'

'Not even for ten thousand dollars in cash?'

'I can't help you, Mr Smith. Goodbye.'

Michael hung up. He looked like he'd seen a ghost. His mouth went dry, and his chest ached. He didn't handle that phone call well, and he knew he'd make a lousy criminal.

His phone rang and kept ringing.

Now despite having an amazing array of technical equipment, and the skills to make it sing, in one area Michael was a dinosaur, a life-member of Luddites' Anonymous. There was no caller ID on his phone. He didn't like having to choose whether or not to answer a call, and he genuinely liked surprises.

So who was on the line?

He let it ring. It might be Jo or his father. He answered the phone.

'Michael Chan speaking.'

'Mr Chan, please don't hang up. I wish to apologise for my rudeness just now and beg you to grant me an audience for just five minutes. If my project doesn't appeal, I will leave immediately and never contact you again. Please sir. I am in Kew and can be with you in half an hour.' Michael paused and the pause killed him. 'That's very kind of you, sir. I have your address as 4 Holden Court. I'll be with you shortly.'

The line went dead and Michael resumed the sweats, to which he added the shakes. His blood ran cold.

He checked and doubled checked his equipment. He had software which enabled him to call the police using a voice command. He tested it. He put Alan in a safe place with an emergency exit to his locked condo. Michael pottered and paced then saw a visitor on his CCTV monitor. Michael opened the door and looked at Cornelius Kruger.

'Mr Chan, I am Tobias Smith.'

'Come in.'

Kruger entered and Michael followed his visitor into the warehouse.

'My goodness, what a fantastic set-up. I heard you were the top professional but this is amazing.'

'You said five minutes, Mr Smith. The clock is ticking.'

Of course. I have a security problem with my company. Somebody has hacked into my accounts and stolen a large sum of money.'

'Define a large sum.'

'To be precise, 210,000 American dollars.'

Michael thought he would vomit. He managed to ask a question. 'What is your line of business?'

'Gold. I buy and sell the precious stuff.'

'So why come to me?'

'Because I'm told you're the best. The police say they recommended you to someone else just last week.'

Michael fought to remain calm. His shoes were glued to the floor.

'As I said I'm not taking any new clients.'

'Please, Mr Chan, I'm desperate. I want you to find the person who hacked my account, and then help me retrieve my money.'

'That's not my area of expertise, Mr Smith.'

'But I was told you did that type of work.'

'The Victoria Police told you I was a criminal?'

Kruger was caught. He laughed. 'I can see you are a smart man, Mr Chan.'

'I'm afraid you've had a wasted journey.'

Michael indicated the door.

Kruger made one final pitch. 'I pay very well. In fact, the right man can name his own price.'

'How about 210,000 US dollars?' Michael wished he could take that back. He meant to send the man away by quoting far too high. Instead, he engaged his mouth without his brain being in gear.

Kruger stared at him. He turned sarcastic. 'Very funny, Mr Chan.'

Michael opened the door. 'I'm not your man, Mr Smith. Good luck.'

He stood back from the door. Kruger shrugged and walked out, stopping beneath the currently not working light from *The 39 Steps*.

'I hope this is not the last time we meet, Mr Chan.'

Their eyes locked and Michael felt a chill on his spine. The chill was so scared it didn't know whether to run up or down.

Like Michael, Kruger was no detective but had rat cunning in spades. Something inside the professional fraudster's mind rang alarm bells. He filed Michael Chan's name in his "Check out this Bastard" file.

Kruger went home to his hidden mansion in Kew. There was no word from the expert back home in South Africa. All that money for nothing. But Kruger had played detective himself and found an expert, someone very keen to lose Kruger. The criminal pondered.

What else can I do? Who hates me? Who wants revenge?

He remembered the advice from Sherlock Holmes. "Eliminate the impossible". Who could he wipe from his list?

Kruger pondered the amount of money stolen. Why did they not take it all? And how did $210 grand relate to his victims? Who could he eliminate? No! Who could he include? Who lost $210K?

Shirley Best sprang to mind. The amount he stole from Shirley was about that amount. Was she the thief? Nah, no way. Ah, but was she the person referred to Michael Chan last week? Then he remembered. Shirley lived in Melbourne.

All his files were non-existent but Balwyn North rang a bell. 'Where's that?' He checked. 'Bugger me, it's the next suburb.'

He looked for phone numbers in Melbourne. There was a Best S N in Balwyn North. It couldn't be. Did the S stand for Shirley?

172

He hired a van and drove to New Street, Balwyn North. Almost all the original homes had been demolished, to be replaced with Georgian McMansions, most complete with ballroom-sized garages and real plastic lawn. He parked some distance from the house in which supposedly Best S N lived. He waited. To avoid looking suspicious, he removed a hardhat, theodolite on a tripod, and a clipboard and pretended to work. It was all a show.

Nothing happened. Had he lived here he would have known. Balwyn North used to be North Balwyn, and, to many, North Boring. It lived up to its name. He decided to call it a day when a small sedan drove past and pulled up outside the Best residence. Out hopped a female wearing a police uniform. Kruger became more than interested.

Into the Best residence went the cop. Kruger kept watch as he packed away his equipment. He dawdled, then got in his van, and pretended to write notes and make phone calls. He wrote down the car's registration. He couldn't sit here forever. The woman wearing a police uniform came out, got in the car and drove off. Kruger followed.

It was tricky as his van stood out. He couldn't hide behind the car in front and he didn't want to get too far behind because with busy roads and many traffic lights, he could lose the cop.

And as she was a cop, the chances of him being recognized tailing her were higher than with your average motorist.

They drove back towards town through Kew, Kruger's patch, and then along the Chandler Highway. Kruger stayed in touch—just. The cop got ahead on Heidelberg Road and Kruger struggled. The lights changed at Station Street. The cop got through but Kruger copped red. He lost her.

On his way to return the van, he went via Michael Chan's abode. He parked, making sure there was a block of flats between him and the warehouse. He took out a newspaper and pretended to read.

He now understood what cops meant when they said chasing crooks is never like it is on TV or in the movies. Most of the work is dead set boring. He decided to call it a day when a car drove past. Kruger watched then really watched.

It was the car he followed from Balwyn North. The car was parked and out stepped the woman in the police uniform. She went into Chan's warehouse carrying a large bunch of flowers, and what looked like a bottle of champagne and a box of chocolates.

'Now that's interesting,' he said. 'What are they celebrating? Surely not the theft of my money?'

He waited and when the policewoman didn't come out, he drove off to return the van. Tobias Smith aka Cornelius "Connie" Kruger now had a lead.

Michael opened his door and Jo saw a ghost.

'Michael, what's wrong?'

He didn't speak, pointed, and Jo entered. She put her gifts in the kitchen and forgot about them.

'You look terrible. What's happened? Has the money been taken back?' Jo didn't know what she was talking about, and her concern for Michael didn't help.

He spoke. 'He was here, today.'

'Who?'

'Cornelius Kruger.'

'Who's Cornelius Kruger?'

'The man we robbed.'

'What?'

'I mean the man who robbed your mother.'

Both were now agitated. Jo's chest felt tight.

'How do you know his name? How do you know who he is?'

'The security guy in the Zurich bank called me Mr Kruger. I conned him into calling me by my first name—Cornelius, Connie. Then today, out of the blue, this guy with a South African accent rang me then came to see me. He told me someone hacked his bank account to the tune of 210 grand.'

'He knew the exact amount?'

'It has to be him. He must live in Melbourne.'

'Did he say his name?'

'Tobias Smith.'

'And you didn't believe him?'

'No, that man was Cornelius Kruger.'

'But how did he find you?'

'The Fraud Squad recommended me.'

'What? How do you know?'

'He told me.'

They stopped for a breather. Both their Fit Bits were exhausted. Jo was doubly worried.

The euphoria of getting her mother's money back was flattened by the reality that she was an accessory to a serious crime and, if caught, getting dumped from the Homicide Squad would seem like good news. She'd be out of the Force and into a cell. Worse, the criminal was no doubt after revenge. She asked the obvious question.

'What did he want?'

'How's this for irony? He wanted me to find the guy who hacked into his bank account and then help him retrieve his money.'

'*His* money?'

'I'm not ashamed to say, Jo, I was scared, really scared.

'So what happened?'

'I told him I didn't do that type of work.'

'And?'

'And he left.'

'Just like that?'

'At the door he stared at me, and his parting words were, "I hope this is not the last time we meet, Mr Chan".'

Jo looked at her terrified friend. He had trouble breathing. In an instant, their plan had produced a very nasty problem. Forget about criminal charges. There was a desperate criminal on the loose, who wanted money and blood.

27

PONZI WAS A CROOK. His friends knew it, his wife knew it, and the cops knew it. When it came to looking for suspects, the Fraud and Extortion Squad had his number on speed dial.

His dalliance with Jo Best was just that. He made a minor suggestion to her one scam. The cash on offer was handy.

But his real job involved creating monster scams. Ponzi had no interest in fleecing lonely women. His expertise lay in creating land development schemes into which desperate first-home buyers and gullible investors poured their savings. Those savings disappeared. Offshore accounts for the fraudsters grew bigger and Ponzi was in the thick of it. His nickname was well earned.

His latest and biggest rip-off was simple. Ponzi and mates bought land, got permission to develop a housing estate then started the scam.

An elderly and naive farmer owned the land. The fraudsters offered more than it was worth. The farmer and his wife were delighted. But the terms, the fine print of the contract, guaranteed problems.

Smooth-talker, Ponzi, got to work on the elderly farmer. 'Listen, Mr Williams, this money will set you and your wife up for life. You can move into a luxury retirement village with all the mod cons and do everything you've always wanted to do.'

Mrs Williams was excited and adored the benefits listed by Ponzi.

'You'll be close to your grandkids. Your darling dog, Max will be there. The expert cleaning service will do your housework. The village restaurant has fabulous food with no more slaving over a hot stove and you'll have constant air-conditioned comfort. Just put your feet up.'

Mr Williams was keen and Mrs Williams ecstatic. Ponzi sold the benefits and ignored the terms of payment within the contract.

All the farmer and his wife could see was the price tag, and the retirement life they used to dream about. If only they'd studied the terms. At first glance, they were fantastic. Ponzi knew the rule. Never mention the fine details. Point to the sparkling lights.

The total price was more than fair but when would the farmer get his money? And how much? Ah, there's the rub, or rather, the sting.

'So it's 10% on signing the contract then 25% once the project begins, and the remainder when the project ends.'

Yes but by never finishing the project—it was never intended to be finished—Mr Williams only gets 35% of the money he's owed, if that.

What happened?

The pitch is what happened. Ponzi and Co spent money on glossy brochures, a spectacular web site, and hired upmarket conference rooms around town.

What were they selling?

A brand new estate with more lies and promises than a desperate politician addicted to pork barrelling.

The title of the project was the *Golden Wattle Village* described as *Glorious home sites in a village atmosphere.*

The estate was just over an hour from Melbourne, which was about the time it took to drive there at 3 am. The estate offered the following.

* Underground cabling
* Library, community centre, public swimming pool
* Bike paths, walkways
* All services

Photos of the proposed "village" featured beautiful, photo-shopped models enjoying the amenities. All the models were a size 6 or 8. In the baking Australian summer, the photos showed the proposed village amenities with vegetation straight out of a Gloucestershire village. Even the flies had digitally disappeared. This was spin on a grand scale. This was bullshit writ large.

The scam worked as follows. Ponzi and Co sold blocks to young couples desperate to get a foot on the property ladder, and sold shares in the management company supposedly developing the estate to investors. The investors were wealthy middle-class folk keen to have a nest egg in retirement.

At the public meetings, the seating and décor were all class. The audio-visual presentation was slick. This was an upmarket religious service where land ownership replaced salvation. Come on down, and give your life savings to the Lord Ponzi and his pals.

The key was to get the money upfront. Ponzi was the driving force. Sell blocks of land. Sell shares in the management company. Get the money up front. GET THE DEPOSIT NOW. Funnel this money into local accounts then into accounts in far-flung places.

The principals got great whacking salaries which found their way into super funds and trust funds in the names of family members. Ponzi and Co had a leave-the-country-overnight plan in place.

The Fraud Squad and ASIC (Australian Securities & Investments Commission) kept watch. As would-be investors, members of the Fraud Squad attended some of the public meetings. So far, no crime had been committed, although the ties and shoes worn by the salesmen sailed close to the wind.

The meetings were packed. Couples with cheque books and platinum plastic were everywhere. Some of them were actors paid to be there. Interested investors saw this huge demand. What better recommendation did they need? Where do I invest?

Now this scam, with Ponzi front and centre, had started before Jo Best persuaded him to join her crime-busting outfit.

Not long after Jo slipped Ponzi a bung in the carpark of the Patterson Lakes library, ASIC went public. It believed the lack of progress on the *Golden Wattle Village* estate was the result of serious underinvestment. It made a detailed study of the company's books and found the project to be hopelessly insolvent. Arrest warrants were drawn up for the principals (if they could be found), and investors were told they'd be lucky to get back any of their money. For them, it was a disaster.

Young couples hoping to move in by Christmas were distraught. The houses where building had started were left unfinished. Older couples who bought shares, applied for the pension. Farmer and Mrs Williams moved out of their luxury unit and into a caravan.

Ponzi's cash was stashed overseas. He was a happy little Vegemite.

The day before ASIC's bad news on the estate went public, a doorbell rang and Carmen Baggio answered it to find two men in suits. They weren't Mormons.

'Mrs Baggio?'

'Yes.'

'We're police officers from the Fraud and Extortion Squad. Is your husband at home?'

Carmen wanted to explode, not at the cops, but at Mr Scam. She had threatened him a lot of late about this exact situation.

'If I find you've been doing that criminal stuff again, I'll leave you and take you to the cleaners. Do you hear me?'

He heard.

Back at the front door, Mrs Baggio managed to keep her cool but her voice had a rich layer of evil in meaning and volume.

'David,' she politely screamed.

The officers looked at one another.

This bloke might be glad to go inside.

'What?' spoke a voice from within.

'You have visitors.'

'Tell 'em we're atheists and anarchists.'

'You tell 'em.'

Silence. Ponzi wandered into the hallway. He didn't like what he saw. He would have welcomed insurance salesmen with open arms but these guys weren't selling.

'Mr David Baggio?'

'Yes' he answered.'

'We're police officers. May we come in?'

The officers held up their ID.

Ponzi had no choice. The cops didn't want to enter the house. As soon as Ponzi came to the doorway, he was nabbed.

'David Baggio, I'm arresting you for obtaining financial advantage by deception. I must inform you that you do not have to say or do anything but anything you say or do may be given in evidence.'

The officer's caution was lost in the tirade of abuse unleased by his wife. The cops were right. Ponzi would definitely prefer the slammer.

Poor old Dave was cuffed and led away. His wife followed and entertained the neighbours with her fruity epithets. She had a nice turn of phrase did Carmen. Mrs Baggio was further incensed, if that were possible, when other officers walked up the drive with a search warrant, and proceeded to turn the Baggio abode upside down.

179

Back at police HQ, Ponzi refused to say anything without his legal representative. When the interview got going, the facts presented by the police were watertight. Ponzi kept consulting his solicitor and using his favourite phrase, *No comment.*

The evidence kept mounting. Ponzi felt trapped. He was going down. He decided to snitch. Why should he carry the can?

To his shock, the other principals in this tawdry scam were no longer in the country. Ponzi fumed. They told Ponzi the time to leave would be next month. They knew better and were gone.

'Keep selling, Dave,' they said as they jetted to safe havens overseas.

Ponzi was hung out to dry. He pondered his position. Dobbing in his missing mates gave Ponzi no bargaining power. The cops already knew their names. And anyway, Ponzi had no idea where his "mates" were hiding. Bastards.

The cops knew they'd struggle to find the escapees, and even if they could locate them, extradition might take forever. The thinking of the police was clear. A bird in the hand is worth a Ponzi in Montenegro, Mauritius and the Maldives. Poor old sod.

He started to drown. He grabbed a floating straw.

'I want to cut a deal.'

The police laughed.

'Ponzi.'

He snapped. 'Don't call me that. My name's David Baggio.'

The police were taken aback by his intense reaction.

'Okay David, why would we cut a deal with someone who has nothing to give?'

'I've got something.'

'But all your mates have fled. Do you even know where they are?'

He didn't have a clue. 'No.'

'Then there's no trade ... Ponzi.'

He raged then dropped his bombshell.

'I can give you a corrupt cop.'

The police looked at one another and then at Ponzi.

'Tell us more.'

'Not till I know what you're offering.'

'Oh Ponzi, please, we need to know what you've got before we can even think about a possible deal.'

There was a long pause. Ponzi wanted to make this work. Without a deal, he was facing a long stretch. His wife knew a cracking divorce lawyer. His mates were home free with him banged up. He spoke using the same amount of exaggeration he used when selling crappy blocks of land in the sticks (the boonies).

'I can give you a cop who is running international scams as big, if not bigger than mine.'

The cops again exchanged glances. If true, this was more than interesting.

'Okay Ponzi, what have you got?'

'Only one cop so far but there are others.'

'Name?'

'Detective Senior Constable Joanna Best.'

28

JO HAD PROBLEMS. Her career in Homicide was over. Michael Chan, her partner in crime, was under major stress. She had evidence about a double murder obtained from an illegal phone tap she couldn't declare.

And these were the issues she knew about. She didn't know a criminal had been following her, and spying on her mother. She didn't know an arrested fraudster had turned snitch, and told Victoria Police she was bent.

She knew Michael was genuinely scared of Cornelius Kruger, and Benny Ross was innocent, but what could she do about it?

Help!

She rang her mother. 'Hi Mum, it's Jo. How are you?'

Instead of a moaning, miserable woman, Shirley sounded bright, almost happy. 'Hello my wonderful daughter.'

Wow. What a difference a day makes.

'I'm going to see Pop today and take him to see Nan.'

'Oh, can I come?'

Jo was stunned. 'Sure.'

'Well don't sound so surprised. You told me to get out and about.'

'That's great, Mum. I'll pick you in an hour.'

'See you then.'

Well, that's one problem I can cross off the list.

Jo had been thinking long and hard about solving the double murder. If she told her former Homicide colleagues she had illegally tapped a phone that could mean instant dismissal and criminal charges. Besides, even if the call had not been destroyed, it wouldn't stand up in court.

She reckoned there were two people to ask. Pop she would see soon, and someone else she could see right now. She rocked up to Dr Gabrielle Strange's abode.

The pathetic pathologist's voice preceded her presence. 'If you're selling, piss off.' The door opened. 'It's the deranged detective.'

She threw open her arms and Jo enjoyed the hug.

'Do you mind me calling unannounced?'

'Mind? Don't be such a pompous prick. Now park your posterior in my parlour, Princess.'

They actually sat in Gabrielle's sunny kitchen and drank coffee. Jo opened up. She told Dr Strange everything except the bank hacking, and the visit from Tobias Smith. Gabrielle was seriously impressed.

'You do realise if you crack this double murder, those dickheads at Homicide will have to eat humble pie and reinstate you?'

'That would be great, but you did use the magic word, *if*.'

'Think positive, my dear. So, what's your plan?'

'That's just it, I haven't got one. If I confront either the old woman or the two boys, and they report me, I'll be up on a serious charge.'

'Why not get someone else to confront them?'

'That would mean telling them about the illegal phone tap.'

'Not necessarily. Make an anonymous call to the Drug Squad saying the boys are dealers.'

Jo thought about it.

'What if they find nothing?'

'Then there's no harm done.'

Jo got thinking. 'But if there *is* something there, that might explain where the cocaine at the murder scene came from.'

'And if they're arrested, that puts them under pressure. Slowly, slowly, catchee monkey.'

'Thanks, I knew you'd have an idea or two.'

'Find a way to put them under pressure. The phone tap worked. What about wearing a wire?'

Jo liked that idea. 'You should have been a detective.'

They laughed and Gabrielle walked Jo to the door.

'Good luck, darling, and keep me posted.'

Jo drove her mother to Pop's place. It's funny how some family relationships flourish while others limp along. Shirley got on okay with her father, Jo got on with the same man like a house on fire. Why? Who knows?

With Pop insisting on riding in the back, the trio headed for the nursing home and Nan. Ida was in her chair in her room. She wasn't fussed on going to the lounge, and sat and watched the world go by outside her window.

One of the nurses led the family down the corridor.

'Ida's very bright today.'

Pop was worried. 'I hope she'll be able to handle all of us.'

'She'll love to see us, Pop.'

Shirley's newfound happiness wavered. She couldn't handle her mother asking, 'Who are you?' whenever Shirley came to visit.

The nurse opened the door. 'Ida, look who's come to see you.'

The nurse left and the family crowded around. Jo had the routine down pat. She kissed her grandmother and spoke clearly making eye contact.

'Hello Nan, it's Jo, your favourite granddaughter. How are you?'

Ida smiled. 'Hello Jo.'

Then it was Shirley's turn. She kissed her mother.

'Hello Mum, it's Shirley, your favourite daughter.'

'Who?'

Shirley hated these moments.

Pop moved in. 'It's Shirley, love, the little girl with the plaits.'

Ida looked at Shirley and then her husband. 'She hasn't got plaits.'

It was a wonderful moment with grins all round. Even Shirley smiled. The family sat and chatted. Ida looked from one to the other. A woman from the kitchen brought in a tray with tea and biscuits. Shirley took over. Jo was pleased.

'I'll be mother, Mother,' she said and Ida looked at her.

'You're not my mother.'

That was not a wonderful moment.

Jo spoke up. 'Mum, why don't you and Nan have a cuppa together? I want to ask the famous policeman a question or two.'

Shirley's heart was still singing and she didn't object. Pop was pleased to take a break. He and Jo settled in the lounge. She wanted to talk about one specific issue—the Elsternwick double murder, including the illegal phone tap.

'That went on in my day. The secret was to not get caught.'

'So what would you do, Pop? What's my next step?'

'I'd concentrate on the bloke who's been charged. So long as DI Steele reckons he's got the right man, nothing will change. Prove the bloke they charged didn't do it, and that'll force 'em to look elsewhere.'

'Okay. How?'

'You're the detective. Follow your hunch.'

Jo glowed inside. *Why didn't I think of that?* 'Thanks, Pop.'

'Has he got any mates? If so, can they prove he didn't do it? You heard the real killer confess. Use that knowledge and nail 'em.'

Jo leaned in and kissed her grandfather. They went back to Ida.

The visit was a raging success in that Ida enjoyed herself, Shirley was out and about, Pop had his family with him, and Jo had ideas to expose the real killer in the double murder. But sleuthing was tricky. She no longer worked for Homicide.

Michael opened his door looking almost normal. Jo smiled.

'You look much better, Michael. Any news?'

'Nothing. I'm praying our friend from South Africa has gone home.'

She looked at him. They both believed Mr Kruger, if that's who he was, would not give up without a fight.

'I want to ask a favour,' said Jo.

'Does it involve hacking into foreign bank accounts or tapping telephones?'

'No, I want to record a conversation by wearing a wire.'

'And?'

'This is police work. I'm desperate to crack that double homicide.'

Michael liked her. He knew she was one of the good guys—gals— and so agreed. He collected material as he spoke.

'This'll be the third crime I've committed since meeting you, Ms Best. Remind me never to cross you.'

Jo laughed. 'No problem, Mr Genius.'

He showed her various items and explained how they worked. She didn't tell him she had no idea who would wear the wire.

With her eavesdropping equipment in a bag, she thanked him again as they walked to the door. Any romantic feelings between them moved into a siding now the fear of death had raised its ugly head.

She was on the graveyard shift that night so had a few hours to spare. She dressed down, removed what little make-up she wore, and messed her hair. She headed to Brunswick and the former abode of the accused murderer, Benny Ross. She knew the address from her interview with the suspect. She parked and found Benny's place.

It was a single-fronted weatherboard due for demolition. There was no sign but had there been, it would have screamed *I'm a Squat* or *Druggies Within* or *Demolition Site—Keep Out*.

Jo entered the property. Two dead wheelie bins lounged in the tiny front yard. Both had serious war wounds and looked like they belonged *in* a wheelie bin. Their smell was threatening.

She looked down the side of the property. It was narrow and packed with junk. Edmund Hillary and Sherpa Tenzing Norgay would have taken a day to reach the back yard. She studied the front door.

It looked formidable. 'Here goes,' she whispered and knocked. She called. 'Benny? Benny, it's me, Sheila. Hello?'

Not knowing where Sheila came from, Jo knocked again. Silence from within. She repeated her knocking and calling routine. She hoped a female voice was less intimidating. It was.

Footsteps. Someone approached. A male voice. 'Who is it?'

'Hi! I'm Sheila, a friend of Benny's. He told me to look him up if I ever came to Melbourne.'

'He's not here.'

Jo was thinking on her feet. 'When will he be back?'

'He won't.'

'What, never?'

'He's gone and won't be coming back.'

'Bugger. Look, can I come in and use your toilet? Please?'

'No. Piss off.'

'Well I'll piss off on your doorstep if you don't let me in. Please?'

Jo hoped hard. Then she heard a bolt and lock being handled, the door opened a little and a face appeared.

It looked worried and well lived in. 'Have you got any gear?'

'I know where to get some. Let me in and we can score together.'

The resident relented. He opened the door and stared at Jo. 'The toilet's down the back.'

'Thanks.'

She checked out the detritus of the house. Everything was filthy with the toilet the filthiest. The sight was sickening, and the smell attacked her. She waited a few seconds then flushed the loo. It made no difference to its "sparkling" bowl.

The man was waiting in the lounge. He looked as rough as the room. He challenged her.

'How do you know Benny?'

'Oh we go back a long way.'

'Describe him.'

Wrong question. Jo had interviewed him when working in Homicide, and could describe him to a tee.

'Fair enough,' said the man. 'I'm Jeb.' Her description of his friend was perfect. He relaxed thinking the visitor was genuine.

'Can I sit?'

He nodded. Jo didn't like her choices. The beanbag had mould and the sofa was a flea farm. She settled for a chair with its seat in tatters. Jeb took the sofa.

'You can't stay here.'

Jo looked sad. 'What's happened to Benny?'

He's dead.'

'Dead? How? When?'

'Not dead dead, he's in jail.'

Jo had been trying to find a way to reveal her real identity. Too soon and Jeb might go crazy. He might attack her, throw her out, almost anything. That would wreck her plan. She needed Jeb. Was coming clean now too soon? If so, too bad, as she jumped in at the deep end.

'I know,' she said and looked at the druggie.

He paused, confused. 'What?'

'I know he's in jail for a double murder.'

He twigged. 'You're a cop.'

'And I know he didn't do it.'

He stood and snarled. 'I can smell a cop a mile away.'

'And with your help, I can prove Benny didn't do it and you will be responsible for having him released.'

Jeb had been ready to go ballistic. He hated cops and hated being conned. But Jo said things he wanted to hear. There was a long pause.

'How?'

'I know who did the murders.'

'Who?'

187

'I mean I know three people who planned the murders and I'm not sure how many of the three did the actual killing.'

'Give me names.'

'Ah there's an old woman called Dora, her godson Bradley, and his boyfriend, Gavin who is the son of the murdered couple.'

Jeb nodded. This woman knew her onions.

'But I bet your name's not Sheila.'

She smiled. Jeb was almost on her team. 'I'm Jo.'

He sat. 'Those two guys took me to a house in Daylesford and kept me there. I didn't know what was happening. When they brought me back, Benny was in jail and charged with killing those people.'

'So the police didn't interview you because you weren't around?'

'When Gavin and Bradley brought me home, they gave me some dough, and said they'd kill me if I ever spoke to the cops.'

'Okay,' said Jo, 'here's the plan.'

An hour later, with Jeb wearing a wire, they parked near Gavin and Bradley's flat.

'Remember,' said Jo, 'I'm right here listening. If there's any threat, I'll come running. If you feel you're in danger, shout *Monte Christo*.'

'*Monte Christo*,' repeated Jeb thinking the woman strange.

'Good luck and stick to the script.'

Jeb exhaled, got out of the car and walked to the flat. He knocked and Gavin opened the door. 'What do you want?'

'I wanna talk.'

Bradley came out of the lounge and turned angry. Gavin grabbed Jeb, dragged him inside and closed the door.

Bradley exploded. 'We told you to never contact us again.'

Jeb was shoved into the lounge.

Gavin spat. 'We paid you well, you little prick.'

'Not enough,' said a defiant but inwardly nervous Jeb.

They called Jeb a series of impolite names but he stuck to his guns.

'I know you framed my mate. I know you planted the jewels from the dead woman's house in our squat. I know you pinched his trainers.'

The conspirators' anger level went from dangerous to extreme.

'I think you know too much,' threatened Gavin.

'Way too much,' added Bradley.

'I saw you bring back Benny's trainers with the dirt from the garden of the murdered couple. You were wearing gloves. I saw you.'

The threats against Jeb got nasty. He kept attacking.

'You took me out of Melbourne so the cops wouldn't interview me. So unless you pay me big time, I'm gunna tell the cops everything.'

Gavin looked calm for someone who said what he said.

'Big mistake, arsehole. You can't tell anyone … when you're dead.' Gavin attacked Jeb. 'Grab him!' screamed Gavin and he and Bradley went for the now terrified visitor.'

Fists and feet got busy. There was a lot of punching and kicking with Jeb giving as good as he got.

In her car, Jo heard everything. Amongst the screams of the fight, she clearly heard Jeb yell, '*Monte Christo*.' He kept yelling it.

She ran. She knew banging on the front door might stop the fight, but would the attackers let her in? She raced along the laneway, opened the unlocked back gate and launched herself against the back door with too much force. It was unlocked and she entered the kitchen a bit like a runaway train. The crashing sounds caused the three pugilists to stop. Real panic set in. Jo grabbed a large kitchen knife, and burst into the lounge.

'Police,' she thundered. 'Stay where you are.'

As all three gents were on the floor in a tangle of arms and legs, staying where they were proved easy. Jo's knife looked threatening.

'Get up, Jeb,' she ordered and the druggie broke free. His attackers whimpered and surrendered. 'Lie on your stomachs,' she bellowed. The men complied. She plunged the knife into the rug between them sending both into the shit-scared category. 'Jeb, in the kitchen, get me some cling film or plastic bags, anything. Go.' Jeb went.

Jo placed her handcuffs around an ankle of each prisoner. Had they been three-legged race champions, they might have stood a chance.

Jeb returned with bin liners. Jo used them to tie Gavin and Bradley's hands behind their backs. She looked up at Jeb and smiled.

'Well done, you. Now, if you wouldn't mind.'

She indicated Jeb's chest. He got the message, undid his shirt and slowly removed the technical equipment stuck to his body. The ankle-cuffed duo saw the wire. They knew what had happened and could put *goose* and *cooked* in the same sentence. Jo pocketed the wire then turned to the rug rats.

'Gavin Hall and Bradley Finch, I'm arresting you for conspiracy to murder, perverting the course of justice, and for attempted murder. I must inform you that you do not have to say or do anything but anything you say or do ...'

Bradley interrupted. 'It wasn't us.'

'...may be given in evidence.'

'Shut up,' yelled Gavin.

Jo had a damn good idea who did the killing.

'Jeb, could you do me one more favour, and help me get these prisoners into my car?'

'Sure. But shouldn't you call the cops to take them away?'

'Normally, yes, but I have a reason to deliver this package myself.'

Jeb helped the two men to their feet. They shuffled out through the partly trashed kitchen, into the back yard and out through the gate. Any locals watching would have seen an unusual sight. A drug addict and a plainclothes cop, female, either side of two residents, handcuffed at their ankles and with hands tied behind their backs using bin liners.

'Shuffle this way, gentlemen,' and shuffle they did.

They made it to Jo's car. The prisoners sat in the back with Jeb in the front beside Jo. They headed to Elsternwick. There was not a lot of chatter during the journey. Jo parked outside Dora Madigan's house and made another request of her new partner.

'This is the last one, Jeb, I promise. Stay here and keep watch.'

'This is not right, me workin' for the pigs.'

'I'll be back. Now can you step outside? I'll lock the car and if they try anything, just yell the magic words.'

'*Monte Christo*,' mumbled Jeb.

'You've got it. Give me five.'

As she knocked on Dora's door, Jo remembered her last visit to this house, and the consequences. She lost her job as a Homicide Squad detective. Dora appeared, looked shocked, and spoke.

'I'm calling the police.' She headed for her phone but stopped when Jo spoke.

'Dora Madigan, I'm arresting you for the murder of David and Larissa Hall.'

'What? You're mad.' She was angry and nervous.

'Bradley and Gavin are under arrest.'

'You're lying.'

'Come outside.'

Dora didn't know what to say or do. Jo beckoned to her. Slowly the woman followed Jo to the front gate. There was the car with Jeb the sentry.

'Look in the back, Dora.' She did. The prisoners looked broken, wretched and guilty. Dora felt faint, and had to lean on her front gate. Jo went to help her.

'It wasn't them, it was me. I killed them,' she said quietly but with force. 'Arrest me, let them go.'

'Save it, Dora. You can talk at the station. Now let's go inside, get your bag and lock the house.' Dora looked at Jo. 'Is there someone you should contact?'

'I only have my godson, and now I've lost him forever.' She cried.

Jo looked at Jeb. 'Two minutes,' she called and helped Dora inside. Jo made sure the house was secure, that Dora had any medication she was taking then helped her prisoner back into the street. Jo's prayer was answered; there wasn't a cat or dog to leave behind. Dora sat in the front seat not willing to turn and look at her fellow prisoners. Jo looked at Jeb.

'I don't suppose you fancy sitting next to those two guys?'

'No way.'

'Or a trip to the cop shop?'

'Forget it.'

Jo handed Jeb a fifty. 'For your fare and hopefully not your fix.'

'Thanks. I might have just met my first half-decent cop.'

'And remember, you're the one who got Benny out of jail.'

29

JO HEADED FOR POLICE HQ, and fancied her next task. She was rapt to have cracked the case but better still would be showing the Homicide heavies they were wrong and her sacking was unjustified.

With luck she found a park, and helped Dora out of the car. The housekeeper looked dreadful and Jo had second thoughts. *Did this elderly woman really murder two people?* Those doubts turned Jo's pride to fear. But there was no turning back now.

The men got out with difficulty. Talk about humiliation. Gavin looked at Dora but godson Bradley couldn't. Jo herded her entourage into the Melbourne West Police complex.

The desk sergeant recognised Jo. 'Senior Constable Best, what brings you here?'

'Hello, Sarge. I have three prisoners.'

'Only three? Rumour has it your average collar is four.'

'Very funny, Sarge. Could you book them in, please?'

'Certainly.' He beckoned to the trio. 'Would you step up to the counter, please, one at a time.'

At first all three were charged with conspiracy to murder but later, after interviews, Dora was charged with two counts of murder, and Gavin and Bradley with conspiracy to murder, conspiracy to pervert the course of justice, and attempted murder.

Other officers in the station took notice. Word soon spread.

None of the prisoners had anything to say. A doctor was called to examine all three. Dora looked like death warmed up, and both the males had facial bruises and scratches having been in a fight as they attacked Jeb.

Jo stood back and let the process proceed. She waited then almost died when the Assistant Commissioner (Crime Operations) John

Crowley, and the Head of Homicide, her former boss, DI Steele, walked into the station. Steele saw Jo and went red.

Jo nodded. 'Sir,' she said.

Steele wanted to tear strips off her for returning to HQ after being banished to booze bus duties in the suburbs. He couldn't vent his rage because of the Assistant Commissioner by his side. To make matters worse, AC Crowley expressed an interest in the gathering.

'What's happening, Sergeant?'

'Three arrests, sir, for a double homicide in Elsternwick.'

Steele veered close to apoplexy. He'd signed off on the case. The date for the committal hearing had been set. Now this junior upstart he'd sacked was back with three new suspects. Steele wondered if police regulations had a charge similar to that of treason.

'And the arresting officers,' asked AC Crowley?'

'Just the one, sir.' He nodded towards Jo. 'Senior Constable Best.'

The AC turned to Jo. 'Senior Constable Best, many congratulations.' He held out his hand and Jo shook it.

'Thank you, sir.'

'How long have you been a detective?'

'Ah, I'm not, sir. I'm a uniformed officer.'

He looked at her clothing. 'I see. And based where?'

'I'm at Flemington, sir.'

'The mystery deepens. So how does a uniformed officer, currently in civvies, and who should be arresting shoplifters at Highpoint West, get to arrest suspects for a double homicide in Elsternwick? Moonlighting are we, Constable?'

Steele had suffered enough. He tried to take control.

'If I may, sir. Senior Constable Best had been working at Homicide but she returned to her local station.'

'Well I'd be looking at getting her back, DI Steele.'

'Sir?'

The Homicide boss hadn't been this miserable since his wife made him judge the flower arranging at their church fete.

The AC kept banging on about Jo and her work. 'Three arrests for a double homicide, and by a single officer, is outstanding work.'

'Thank you, sir,' said Jo wondering how this would end.

'I tell you what, Senior Constable, if DI Steele won't have you at Homicide, and he'd be mad to let you go, I'm always on the lookout for capable, young officers. I'd be happy to have you working for me.'

Jo was both thrilled and terrified.

The offer pushed the enraged DI Steele towards naked fury. He was between a terrorist and a drunken sniper. To invite Jo back would be so humiliating. To see her appointed by the Assistant Commissioner to the AC's personal staff would haunt him until retirement. He chose the lesser of the two grovels.

'I think we might be able to reconsider Senior Constable Best's request for a return to Homicide.' He gave the worst example of a forced smile in the history of insincerity. 'That's if she wants to return.'

Steele hoped like hell she'd refuse.

'I'd like that very much, sir,' she said.

'There you go, Senior Constable,' said AC Crowley. 'My loss is Homicide's gain. Good luck,' he said, departing for higher floors and higher matters.

There were witnesses around, and Steele needed to get cracking. 'Report to my office at 0800 hours,' he snapped and hurried after the Assistant Commissioner.

Jo looked at the desk sergeant. He winked and pursed his lips.

'Oooo, who's a clever clogs?'

Shirley heard her doorbell. Two days ago she would have ignored it. Now she had a spring in her step and a smile on her lips. She opened the door to a complete stranger.

'Hello Shirley.'

'Who are you?' She felt uneasy.

'Aren't you going to invite me in?'

'I don't know who you are or what you want, so please go away.'

She began to close the door but the man used his foot to block it. With a hand, he gripped the frame. The door froze.

'Now Shirley, that's no way to treat the man you said you loved.'

Shirley felt sick. The unusual accent seemed scary. The man's forced smile, his determination to come inside without raising his voice or being physical gave Shirley the creeps. She sensed terror.

'If you don't leave, I'll call the police.'

That provoked a serious reaction. The man pushed his way inside, shoved Shirley and closed the door. Gone was his smooth chat-up line.

'Just get inside you stupid bitch or I'll break your fucking neck.'

Right, now she understood, now there were no secrets. The visitor was evil, with criminal intent, and Shirley had no doubt he could and would hurt, even kill her. He pushed her into the lounge.

'Sit, Shirley, and be a good girl.'

She sat. 'What do you want?'

'We'll get to that. Now who helped you steal my money?'

Shirley realised. She knew this man. He was, is the smooth-talker who lied to her, tricked her online, and stole her money. Now she knew the cause of his outrage. Strangely, she felt better, if that were possible, and she challenged him.

'What's your real name?

'Does it matter?'

'You know my name. Why shouldn't I know yours?'

'I'll say this once, Shirley. I want my money, bitch, and if you won't give it to me, I'll kill you—slowly. Now, do you understand?'

Shirley was petrified but for some inexplicable reason, chose to stand up to the bully. Maybe she thought he would kill her anyway. Maybe she didn't want to die begging for her life so fired back at him.

'You want your money back? It's not your money. It never was your money. It was and still is *my* money.'

'You gave it to me, you stupid, ugly old cow.'

Shirley looked at Cornelius Kruger. 'Oh, please forgive me. I didn't recognize you—George Clooney.'

Kruger's blood got warmer. He wanted a quick kill. Get in, get money, get out. But the more he argued with the woman, the longer it would take to pocket the cash.

'Listen to me, bitch. I know you hate pain. So be told, I'm brilliant at inflicting excruciating torture.' He moved closer to her, his eyes smouldering with rage. 'Let's cut to the chase. I want the names of the people who stole my money, and I want the full amount transferred to my account, now. So think very carefully before you answer this next question.'

'If I get it right, do I win a prize?'

Without trying, she was mocking him, ridiculing the monster. Kruger became enraged. He strode to Shirley who cowered in fear. She felt his breath as he grabbed her hair and dragged her face against his. His spittle went free range.

'You are asking for it, bitch. Keep this up and you will quickly beg for mercy.' He roared into her face. 'Give me my money.'

With her face up against his, and despite being terrified, she spoke in a motherly voice.

'Say please.'

For a moment Kruger thought he would snap, and Shirley expected him to snap. He shoved her hard against her chair and stepped back.

'Nice one, Shirley, I like your balls. But all your smartarse answers won't stop me getting my money.'

Somehow she seemed emboldened. 'You've shot yourself in the foot, my son. I don't care. I've got nothing to live for. My husband's left me for a child bride, my mother's got dementia, and my grandkids prefer their mates to the one you call a stupid, ugly old cow.'

He roared in a crescendo. 'I want my money.'

She said nothing. If her smartarse answers drove him nuts, maybe saying nothing might have even more of an impact.

He tried another tack. 'Think how your family will feel discovering you dead with torture marks all over your body. The distress will haunt them forever.'

'Malcolm X will be over the moon.'

Kruger paused. He'd heard of Malcolm X but not in this context.

'What about that lovely young policewoman who pops in here?'

Shirley flinched ever so slightly and Kruger noticed. 'Ah, someone who cares. Now we're cooking. Just imagine her finding you gurgling with blood and snot oozing out of various orifices.'

Shirley found her second wind. 'Can we please get on with the torture? I'm getting bored.'

She saw the rage reignite in his eyes.

'Right, bitch, you asked for it.'

30

JO WAS THRILLED. She almost skipped back to her car. She was back at Homicide, starting in the morning. She could have had a job working for the Assistant Commissioner (Crime). She solved a major murder, which the experts got wrong. She was on top of the world.

She wanted to tell her mother and definitely Pop but before them came her friend, Mr Michael Chan. She drove straight to Northcote.

As always he knew she was on his property, and opened the door just as she got there.

'Michael, I have the most fantastic news.'

'Great,' he said without showing any enthusiasm.

Jo was immediately worried. 'What's happened?'

'Nothing but I can't help thinking our friend from South Africa will be back at any time. Sorry, what's your news?'

'I'm back at Homicide.'

'Wow, congratulations. But how?'

'And it's all thanks to you.'

'Me?'

'Your listening device trapped the killers and I made three arrests.'

'Only three; you're slipping.'

She smiled at the joke she heard at the station. 'I report back to Homicide in the morning.'

'I thought you were on night shift tonight.'

'Oh God,' said Jo. 'I have to ring Flemington.'

She reached for her phone but as she did it rang. Jo looked at the caller ID and answered with a cheerful voice.'

'Hi Mum. I've got some brilliant news.'

'Well so have I,' said Cornelius Kruger.

Jo nearly dropped the phone. Michael saw the fear in her face. He mouthed, 'What's up?'

Jo hit the speaker button, put her finger to her lips for Michael to remain quiet, and tried to speak normally.

'Who's speaking?'

'I think you know, Senior Constable Joanna Best of Victoria Police, and daughter of the lovely Shirley Best, here in Balwyn North.'

Michael knew who was speaking. He pointed and mouthed, 'That's him.'

Jo realised and fought to control her panic. 'What do you want?'

'I'm with your dear mother, Joanna, and I'd like you to listen to what she has to say.'

There was a dreadful pause. Jo thought her heart would explode. Michael got back his sweats and shakes.

Shirley spoke. It was difficult to understand her words. 'I'm okay, Jo. I've told him nothing.'

Jo and Michael exchanged glances. He picked up his phone. Jo waved frantically. She scribbled a message while conducting a phone call with a maniac about to kill her mother.

Kruger grabbed the phone. 'Now Jo, I know you love your mother dearly, but she's a smartarse bitch who thinks she can get away with stealing my money.'

Jo scribbled. *Call AC Crowley.*

'You stole her money, you bastard,' snapped Jo.

It was Michael's turn to wave a hand. He made a calming gesture wanting Jo to keep her cool. She nodded, her pulse now racing. He looked at her scribble and mouthed *Number?* She wrote.

'I'll put this in simple terms, Jo,' said Kruger. 'Unless I get all my money back within the next ten minutes, your mother will suffer terrible pain and slowly bleed to death. Have you got that?'

Jo wrote Crowley's number and her mother's address. Michael went to the kitchen and made a call. Jo took Michael's advice and turned on the respect.

'I understand. I want to help but please do not hurt my mother.'

'Smart girl,' said Kruger. 'Just tell me your mother's banking details so I can transfer the funds back where they belong.'

'I don't know her banking details.'

Kruger's voice swelled with rage. 'That's not the right answer, Joanna. Listen to this.' Kruger went to Shirley and twisted her arm. She tried not to cry out but the pain became too much. She screamed. Jo heard the suffering from miles away.

'All right, just stop that, please stop!' Shirley stopped screaming.

'Give me the details, Joanna, and your Mum will be okay.'

'How do I know I can trust you?'

'You don't. But try hanging up or stalling and the only thing certain will be the torture and death of your bitch of a mother.'

'Do that and you'll get nothing.'

'Ah, not true, Joanna. I'll get the satisfaction of seeing your mother pissing and crapping herself as she dies a painful death.' He paused. 'Your call, copper.'

Jo paused. 'I'll have to look for them.'

'You do that, Joanna, but I've got a plane to catch so unless that money moves in five, Shirley suffers—big time.' He shouted. 'Do it!'

Jo put down her phone and moved to Michael and whispered.

'Did you get through?'

He whispered. 'Yes. He knows it's a hostage situation.'

She squeezed Michael's arm then picked up her phone. 'I'm still looking.'

Michael moved to his work desk to make another call.

Kruger fumed. 'Waste my time Jo, and you'll be responsible for your mother's torture and death.'

Jo tried to sound frantic. She *was* frantic. 'We changed the banking details after you stole her money.'

'I didn't steal it. She gave it to me.'

Her mind was racing. *Don't rile him, Jo.*

'The bank insisted on my mother having new account details and a new password. I don't know them off the top of my head and I've filed them somewhere safe and can't remember where.'

'Right, that's it. I'm torturing your mother right now.'

There was a dreadful scream and Jo nearly died.

Then they heard the sound of a phone ringing and Shirley stopped screaming. Kruger started speaking.

'Hello? ... Yes, Kruger speaking ... In Zurich? ... What's happened?' Kruger sounded desperate. 'What do you mean hacking my account? What is the matter with you people?'

Jo looked at Michael who seemed otherwise engaged. He was busy working his digital magic simulating a hack attack on Kruger's accounts in Zurich. He wasn't trying to steal Kruger's money, just putting on a powerful show of smoke and mirrors.

More shouting came from Kruger who grew ever more furious. Shirley was silent and Jo could only hope she was safe. The seconds ticked by. Jo didn't have the new banking details with her. If she guessed, his transfer wouldn't work and her mother would be killed. If she said she couldn't find them, her mother would be killed. Her mind caught fire. There seemed no solution. Her mother faced torture and death and Jo could do nothing to help.

Could the police get there in time?

Kruger raged, Michael hacked and Jo was in torment. Suddenly, from the phone, she heard a blood-curdling scream. She and Michael stared at one another. The pain in Jo's chest turned nasty.

'Mum!' she screamed. 'Mum, are you there. Mum, speak to me.'

Silence. The tension in the Northcote warehouse was unbearable. Jo started to cry. Michael felt so, so sorry.

Then someone spoke. It was soft. Who was it? It croaked again.

'Jo, Jo, I'm okay.'

'Mum?' Jo screamed. 'Mum? Are you okay?'

There was another pause and then, 'Nothing a G and T won't fix.'

'What's happened to Kruger?' Pause. 'Mum?'

'You know that dreadful sculpture my cousin made.'

'Mum?'

'I gave it to Mr Kruger.'

They heard sounds of people outside.

'Hang on, said Shirley. 'Did you call the police?'

They heard door banging sounds, and then armed officers who entered via the back door were looking at Shirley.

'I did, Mum.'

'Well they've just arrived. Can I tell them my daughter's the top cop in Victoria?'

Jo and Michael breathed a mighty lot easier.

'Yes, Mum,' said Jo. 'Just stay put. I'll be there as soon as I can.' Jo went to hang up but stopped. She paused. 'I love you, Mum.'

She hung up and burst into tears. Michael shed a few too.

The wash-up was pretty simple. AC John Crowley sent a SOG (Special Operations Group) team to Balwyn North but they weren't needed. Kruger became enraged and distracted when his bank rang him, as per his request, if his account ever came under a hack attack again.

It was a fake attack. It was Michael Chan from Northcote, Australia playing games with the Swiss bank's security. He was brilliant, was Mr Chan. He'd make a master criminal if he ever set his mind to it.

When Kruger lost it with the bank and took his eye off Shirley, she grabbed the family sculpture, an artistic monstrosity, and clobbered the South African scammer on his nut. He screamed then went down like a stunned elephant, and was still out cold when the SOG arrived. Unsurprisingly, the hacking stopped soon thereafter.

Kruger's two injuries were a blinding headache and a shattered ego. He faced a number of charges in Australia with worse to follow. Once listed, his name threw up red flags around the globe. After his stint in an Aussie jail, his extradition to South Africa looked a formality. There were incarcerated inmates in Kruger's hometown who were excited at the prospect of meeting Connie again although, unsurprisingly, Connie didn't share their excitement.

Jo went to the hospital where Shirley remained overnight for observation. It was an emotional visit. Both women were exhausted.

Later, at home, Jo couldn't sleep. She was due at Homicide by 0800. Through the night she kept looking at her bedside clock, and trying to comprehend all that happened in the last 12 hours. Her mind kept racing. The Elsternwick double murder arrests saved her career. Her mother fought a murderous bully and won. Jo pinched herself.

When she walked into Homicide next morning, the word had already spread. Billy Hughes and Richelieu were kindness personified. Baldwin was delighted that Jo had been right all along, and graciously congratulated her. Others were magnanimous although not everyone spread the good cheer.

Payne said nothing. He was furious. His delight in seeing Jo kicked out of the squad now saw him consumed with jealous rage. She had caused the current prisoner, Benny Ross, to be released, a new set of prisoners to be charged, and she, the bitch from the Department of Accelerated Promotion was back in the Squad. Steele said nowt.

When the trio arrested by Jo finally got to be interviewed, the whole story came out.

The murdered couple had great difficulty in accepting their son's sexual orientation. They argued with each other and with their son.

'I am what I am,' he said to them.

He tried to explain that being homosexual wasn't a lifestyle choice. But his ultra-conservative parents tried to have him treated for some sort of mental illness. The relationship between Gavin and his parents turned sour then bitter. David and Larissa refused to meet Bradley or even have his name mentioned in their house. Visits by Gavin to his parents became less frequent. A truce of sorts was agreed. The parents tolerated Gavin's behaviour provided he kept it quiet. But when Gavin and Bradley decided to marry, and Gavin told his parents hoping they would relent and attend the wedding, a blazing row exploded.

The parents claimed a public marriage would humiliate them. David threatened to change his will and disinherit his son. Gavin loved Bradley and refused to be bullied.

Gavin didn't want to be disinherited and Bradley wanted funds to start his own art gallery. They had motive aplenty. As did Dora.

Working in the house, she overheard confrontations between David, Larissa and Gavin. Dora was godmother to Gavin's boyfriend, a fact she never told her employers. That was how she got the job.

Dora loved her godson Bradley, and here he was being described in appalling terms when Gavin was at home, and horrendously so when Gavin was absent. Dora suffered. Her employers were horrible. They said the most dreadful things about her godson, the young man she had nurtured and supported all his life. Dora grew to hate Mr and Mrs Hall. How dare they think and say such things about her boy. He and Gavin deserved the blessing not condemnation of Gavin's parents.

At a dinner party, when David's cousin, George, told David and Larissa that his son Benny was a drug addict, and a minor criminal, Dora overheard. George talked about his despair for his son living in a squat in Brunswick, now due for demolition. Dora hatched a plan.

If the Hall parents were dead, Bradley and Gavin could marry without the hate of Gavin's family. Gavin would inherit the house and the boys would have a secure future together.

She told Bradley her plan. Gavin joined the conspiracy. The three hatched a murder plot framing drug addict Benny. He knew the layout of the house. He was desperate for money. He had a criminal record and was the perfect fall guy.

The plan would work on a night when the Halls were entertaining. That night arrived and Dora was in the kitchen helping with food preparation and the cleaning up.

Dora had been pinching David's heart medication over time and had a small collection. The boys filled the capsules with cocaine. With the dinner party in full swing, Dora slipped upstairs and swapped the real ones with the cocaine capsules.

Larissa Hall took a sleeping tablet after a late night. Tonight was such an occasion. Dora again built up a small supply over time. At the dinner party, Dora slipped some crushed sleeping tablets into Larissa's coffee. When the hostess came into the kitchen to collect the tray, Dora pointed out Larissa's cup. She took sugar in her coffee.

'That's your coffee, Mrs Hall,' said Dora who then held the door for her employer.

The dinner guests departed, Dora finished her domestic duties, said goodnight and left. Two hours later she returned. The house was in darkness but Dora could find her way around blindfolded.

She went upstairs and knocked softly on the Hall's bedroom door. No sound. She crept in. She spoke in case they were awake. No response. She turned on a bedside light. Both were motionless. David was dead and Larissa in a deep sleep. Then came the difficult part.

Dora wasn't squeamish but she was small. She collected a really soft and bulky pillow, climbed on the bed and did the deed.

The lady of the house involuntarily responded but Dora was nothing if not determined. The writhing stopped, the pillow was removed, and Dora read the last rites.

'That's for Bradley and Gavin you evil, evil people.'

Wearing gloves, Dora replaced the heart pills with the real thing, left a small amount of cocaine, trashed the room, stole jewels and left.

The boys were waiting in their car in the street. Gavin, who took a size 7 shoe, went to the front of the house, and slipped into Benny's stolen size 9 trainers. Standing in those shoes, Gavin made a forced entry using a screwdriver. Bradley took the jewels from his godmother then the boys drove Dora home before calling in at Brunswick to return the trainers and plant the jewels.

Benny was on a bender but Jeb, in a drug-addled stupor, saw them. The boys didn't expect anyone to be there. Jeb then got the VIP treatment in Daylesford to prevent him being interviewed by the cops, and from giving Benny an alibi.

After the double-murder, Bradley helped Gavin rehearse his lines to express his grief at the awful death of his beloved parents. For both the lovers, it was game, set and match.

Weeks earlier, to add some red herring insurance, ventriloquist and impressionist Gavin rang Graham James the local TV technician, and imitated his father. Gavin ordered a new antenna when his parents were away. Dora was on hand to let the technician in the house. Naturally, David refused to pay for something he knew nothing about.

Dora and the boys thought they'd pulled off the perfect crime.

Jo was never happy with the neatness of Benny being the culprit. Why were his footprints uneven? Why would he kill two people for a few jewels? If Dr Strange reckoned the murderer had more strength in their left hand, that wasn't Benny. When Jo asked Dora to write her DOB, the woman wrote with her left hand. If Winnie the nosy neighbour knew about the family conflict in the Hall household, how did Benny fit into that scenario? He didn't. If Winnie thought she saw a car parked outside at midnight on the night of the murder, and told the uniformed officer, why was she labelled a busybody and ignored? Jo had a hunch, a feeling. She followed her hunch.

The arrested trio told different tales. Dora accepted total blame and said the boys had nothing to do with the murders. The boys denied everything. There was no evidence linking either of them to the murders. They each gave the other an alibi.

But Jeb's statement included his trip to Daylesford, where he and the boys had been seen. And how could Jeb describe the interior of the Daylesford house so well? The boys struggled to explain. They crumbled and, in turn, blamed each other. The truth came out and all three were charged.

And speaking of charges, the five people arrested in relation to the death of Larry Devine, who "fell" from Puffing Billy, produced mixed results. Senior ranks looked at the charges and were not convinced. It was thought that proving a charge of murder would be difficult.

Chloe and Jason were released without charge. Nina and Simone were found guilty of interfering with a corpse, and copped a fine. That left poor old Colin to carry the can. He was charged with involuntary manslaughter as he broke some Transport Safety Victoria regulation by allowing the van door to be opened while the train was in motion. He copped a suspended sentence and a tongue lashing from Puffing Billy.

Brunel was over the moon.

And with the stabbing death of Robert Gregson in Frankston, Ponzi was never charged. Ola Hatton pleaded guilty to involuntary manslaughter, citing provocation that her brother, the victim, had abused her son, his nephew. Her husband, "Jowls" Hatton, was charged with making a false report to police.

31

JO WAS BACK IN THE INCIDENT ROOM. Applause and friendly banter greeted her. She felt great but nervous. She was back where she wanted to be and was there on merit. Her grandfather's name didn't crack the case. Being a woman with a law degree, didn't crack the case. No, she did so by observing things, examining evidence in fine detail, and questioning anything which seemed suspicious.

There's that word again—*seemed*. Jo believed there would always be a place for one's hunches. If only they worked for her in the future.

Steele didn't bother to welcome Jo. He hated the humiliation he faced in signing off a case in which he was wrong. And he especially hated the fact that Jo's determination, which had uncovered the truth, caused Steele major embarrassment.

As Jo was enjoying her reunion, Steele got a call. DS Barry Craven from the Fraud Squad wanted a chat about possible corruption in Homicide. Steele needed this sort of news like a hole in the head. He already had a nasty taste in his mouth thanks to Jo Best.

Craven entered Steele's office. Bagman Stephen Payne joined them. The men shook hands. The visitor opened a file and explained.

'We recently arrested a bloke, David Baggio, aka Ponzi, on fraud related charges. We had him banged to rights, and were about to charge him when he asked for a deal. We thought he had nothing to trade so had a laugh until he came up with something interesting. He claimed to be working with a crooked cop who's running scams and stealing large sums of money.'

Steele tensed. 'And the cop works here in Homicide?'

Craven nodded. 'Correct.'

Steele and Payne looked at one another.

'And?' Steele felt his breathing change gear.

Craven looked at his file notes. 'Detective Senior Constable Joanna Claire Best. Is she a serving officer here?'

'She is.'

Steele purred, thinking his day had just become slightly better than wonderful. Payne pondered changing his name to Cheshire Cat.

Steele hated alliteration but he'd been bitten by Best before. 'Do we know if it's true?'

Craven produced a document inside a plastic folder. 'Baggio claims this is a screed detailing a scam Best was running, and claims she gave him this document at his home in Patterson Lakes.'

Steele read the screed and handed it to Payne.

'Forensics?'

'There are three sets of prints with Baggio's one of them.'

'And the others?'

'Still checking, sir.'

Steele wanted all bases covered. 'Who have you told about this?'

'Apart from my DI, you're the first, sir. We thought that as the officer named is with Homicide, you should be given priority.'

'Right, thank you DS Craven. I'll be advising your DI about this excellent work. And I'll take responsibility for informing IBAC.'

'Thank you, sir.'

'I might also speak to your boss about running a joint operation. Is this Baggio on strict bail conditions?'

'Yes sir.'

'Then we might offer him a better deal if he agrees to keep working with Best to build a substantial case.'

'That sounds promising, sir.'

Steele stood and Craven realised the meeting was over. The three shook hands and Craven left.

Steele and Payne looked at one another. Both were rapt.

'You want me to inform IBAC, sir?'

Steele had his back to Payne and looked out the window.

'No, Detective, you'll say nothing. I'll inform the Independent Broad-based Anti-corruption Commission.'

'It's brilliant, sir. She weasels her way back in, and five minutes later gets booted, permanently this time, and finds herself in court facing serious charges.'

'Were you listening, Payne?'

'Sir?'

'Just now. Did you hear what I said about keeping Best and setting up a sting to put her away for years?'

Payne landed back on Earth. 'Oh right, boss, gotcha. Brilliant.'

'Now we know she's bent, let's give her plenty of rope.'

'I like it,' smirked Payne.

'We'll watch her like a hawk, build a case, and make sure our Detective Senior Constable Best gets 20 years.'

Both men grinned. Steele led Payne to the incident room where Jo had the squad hooked relating her exploits. Richelieu was super impressed. He liked her from the start and had been sad to see her go.

Steele entered and called. 'Ladies and gentlemen, if I could have your attention.' Silence settled. 'Merci,' said Steele, and his joke fell flat. 'As you know, DSC Best has returned to Homicide, and I want to congratulate her on how well she handled the Elsternwick double homicide. Welcome back, Detective.'

'Thank you, sir,' said Jo. She wasn't the only one surprised.

'I'm sure we hope your stay this time is much longer and, shall I say, even more successful.'

To say the silence was deafening would be an understatement.

'Hear, hear,' said Payne the liar.

Jo didn't know what to say. Nobody did.

She nodded. 'Sir.'

'Carry on,' said Steele who turned and left. Payne had trouble removing his smirk. Several officers wondered if Jo had compromising photos or a revealing video of the head of the Homicide Squad.

'Watch yourself, my girl,' said Billy Hughes. 'I smell a rat.'

'Très intéressant,' murmured the blue-eyed Frenchman. Jo looked into his eyes and felt glad to be home.

If only she knew.

To be continued

The Detective Joanna Best Mysteries

www.cenfoxbooks.com

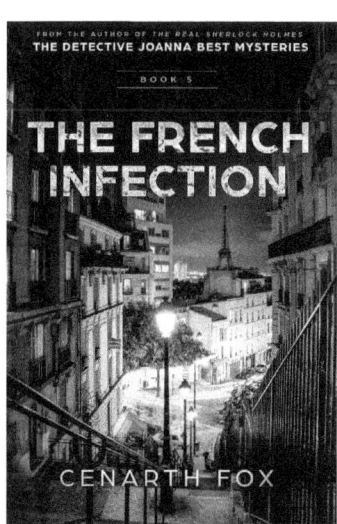

www.ingramcontent.com/pod-product-compliance
Lightning Source LLC
Chambersburg PA
CBHW071108100726
47908CB00008B/2306